# BLOOD
# ON THE
# SHRINE

**By Chris O'Donoghue**

A DI Sonny Russell mystery

*Best wishes*

*Chris O'Donoghue*

First published in 2018
by Boghopper Books with Printed Word Publishing
Second Reprint 2021
Copyright © Chris O'Donoghue 2018

A catalogue record of this book is available from
The British Library
ISBN 978-1-91069-378-0

Typesetting in Minion Pro by Edward Sturgeon
Cover Illustration © Paul Harwood

Printed in Great Britain by Printed Word Publishing
Part of the Scantech Group, Hastings

PRINTED WORD PUBLISHING

*"Every man at the bottom of his heart believes
that he is a born detective."*
John Buchan


*Do you find it easy to get drunk on words?"*
*"So easy that, to tell you the truth, I am seldom perfectly sober."*
Dorothy L Sayers – *Gaudy Nights*


*My thanks go to my wife and soulmate, Greer,
for her continuing support and expertise in editing
my manuscript and to Paul Harwood for the great job he has done
in designing the cover of the book*

# Chapter 1

*__Shrine__ – a holy or sacred place that is dedicated to a specific deity or similar figure of awe and respect in which they are venerated or worshipped.*

THE ROBED figure was seated bolt upright on the meditation cushion. He was perfectly still, a thick grey blanket swaddling his body from his neck downwards. Candlelight reflected off his shaven head; his eyes were closed, his face impassive. All was serene… except for a scarlet trickle that ran from his exposed neck, flooding into the coarse material, turning the dark fabric darker.

'I'm not sure this is a good idea,' Russell mumbled to himself as he peered through the windscreen of his car at the large flakes of snow, lazily falling. 'Either travelling in this weather… or the destination,' he added gloomily.

Detective Inspector Sonny Russell was driving across the county to a Buddhist retreat centre. It had been an unusually mild winter but spring was taking its time in getting started. He had set off from his railway carriage home near Collinghurst in brilliant sunshine. That was more than an hour earlier. Gradually, as he drove through the country lanes, the sky had darkened, the cloud cover had thickened and, surprisingly, snow had begun falling. At first it was just a light swirling mist but now it was coming down as if it meant business.

'I wonder how much further it is?' he said out loud, bringing the car to a halt at the side of the road. He peered at the map, open on the passenger seat. 'What was the name of that last village I passed through? Ah, Buxted.' He ran a finger along the map, tracing the route. 'Got it! Looks like I'm nearly there. If I continue along this road… for about half a mile… then turn right up Hurstwood Road – it's about a mile further on.'

The flakes were becoming thicker and the light was going from the sky. Russell switched on the headlights, creating twin cones of twisting white. The snow was settling on the tarmacked surface of Chillies Lane, indicating that his was the first vehicle to pass this way since it had started falling. 'Too late to turn back. Have to press on. Must be nearly there.' He leaned forward over the steering wheel, rubbed a circle in the condensation that was forming on the screen and peered myopically forward. 'Have to look out for the sign, *SHAMBHALA*, whatever that means.'

Visibility was down to a few feet. He was keeping the car moving slowly, fearful of driving off the road. Suddenly a large white sign with black lettering appeared on the right. Russell turned the wheel, the car crabbed sideways and slithered to a halt in front of a large brick house. He sat back in his seat and exhaled loudly. 'Phew! Made it. Right, let's see what I've let myself in for.'

~o~

It had been Superintendent Vic Stout's idea. Russell had been sitting in his boss's office discussing the last big case they had handled. Three Waffen-SS officers had been brutally murdered by a pair of vengeful German brothers named Müller. One of them, Ludwig, was in custody, awaiting sentence, while the other, Wolfgang, was still at large. It had been a challenging and exhausting case. Partway through Russell had been suspended and Weeks, his DC, kidnapped. He had been lucky to escape with his life. By way of a 'reward' Stout was sending Russell away for a break. He was aware of the Inspector's interest in eastern philosophy, discovered when he was serving in Asia during the war, and that he had developed a curiosity about Buddhism. Stout knew just the place to send him.

'I think you could do with a couple of days of peace and tranquility,' he said. Russell was suspicious. It wasn't like his boss to be so generous. 'You need to get away, somewhere peaceful, where you can leave your police work behind. I've had a splendid idea!' This conversation had taken place in the summer of the previous year. Instead of getting away then, Russell had been given more than enough work to keep him busy for the next nine months. So, it wasn't until early spring that he could take up the Super's dubious 'reward'.

Before he left Stout shook his hand and wished his DI a good break. But as Russell left his office and closed the door behind him, the Superintendent muttered under his breath: 'Yeah, enjoy yourself, with all the other misfits!'

'Do you think he's all right?' Sanghaketu asked anxiously, peering round the door to the shrine room. The speaker, robed in maroon, looked to be in his mid-twenties or early forties – it was difficult to tell. His domed head was neatly shaved and the skin on his face was smooth, almost without a wrinkle. His cornflower-blue eyes were clear and sparkled in the candlelight.

'I don't know. How long has he been there?' Vidyatara replied. He too was dressed in maroon. Also shaven headed, he looked all of his 60 years. His skin was drawn back across his skull, accentuating his high cheekbones and sunken eye sockets. He had the look of a man who'd had a life in the outside world before joining the order. They were half of the four-man team that lived at the centre and looked after the retreatants.

'He was there when I came to do my practice after lunch. I think he's been sitting since then.'

'Should we be worried?' A shadow passed across Vidyatara's face.

'I'm not sure... He's a very experienced meditator.'

'But he's been sitting a very long time. What time is it now?'

Sanghaketu pulled back the cuff of his robe to reveal an old wristwatch almost unreadable through a heavily scarred glass. 'Umm, Just after five.'

'Perhaps give him another hour then.'

'Very well, I will go back and look again.'

Vidyatara took a deep breath, then exhaled noisily. 'Anyway, I think someone has just turned up for the retreat. I suspect they may be the last as the snow is starting to settle. Let us go and meet whoever it is.'

~o~

Booked for the weekend meditation retreat, Russell was looking forward to it. Unusually for a policeman he was a vegetarian of many years standing and with his interest in Eastern philosophy he was intrigued to see how those, far more committed to an alternative lifestyle, lived. The *Shambhala* retreat centre had been set up initially to provide a refuge for monks fleeing the Chinese invasion of Tibet in October 1950. The benefactor was Gareth Temple, an English barrister, who had a deep interest in Mahayana Buddhism and had written several books on the subject. In the 1930s he had travelled extensively in Tibet, living among the people. He so loved the country that he wanted to help the exiles as much as possible.

The building that *Shambhala* occupied had been built in the late nineteenth century as a vicarage with schoolroom attached. It was a substantial brick structure, pleasing to look at, with decorative pegtiles on the upper elevations and ornate bargeboards on the gable ends. When the barrister had bought it, just after the war, it was in a rundown condition. But, with a cash injection and the labour of enthusiastic exiled monks, it had been turned into a refuge for them as well as a retreat centre for lay people who had an interest in Tibetan Buddhism. The donations from a steady stream of retreatants had provided a useful income.

The upper floor of the main house had been converted into dormitory rooms, and downstairs there was a kitchen, dining room and two lounges. An attached cottage provided accommodation for the four resident monks and the annexe, where the village children had been taught, became the shrine room where meditation took place. This had a raised dais at one end with a life-sized image of the Buddha in gleaming gold. Fresh flowers and candles added to the calm and welcoming atmosphere. A mound of circular cushions was piled neatly on the floor and two piles of folded blankets were lined along the wall, ready for use by the meditators.

Russell was greeted at the front door by the two monks who smiled warmly. Each clasped his hands together and bowed to the visitor. 'Welcome to *Shambhala*.' Sanghaketu said. 'I do hope you have had a good journey.' His voice was light with a distinct accent.

Russell stamped the snow off his shoes. 'Not bad thanks, until the last half hour, when the snow started.'

'Have you come far?' Vidyatara asked. His voice was more guttural, each word carefully enunciated.

'From Collinghurst, on the other side of the county. About an hour and half away. Are there many of us?'

The two monks exchanged a glance. Vidyatara spoke. 'We were expecting 15 or 16 but as the weather seems to be getting worse I think it could be only 12.'

'Oh.' Russell raised his eyebrows. 'Is that a problem?'

Sanghaketu chuckled. 'No. One or one hundred, it does not matter. All that counts is the intent,' he said enigmatically.

Vidyatara picked up a clipboard from a side table. 'Could I have your name, please?'

'Of course,' he smiled, 'I'm Sonny Russell.'

'Thank you.' The monk peered at the sheet on the clipboard then underlined a name. 'Ah. The policeman,' he said, knowingly.

Russell nodded and smiled. 'Perhaps best if you don't mention it to the others.'

'I understand. Now, please come with me and I will show you to your room.' He inclined his head to Sanghaketu, who set off along the corridor, then led the way to the bottom of the staircase. 'Please would you take off your shoes?'

'Oh, of course.' Russell bent and untied his laces. 'Is this part of your religion?'

Vidyatara smiled. 'No. We have just had a new carpet fitted.' He led the way up the staircase. Russell followed and soon they were on a landing with several doors opening off it. The monk showed him into a room that contained four single beds, with a small cupboard next to each one. 'This is where you will sleep,' he said. 'You will be sharing with another man.' He looked down at his clipboard.' His name is Laurie. You will meet him later.'

'What about the other two beds?' Russell asked.

'I doubt the others will make it in this weather.' Russell walked over to the window. The snow was falling heavily now. The light was almost gone but he could just make out the grounds, fast disappearing under a quilt of white. 'Supper will be in half an hour. We will ring a bell. The bathroom is at the end of the corridor.' Vidyatara bowed and backed out of the room.

When he had gone, Russell looked round the room. It was the plain side of spartan but he felt quite comfortable with it. Leaving his bag he walked to the bathroom to freshen up.

A little later he found this way down to the dining room. There were half a dozen plain tables, some laid for supper, with four wooden chairs arranged round each one. In the recessed fireplace sat a solid looking stove, an orange glow shining through the glass front and warmth coming off its iron body. A handful of men and women were standing or sitting, quietly chatting. Russell stood slightly awkwardly, just inside the door. Then one of the women broke off from the conversation she was having and walked over to him, holding out her hand and smiling. 'Hello, my name is Helen.' She was as tall as Russell, with shoulder-length dark hair, pale skin and round spectacles.

He took her hand, which was slim and warm and introduced himself.

'Is this your first visit?' she asked.

'Yes. Is it yours?'

Helen gave a sweet smile and spoke softly. 'No, actually it's not, though I feel like I'm coming home when I step through the door. It is as if a big weight is lifted off my shoulders.' She smiled again. 'You do know the food is vegetarian, don't you?'

Russell grinned back. 'That's one of the reasons I was keen to come. The only decent vegetarian food I get normally is when I cook it myself.' The ringing of a bell in the hall briefly put a stop to the conversation.

Helen invited him to sit at the table with her. 'Oh, and this is Laurie. I believe you are sharing a room.' Laurie stood and they shook hands. He was small and neat with hair that looked as if it had been cut using a pudding basin, or by a monastery barber – unusual for man in his middle years. However, his smile was pleasant and as they sat Russell felt comfortable in their company.

~O~

Sanghaketu gingerly pushed open the door of the shrine room. Slipping his feet out of his sandals he walked noiselessly across the wooden floor, approaching the still seated figure. As he grew nearer his anxiety increased. 'Tara Rinpoche...' he called out quietly. No response. He coughed. 'Tara Rinpoche.' Louder this time. Still nothing. Reaching out he touched the man's cheek. It was cold. Moving in closer still he gently shook the seated man's shoulder. There was no reaction. Sanghaketu was scared.

Tara Rinpoche had been like a father to him; guiding and nurturing when he first came to the retreat centre. When, a few years earlier, Sanghaketu had fled Tibet, he'd left his Gompa, and all the monks he'd trained with. The men, young and old, had not only been companions during the long hours of meditation and study, but many of them had become close friends. Some had stayed in defiance of the Chinese invasion while others had fled to other countries. Sanghaketu had met Gareth Temple when he was travelling in Tibet. He had been entrusted with the task of escorting the Englishman round the Gompa and showing him the ancient scrolls that contained the texts which had been handed down, reputedly from when the Buddha had first shared his experiences with his followers. At first the monk was wary of the Englishman, not quite trusting a foreigner who was able to speak their language. But in time, the man's obvious enthusiasm and respect for the teachings had won him over and they developed a mutual understanding.

So, when the Chinese soldiers were marching towards his home, he escaped, first to India, where he stayed for a few months, then to England, where he helped set up what was to become *Shambhala*. Sanghaketu grew to love the Sussex countryside and although he missed the wilds of Tibet, he was glad to be away from the winds and the biting cold of winter. The snow that was now falling heavily reminded him of home but it wasn't the weather that was making him sad, but his fear for his friend and mentor. He hurried out of the shrine room, looking for Vidyatara. He found him in the dining room, eating at the same table as Russell and Helen. He bent and whispered in the monk's ear. Vidyatara got up quickly from his chair, nodded to the others and followed his companion.

'What is it Sanghaketu?'

The other man was pale and shaking. 'It's Tara Rinpoche. I think he's... dead.' His voice quaked.

'Show me.' They hurried out into the cold, crunching through the fresh snow that had built up on the path, and entered the shrine room. The only light was from two candles that cast glittering reflections on the golden Buddha. Kicking off their sandals they made their way across the room. Vidyatara crouched down by the seated figure and touched his neck. He felt dampness and quickly withdrew his hand. He held it out towards the candle, palm upwards.

Sanghaketu gasped. 'Blood!'

Vidyatara exhaled noisily. 'What does this mean?'

'I don't know.' He paused, thinking. 'The policeman. Perhaps we should tell him.'

'Yes. That would be wise. Go and fetch him… But don't alarm the others.'

~o~

'Is there anything brighter than candles in here?' Russell had been dragged away from a most enjoyable vegetarian meal and lively conversation with good company so was a little annoyed. He was standing in the dimly lit shrine room, looking down at the still figure. Sanghaketu walked back to the door, flicked a switch and the room was suddenly flooded with electric light. Russell crouched and peered at the man. He reached out and touched the top of the blanket that was wrapped round him. Holding his hand up to the light he could see fresh blood on his fingers. Leaning forward he peered at the man's neck. Reaching out again he ran his forefinger gently down the flesh. 'Ouch!' He pulled his hand back quickly and rubbed finger and thumb together. 'Something sharp.' He pulled a handkerchief out of his pocket and moved even closer. Holding the cotton fabric between his fingers he put it on the man's neck and plucked something from it. He held it out and the two monks leaned in closer. 'Glass.' The thin shard was less than half an inch wide and about an inch long.

Vidyatara breathed in sharply. 'Is that what killed him?' his voice, almost a whisper.

'It didn't help.' said Russell, rising from the floor. 'I'm afraid I'm going to have to seal this room off.' The two monks exchanged a worried look.

'But what about the retreat?' Sanghaketu asked. 'The shrine room is central to the whole weekend.'

Russell shrugged his shoulders. 'I'm sorry, but I can't see any way round it. This man is dead and we don't know how it happened.'

'Could we move him?'

'Hmm. Let me think.' Russell folded the glass shard into his handkerchief and carefully placed it in his pocket. 'There are two other monks here, is that correct?' Sanghaketu nodded. 'Are they likely to have been in here while this man…' he nodded towards the dead monk, 'has been in here meditating?'

The two men exchanged a glance. Vidyatara spoke. 'Er, Dharmasiddhi was in here this morning, cleaning the room. Karunavadra, I don't know about.'

Russell couldn't see how there could be foul play in a Buddhist centre but he needed to make sure. 'We'd better have them in here so I can talk to them.'

'But what about the others on the retreat?' Sanghaketu asked, his domed forehead creased with concern. 'They will be expecting to come in here. It's what we do on the first night – introduce them to the meditation practices and dedicate the shrine.'

'I'm afraid it won't be possible. You'll have to make some excuse and ask them to stay in the house. Now, please will you get your companions?'

The two monks left quietly, one to speak to the retreatants, the other to fetch his companions. Russell clasped his hands behind his back and walked slowly round the room. He stopped in front of the shrine. The almost life-sized golden figure was sited centrally with two tall candlesticks placed symmetrically either side. In front of each was a vase containing fresh flowers, again placed in perfect symmetry, the carefully arranged blooms mirroring one another. Russell smiled in satisfaction and was just about to move on when he stopped and looked again. Peering closer he could see that the vases were very slightly different. Although both were made from clear glass, the one on the left had a geometric pattern engraved into the surface while the other had a series of spirals cut into it. Curious, he thought and moved on. When he reached the two piles of grey blankets he stopped. Something had caught his eye. Something small sparkled, picked out by the overhead electric light. He crouched again, reached down and picked it up. It was another shard of glass. As he stood upright, two new figures came into the room. One was tall with a serene face, the other shorter, a stubble of dark hair on his head and a shadow round his jaw.

'Which of you is, er, Dharmasiddhi? Have I got that right?'

The smaller man took a pace forward. 'Yes, that is me.' His accent was strong, words carefully chosen.

'I understand you were cleaning in here earlier today.'

'That is right.'

Russell tilted his head to one side. 'Did anything get broken?'

A flush rose up the man's neck and coloured his cheeks. He looked down towards the floor and mumbled. 'Yes.'

'Was it a vase by any chance?'

The monk looked him in the eye. 'It was. How you know?'

Russell held out the shard of glass. Dharmasiddhi swallowed. 'I was carrying both vases. I caught my foot on the blankets. I tripped and dropped one and it shattered.'

'Where did the glass go?'

'Everywhere.'

'On the blankets?'

'Yes. I thought I had cleaned it all up. I must have missed that piece.'

Russell looked thoughtful. 'I don't think it was the only piece you missed.' He turned to the taller monk. 'You are?'

'Karunavadra.' His voice was deep and sonorous.

'And did you come in here today?'

'Yes. I did.' His faced remained impassive.

'When was that?'

The monk was quiet for a few moments before he spoke. 'About four o'clock.'

'What did you do?'

'I came in to meditate. I saw Tara Rinpoche and went over to check he was okay.'

'Why did you do that?' Russell asked, intrigued.

'He is – was – a very experienced mediator. I know that he was able to go very deep and was concerned as it had become very cold. So I wrapped a blanket around his shoulders.'

'Where did you get the blanket from?' Russell asked. Karunavadra pointed to the pile on the floor. Russell pursed his lips and rubbed his chin. 'Hmm. Thank you. Can you show me where the telephone is?'

Dharmasiddhi spoke. 'It is in our community – the cottage where we live. Come, I will take you.'

~O~

13

'Do you think he died of natural causes?' Russell was in the monks' compact office in their private quarters. He was speaking to John Crooks, the pathologist back in Collinghurst.

'Difficult to say, without being there. Tell me again how you found the poor unfortunate.'

'He was sitting very still, and had been for some hours apparently. He was cross-legged, in the Lotus position, with his hand folded together in his lap. One of the other monks, seeing that the temperature had dropped, had wrapped a blanket round his shoulders. I think there was a sliver of glass caught in the material and when Karunavadra put the blanket round it went into his jugular. What I don't understand is why he didn't feel it and react. Instead he just seems to have bled to death.'

'Did you say he is – or was – a very experienced meditator?'

'Yes, as far as I can make out he'd been meditating for many years and had perfected the ability to go into a deep, trance-like state.'

Crooks was quiet for a moment and there was just the sound of crackling on the line. Russell was about to speak again when the pathologist answered. 'Ah … that could be the reason. It is my understanding that through meditation, some yogis are able to reduce heart rate and pulse to such a low level that the body goes into a sort of hibernation. I would imagine that when they are in this state, they can remain unaffected by external conditions or stimuli.'

'Then he may have been unaware of the glass going into his neck?'

'Quite possibly. I may be able to give you a better idea when I can see the body. However, I fear that won't be for a while, if this weather continues.'

Russell looked out of the window and although it was now dark he could see the snow still falling, lit by the light from within the room. 'I think you're right, John. The monks here are anxious to use the shrine room where the body is. What do you suggest?'

'Well. From what you've told me, there is no hint of foul play – just an unhappy accident. I presume there must be an outhouse or shed there?'

'I would imagine so. Just a moment, I'll ask.' Russell put his hand over the mouthpiece and called out. 'Hello…'

Vidyatara appeared in the doorway to the office. 'Yes?' Russell passed on the pathologist's request. 'There is a brick store where we keep materials for repairs and so on.' Russell passed the information on to Crooks.

'That sounds fine. With this weather it shouldn't be difficult to keep the body cool – until I can get over to see it.'

'Thanks, John. I'm sure they'll be happy with that.' He was looking at the monk as he spoke. Vidyatara nodded and formed a faint smile with his thin lips. 'I'll make sure the body is secure until you can get over here – whenever that will be.'

'Right-ho,' Crooks said cheerily. 'Keep in touch… And enjoy your retreat – if you can.' With that there was a click and he was gone.

~O~

Back in the shrine room the other monks had removed the blood-stained blanket from around the dead man's shoulders and wrapped him in a fresh one. They had also unfolded his arms and legs and laid him out flat, with his hands, one over the other on his abdomen. His face was serene – he looked to be at peace.

Vidyatara turned to the policeman. 'When we have moved the body we will need to perform certain rituals – to help him move on to the next life and to ensure he has a peaceful passing.'

'I'm sorry that you'll have to do it in a cold, uncomfortable outhouse.' Russell was beginning to feel bad about getting them to move the body out into the cold.

Vidyatara held up his hand. 'Normally the ceremonies would take place here but do not worry, we are used to the cold. Where we come from this weather would be considered mild.' He gave a thin smile. 'At least one of us will stay with him for the next 24 hours. The others will make sure the retreat runs as smoothly as possible.'

Russell smiled back. 'Thank you, I'm sure those here will appreciate that. But I think it's best if you delay the dedication here. Could you do it in the morning?'

'I think that would be in order. I will go and speak to them.'

'I'll come with you. I may be of some help.'

Between them Russell and the monk explained as delicately as possible what had happened to Tara Rinpoche. Initially shocked, the retreatants took the news philosophically and were grateful that the retreat would continue as expected.

At seven the following morning, wearing coats, hats and scarves, they made their way the short distance from the house to the shrine room through the snow, which overnight had settled in a thick blanket. In the vestibule they shrugged off their outer clothing and slipped out of their shoes. As they entered the main room they bowed towards the shrine and collected cushions and blankets. Arranging themselves in lines, they settled, cross-legged or sitting back on heels, along the long walls. Each carefully wrapped a blanket around their body against the cold and then sat quietly, waiting for the instruction to begin. Russell followed their lead although he found it difficult to get comfortable. Vidyatara, sensing his discomfort, came over and, using folded blankets to support his knees, helped him to settle. Smiling, he left Russell and returned to his place at the side of the shrine; once he was seated he struck a small gong.

'We will start by dedicating the shrine.' His voice was deep and melodic. 'Please stand.' The 12 men and women rose to their feet, shrugging off the blankets. Russell looked round and seeing the others putting their hands together, as if in prayer, followed suit. Vidyatara intoned: 'We dedicate this shrine to the Three Jewels.'

'We dedicate this shrine to the Three Jewels,' the retreatants replied in unison, Russell hesitantly joining in.

The monk went on: 'To the Buddha, the Ideal of Enlightenment to which we aspire.' Again the others responded. This continued for several minutes until they reached the last stanza: 'For the happiness of all beings, for the benefit of all beings, with body, speech, and mind, we dedicate this place.' Their voices faded away and Russell was aware of the almost total silence. The atmosphere in the shrine room felt magical: the lambent light of the candles on the shrine; the glittering surface of the gold Buddha and the reflected sunlight shining through the small windows, overlooking the white-carpeted garden.

'We will now practice The Mindfulness of Breathing,' Vidyatara said. 'Please make yourselves comfortable on your cushion. Let your body relax, close your eyes and become aware of your breath.' Russell sneaked a look around the room. All the others seemed serene and relaxed. He tried to make his limbs stay cross-legged without aching or going to sleep so he could concentrate on his breath but was finding it hard. However, with the monk's guidance he found his muscles softening and his breathing slowing...

# Chapter 2

*Shambhala – In Buddhist and Hindu traditions
it is a mythical kingdom or pure land, a fabulous place
whose reality is visionary or spiritual as much as
physical or geographic.*

THE LANDSCAPE looked picture perfect. The fields were covered with a pristine coating of white, sparkling in the winter sun. It was deep enough so that the fences and hedges that formed the boundaries were reduced to amorphous mounds. Trees, skeletal in form, were festooned with shimmering coatings of snow, an occasional bird landing on a branch sending a cascade of flakes spiralling to the ground. In the distance a plume of smoke rose lazily from a chimney but there was no sign of anything moving. Sheep and cows were either under cover or huddled in field margins, waiting for the farmer to bring fodder.

There was just a single set of tracks in the snow that had built up in the lane, made by a tractor that had passed by earlier. The tracks disappeared as the road turned a bend at the bottom of the hill but there was movement in the distance. At first it was just a dark speck against the white but gradually the shape became a figure, struggling up the hill, following in the track made by the tractor. And as the figure grew closer it took the shape of a man, wearing a coat that was too thin for the weather and shoes unsuitable for the conditions. When he reached the entrance to the retreat centre he paused, wiped the snow off the sign with his sleeve and revealed the name, *SHAMBHALA*. Trudging up to the front door he knocked and waited.

Hearing the knock but feeling baffled that anyone would turn up in this weather, Sanghaketu cautiously opened the heavy wooden door. A young man was standing there, bare-headed and shivering, his laboured breathing causing clouds of vapour. 'Is this the retreat centre?' he asked, his voice, a shaky guttural growl.

'Ye-es,' the monk answered hesitantly. 'What did you want?'

'I'm a traveller,' the man went on, 'and I thought, as this is a retreat, you'd take me in.'

Sanghaketu smiled. 'It is not normally something that we do, but...' he gestured outwards with his hand. 'As the weather is bad you had better come in out of the cold.'

'Thanks,' the man said, and stepped into the hallway.

'Are you hungry?'

The man's face lit up. 'Starving!'

'I will find you some food. Then I will talk to the others to see if it would be in order for you to stay.' He led the man into the empty dining room – the others were still meditating – and told him to sit. Going into the kitchen, he filled the kettle then placed it on the stove. He brought out a tray with bread, margarine and jam.

The man grabbed at the bread, smeared it with spread and jam and started hungrily wolfing down great mouthfuls, barely pausing for breath between bites. Sanghaketu also gave him a steaming mug of tea and a plate of biscuits. In no time the plate held nothing but crumbs and the scalding tea had been emptied down the man's throat. He sat back in his chair, closed his eyes, took a deep breath and belched noisily. Then looking up he saw the monk staring at him. 'Sorry! I haven't eaten anything since yesterday.'

The monk nodded. 'I am glad you found it satisfying. Now if you would wait here I will see what can be arranged.' He gave a small bow and left.

The man looked around the high-ceilinged room. It was plainly decorated, the walls maroon below the dado and cream above, reminiscent of the livery of a pre-grouping railway carriage. The tables were laid with knives, plates and spoons. Looking through the large serving hatch to the kitchen he could see a catering-sized saucepan on the stove and he could hear the hiss of gas and the sound of bubbling coming from the pan. A stack of earthenware bowls stood on the countertop. Looking the other way he could see the glow from the coal stove and he turned his chair towards it and held out his hands, feeling the warmth. He smiled; this was better than the bed and breakfast he thought he was going to stay at in Uckfield.

Russell followed the instructions, concentrating on his breath and almost forgot the cramp in his calves. But, after half an hour, when the final gong had sounded, he was relieved to be able to stretch and ease the tension in his legs. However, he was pleasantly surprised to find his mind was much clearer than it had been before and he felt relaxed. He looked around and could see by the serene look on the faces of the others that they too had benefited from the meditation. Quietly they got up and made their way to the anteroom where feet were pushed into shoes and shoulders shrugged into coats. Outside the sunlight sparkled on the crisp white snow as they made their way along the cleared path, back to the house for breakfast. Filing in, they noted the newcomer sitting warming himself by the stove. The nature of an all-welcoming retreat centre rendered them only mildly curious. Russell, however, with the nose of a policeman, was a little more interested. He nodded to the man then took his place in the queue for porridge. This was ladled out from the pot that had been simmering on the stove. Honey, brown sugar, a bowl of dried fruit and milk were on a side table, to be added to taste. When he had been served he found a chair next to the man and sat at the table.

'Hello. Have you come to join us?'

The man squirmed uncomfortably in his seat. 'Not exactly…'

Russell raised an eyebrow. 'You could hardly be just passing…'

The man gave a sheepish grin. 'No, I walked from Buxted station. I was heading for Brighton on the early train but the line's blocked near Uckfield so that was as far as it went.'

'But that's a good mile and a half away. What made you head for here?'

'There was a poster advertising this place. I guessed if there were monks of some sort they'd offer me their hospitality. I didn't realise how far it was until I was halfway. Then it was too late to turn back. I just kept going in the tracks made by some farmer on his tractor.'

'Mmm. I see. You'd better get yourself a bowl of porridge before it's all gone.' The man was getting eagerly to his feet when Russell asked: 'By the way, what's your name?'

'Oh, Dave… Dave Elsdale.' As he stood he glanced across the heads of those eating and Russell saw him start as he caught sight of someone on the other side of the room. For a moment recognition stopped him in his tracks and he blanched, but then quickly he composed himself and moved to the serving hatch. Curious, Russell looked round and stared straight into the eyes of the man who had caused such shock – his roommate, Laurie. The man blinked then looked back at his food.

~o~

After breakfast most of the retreatants had drifted off to their rooms or to sit in one of the lounges to read. Two, whose names were on the rota remained to clear away the breakfast things and wash up. Russell could hear them going quietly about their work in the kitchen. He and the new man, Elsdale, were sitting in relatively companionable silence by the stove when Sanghaketu returned with Vidyatara.

He addressed Elsdale. 'We have had a discussion and decided that you can stay – at least until the road is cleared. Perhaps you would like to join the retreat?'

'Well… I don't know…'

'It will be difficult if you do not,' Vidyatara added. 'You see, we act as a community and if one person is not taking part…' He let the sentence hang in the air.

'Perhaps you would like to share a room with, er, Sonny?' Sanghaketu said, nodding towards Russell.

'Oh, er, I don't know. I'm not used to sharing.' Elsdale paused and thought for a moment. 'Is there anyone else in his room?'

'Yes, Laurie.'

'Oh – no.' He was obviously flustered. 'I mean… Could I possibly have a room on my own?'

The monks exchanged a glance. Vidyatara spoke: 'We like people to share. It is part of the community spirit but I suppose, in this case…'

'Yes, there is a single room,' Sanghaketu continued. 'Come with me and I will find you some bedding and towels and so on.' With that the two men left. Vidyatara bowed to Russell and followed them out.

Russell sat alone by the stove. The peace that had descended on him after the meditation had quickly evaporated as the policeman's instinct took over. Elsdale had apparently been rattled by something, or someone. Laurie perhaps? He obviously did not want to share a room with him, that was certain. Perhaps it meant nothing. Russell shook his head. No, he thought, I've come here to get away from work. But... but, something was niggling at the back of his brain. The trouble was, as much as he had been looking forward to a break he felt out of his depth – no, not that – he felt alone, that was it. Normally he would have the support of his DC, Johnny Weeks. Someone he could discuss things with – use as a sounding board. But discuss what? He shook his head again. Come on, he said to himself, you're here to relax. With that he got up and wandered off to the lounge.

Being closer to the coast, the snow in Collinghurst was much lighter. Even so, Detective Constable Weeks felt oppressed by the weather. Pushing back the mop of dark curly hair that flopped over his forehead he flicked listlessly through the papers in the folder open on his desk. He was finding it difficult to concentrate, there were so many thoughts swirling round his head. Normally the subject would have held his attention but none of the information was making much sense. He found his focus blurring, the words on the page becoming nothing more than a series of swirling shapes – mere Rorschach inkblots. After what he had learned he needed guidance from his boss – but *he* was over on the other side of the county, quite possibly snowed in and undoubtedly having a peaceful time. He shook his head, stretched his arms wide and yawned. Taking a deep breath he turned back to the first page.

The file concerned what became known as the Eastcastle Street robbery that had taken place four years earlier. It was very different from others that had happened before, in that it was meticulously planned. The thieves had rehearsed for weeks in advance, avoiding suspicion by pretending that they were making a film. They escaped with £287,000. The mastermind behind the raid was a notorious London criminal, Billy Hill and the gang included George "Taters" Chatham and Terry "Lucky Tel" Hogan. The robbers were never caught and the case remained open. The surprise was that the files had found their way from the normally protective Metropolitan Police to the sleepy Sussex backwater of Collinghurst. The reason was that a small-time crook had been heard boasting in a local pub that he was part of the gang.

Weeks had been having an after-work drink in The Queen's Head, sitting discreetly in a shady corner of the bar, nursing a pint of bitter and poring over the crossword in the evening paper. The felon, Tommy Atkins, had already done the rounds of the local hostelries and was well oiled by the time he staggered into The Queen's. He had started chatting to a young lady at the bar, apparently trying to impress her with his prowess but actually rather annoying her. When he said the words 'Eastcastle Street' rather loudly, Weeks's ears pricked up, pen poised, the crossword forgotten.

'See,' Tommy said to the girl, 'before that, all robberies was "Wham, bam, thank you Mam".'

'You what?' She was obviously not the brightest.

Tommy rolled his eyes, and then went on, speaking slowly and deliberately. 'They weren't planned – well not properly. A couple of blokes would get together an' decide to rob a bank. Then they'd nick a car an' get another mate to be the getaway driver. They'd pull nylon stockings over their faces, get tooled up an' burst into the bank.'

'What's "tooled up" mean?'

'Blimey! Don't you know nuffink?'

''Ere! Cheeky!' she said, thumping him on the arm.

He rocked on his stool, just managing to stay upright. 'Steady on! Just means they 'ad guns – sawn-off shooters maybe.'

'Why didn't you say that then?' The girl tossed her hair and reached for a cigarette from the pack on the bar.

Tommy ploughed on. 'Anyway, sometimes they'd get away with it an' get a few quid – an' sometimes some bright spark would ring a silent alarm under the counter, the rozzers would turn up an' cart them off to clink.'

The girl was rapidly losing interest. She drew hard on her cigarette then blew a plume of smoke towards the ceiling. 'So what are you saying?'

'At last.' She gave him a withering look that he barely noticed. 'What I'm sayin' is that Billy Hill's blag was carefully planned. 'Im an' 'is mates, Taters Chatham an' Lucky Tel Hogan among 'em, pretended they was making a film when they was really plannin' the job.'

The girl looked up. 'Who was starring in it then?'

Despite his inebriation, Tommy couldn't believe his ears. 'Starring in it? They were only *pretending*, you silly cow.'

'You what?!' She whirled round and slapped his face – hard. 'You're full of shit! I've 'ad enough – I'm going!' With that she grabbed her bag, scooped up her cigarettes and stormed out of the pub, slamming the door so hard the windows shook and the glasses rattled on the shelves behind the bar.

Tommy was shaken. He sat on his stool, speechless. The barman pretended not to notice. Weeks took the opportunity to leave his seat and walk to the bar to order another drink. 'Women!' he said, standing next to the crook.

Tommy seemed not to hear at first. Then he shook his head, as if trying to get water out of his ears. 'Sorry mate, what did you say?'

'Buy you another?' Weeks pointed to the empty glass.

Tommy looked down, then up at the other man, still stunned. 'What? Yeah. Thanks, matey.'

Weeks signalled to the barman who refreshed their glasses. When they were filled he chanced his arm. 'I couldn't help hearing you talking about the Eastcastle Street robbery.'

Tommy looked up sharply, suddenly sober. 'You a copper?'

Weeks held his hands out, palms forward. 'Me? No. Far from it!' He gave a dry laugh. 'It's just I admire the way they pulled it off.'

Tommy's face relaxed into a grin. 'Clever, weren't it?' He paused, then spoke again. ''Ere, what's your name?'

Weeks thought quickly. Better to stick to the truth, as far as possible, without giving too much away. 'Johnny,' he said. This seemed to satisfy the other man. Feeling he was on safer ground the DC warmed to the subject. 'Yeah, all that careful planning paid off. Nearly three hundred grand, wasn't it? I wouldn't mind being part of something like that.'

'An' they never got caught. Cheers Johnny.' Tommy lifted his glass in salute then took a swig. Leaning forward he lowered his voice conspiratorially, taking Weeks into his confidence. 'D'you know what?'

'What?'

'I was one of the team.'

'*You weren't*?' Weeks was astonished. The booze had made the man careless.

Tommy tapped the side of his nose with a none-too-clean forefinger and peered both ways along the bar before speaking. 'I was the look-out,' he said in a whisper.

'Really?'

'Shh! Keep yer voice down.'

'Sorry.'

'S'alright. Learnt a lot from Billy and Tel.'

Weeks cocked his head to one side. 'Yeah?'

'Yeah. I learnt that the most important thing in doing a job is ... plannin'. Don't matter 'ow long it takes, you've got to plan – make sure you don't forget nothin' – look after every little detail. That's what they taught me.' He lowered his voice even further so it was not much more than a whisper. 'And d'you know what?'

Weeks had to lean in close, just to hear. 'What?'

'I'm plannin' me own job.'

Weeks couldn't believe his ears. He swallowed, trying to keep his voice neutral. 'Really? Tell me more.'

Tommy stood up unsteadily. He gestured to the corner where Weeks had been sitting. 'Let's go an' sit over there – so no one can hear us.' He picked up his glass and weaved his way across the bar. 'Right,' he said, sitting down heavily on the dusty, plum-coloured banquette. Weeks pulled up the chair on the other side of the table. 'You know that Billy robbed a post office van?' Weeks nodded. 'Well *I'm* gonna rob a *mail train*.' He sat back, a triumphant grin spreading across his face. 'An' this is how I'm gonna do it…'

~o~

Dave Elsdale sat on the narrow bed in the narrow room that the monk had shown him to. He shuddered. It really was a miserable little cell but at least he wouldn't have to share with Laurie Baker. He couldn't believe his eyes, when he saw him in the dining room. That horrible little man with the silly haircut – bosom pals with Tommy Atkins. Thick as the thieves they were. Dave liked to think that he wasn't jealous, but he was.

He and Tommy had grown up together during the war. As boys, neither had enjoyed school and although Tommy had shown a genuine talent for drawing he had preferred scrambling over the rubble of bombed-out houses, looking for valuables that had been left behind by the unfortunate householders. The pair became adept at dodging the rozzers, firefighters and ARP wardens. The things they found – watches, jewellery, photo frames – more than made up for the grazed knees and bruised elbows.

He remembered Tommy's dad as a shadowy figure, still young enough and fit enough to be called up but somehow avoiding enlistment. He didn't spend much time with his family, preferring the bars and dives where he mixed with the other lowlife in the city. But he was useful to the boys. He knew the right people who would fence the trinkets they looted, giving them pocket money for their finds. Dave was bright enough to realise that the man probably gave them only a fraction of the value of their pilfered spoils but the boys were glad of the coppers and occasional half-crowns that kept them supplied with sweets, when they were available, and cigarettes. That was then. Now, and for the past few months, Tommy didn't want to know him. They hadn't grown apart, as boys becoming men often did. Tommy had actively pushed him away. Dave was pretty sure the reason was because he'd gone straight. Got a proper job. Up until then they had passed from being naughty boys – pinching what they could – into manhood, becoming outright, small-time villains. They hadn't been very good at it, never hitting the big time, just scratching a precarious living. After a few years Dave had grown tired of the brushes with the law and decided to go straight. It was from then that he had definitely been given the cold shoulder.

He'd started working as a clerk for the Southern region of British Railways. At first Tommy jeered at him and said he was 'going soft' but still kept his company. Then, Laurie Baker came on the scene. He was a sneaky little man, a bit older by a couple of years, and Tommy took to him straight away, carelessly brushing his long-term friend aside. When he first started his job, Dave was tolerated by Tommy and his cohorts but quickly it was made known that he wasn't welcome. This really hurt. At first he was angry at being cast off so glibly. Most of his frustration was directed at Laurie who, he felt, was the main reason for his exclusion. Gradually, as he settled into his job, he found he quite enjoyed the routine, even though it was lowly and poorly paid. Eventually he began making new friends and gradually the hurt he had felt at being rejected began to wear off. Then something happened that made him hanker for the buzz of his old life.

He was having a drink with one of his fellow clerks, a pleasant enough, but slightly flash chap called Simon, a little older and more senior but very much a Teddy boy. After a few pints they got to talking about unusual loads that the railway carried and Simon let slip that there was a regular consignment of mail bags that went from Brighton up to London containing bank notes. As soon as he mentioned it the older man realised he'd said too much and clammed up. Dave knew better than to push him for more details and let it go. However, the next time they met, he managed to steer the conversation round to the subject and Simon, probably having drunk more than usual, opened up. Dave found out when the consignment was sent, on what train and how often. As he weaved his way back to his digs – he'd drunk quite a bit too – he started working out how he might be able to get back in favour with Tommy.

First, he needed to find out more about the journey the mail bags took from the coast to the metropolis. On his next free day and using his railway travel pass, a perk of the job, he set off for Brighton. It was when the snow began falling heavily that his troubles started and his journey ended at Buxted station, which was how he came to find his way to *Shambhala*.

Russell walked into the blue lounge. Along one wall was a floor-to-ceiling bookcase with works on Buddhism, meditation and Tibet filling the shelves. A cheery blaze sent out waves of heat from within a large ornate fireplace with tiled surround and heavy overmantle. A couple of armchairs faced the fire. Sitting on one of them was the woman who had welcomed him the previous day. She elegantly uncurled her legs that had been tucked beneath her, stood and said: 'Hello, Sonny. Can I help you choose something to read?'

Russell smiled. 'Thank you, Helen, that would be very kind.'

She crossed to the bookcase and ran her finger along the spines of the books. Stopping, she gently pulled out the Manual of Zen Buddhism by D. T. Suzuki. She held it towards him and said, 'This should be a good introduction. There are simpler "How to meditate" guides, but I think this would be more your style.' She smiled knowingly and much to his surprise Russell almost blushed. He was obviously more relaxed than he realised. She returned to her chair, Russell sat in the other and flicked through the pages of the book she had chosen for him.

After a few minutes of companionable contemplation he lifted his head from the book to see Helen looking back at him, an enigmatic smile playing about her lips. Russell returned the smile and spoke: 'How well do know Laurie?'

'Laurie?' She looked puzzled.

'The man sharing my room. He was at our table for supper.'

'Hmm, not well. I only met him yesterday evening. Not long before you turned up.'

'Oh, I thought you were old friends, the way you were chatting.'

Helen coughed and looked down. 'Er no, we just seemed to click. It's like that in a place like this,' she added quickly.

'I see. What do you know about him?' he asked.

'Well,' Helen began, 'I don't think he's been on a Buddhist retreat before, or any other retreat, despite his appearance.'

'You mean the hairstyle?'

'It is rather distinctive.' She laughed. 'But I don't think he's a monk.'

'What makes you say that?'

She thought for a moment. 'He was quizzing Sanghaketu and Vidyatara.'

'What about?' Russell leaned towards Helen, closing his book and putting it on his lap. He had regained his composure and his policeman's inquisitive nature had come back to the fore.

I think it was something to do with trains.' She paused. 'Yes, I remember, he was asking how far this place was from the Brighton line.'

Russell frowned. 'A strange sort of question.'

'That's what I thought. Probably why I remembered it.'

'Can you recall anything else about him?'

'You seem rather interested. I thought you'd come here to get away from detective work?'

Russell smiled sheepishly. 'Sorry. Force of habit.'

'Don't worry, I quite understand.' The easy silence between them returned, only broken by the crackle of the fire. Somehow, the room and indeed, the whole of *Shambhala* was imbued with an atmosphere of calm and tranquility which Russell could feel working its way into his whole being. After a few minutes Helen spoke again. 'Tell me about you. Where do you live?'

'Ah.' Russell wasn't used to being on the receiving end of questions but was happy to open up to this woman. 'I live in a converted railway carriage by the coast, on the other side of the county.'

'How fascinating. Is there a Mrs Russell?'

He laughed. 'No. I guess you could say I'm wedded to the job.'

'Any family?'

No. My parents are both dead, I've got an older sister and a nephew, Christopher, who I'm rather fond of. He's a bright boy – actually helped out on a case last year.' He looked a little wistfully into the glowing embers of the fire. 'There may be some distant cousins but we don't keep in touch.'

'Oh. That's a shame.' Helen's eyes were full of compassion.

'It's what I've got used to.' He looked up and beamed. 'But I do have a little terrier, Aggie.'

'That's a nice name. Is it a girl?'

'Yes, Agatha Christie… in full.'

She smiled warmly. 'The queen of crime.'

There was another long pause then he spoke. 'How about you?'

'Me?'

Russell chuckled. 'Yes you. You said you felt at home here.'

Helen threw back her head and laughed. 'This is about as far from home as you could get. I work in the City.'

'Oh yes? What do you do?'

She took a moment before answering. 'Oh you know, secretarial work – nothing of importance.' Russell was about to speak again when a bell rang summoning them to their first workshops. Uncurling her legs, Helen got to her feet and, smiling at him said: 'C'mon, we're going to have our first lesson in mindfulness.'

~o~

'So he told you he's going to rob a mail train then?' DI 'Bonnie' Parker sat behind his desk, flakes of grey cigarette ash peppering his jacket and tie; a Capstan Full Strength smouldering in the ashtray sending a lazy plume of smoke snaking towards the ceiling.

'Yes, Sir,' Weeks replied hesitantly.

Parker guffawed. 'And you believed him?'

'He was very definite.'

'He may well have been.' The DI paused. 'Tommy Atkins,' he went on, 'is a greasy little toe-rag. I wouldn't trust him as far as I could throw him.' Parker picked up his cigarette and took a long drag, blew out a stream of smoke and coughed, phlegm rattling in his chest.

'But he told me the dates, the location, everything.' Weeks looked crestfallen.

'More fool you.' Parker waved his hand towards the door, ash flying off the end of the cigarette. 'Go on. I'm sure you've got work to get on with.' As Weeks turned the DI's voice softened. 'Don't take it too hard, lad; they're not called cons for nothing.'

Weeks went back to his desk and sat behind the pile of files, teetering on its surface. Yet again Parker had refused to take him seriously. He recalled this had happened when his usual DI, Sonny Russell, had been taken off the last big case they had worked on. Owing to Parker's cynicism on that occasion, Weeks had been abducted and taken to France. By pure luck he'd escaped with his life – and prevented a man from being hanged. Parker obviously had a short memory, he reckoned.

He thought back to the previous Friday evening when the 'con' had taken him into his confidence.

~o~

They were sitting in the corner of the saloon, as far from the bar as possible. Tommy had picked up his glass and taken a deep swig. He banged the glass down then belched noisily. 'It's like this, see,' he began. 'Every week, the Post Office sends a load of mailbags from Brighton up to London. Now I know – don't ask me how,' he leaned forward and tapped the side of his nose with a grubby forefinger, 'but I know that some of them mailbags is stuffed with banknotes.'

Weeks raised his eyebrows. 'Really?'

'Yeah, really. Somebody – and I ain't tellin' you who – told me that they're heading for the London headquarters of the banks down there. It's all the takings from the previous week plus the weekend. Money from the shops an' the races an' that.'

'Isn't that a bit unusual?'

Tommy scowled. 'Wadyer mean?'

Well I thought they usually sent cash in some sort of armoured van.'

'Ah, well, that's where this is different, see.' The amount of alcohol he had consumed turned the wink he gave Weeks into more of a leer. 'My mate says they reckon that sending the dosh by train, anonymous like, is more secure; less risky.' Weeks nodded sagely. 'And this mate of mine knows which days the money is on the train,' Tommy went on. 'And not only that, he knows which train it's on.'

'How...?' began Weeks, but was immediately cut off by a growl from Tommy.

'Don't ask, Johnny! I ain't gonna tell you no details 'til I know I can trust you.'

Weeks held his hands up. 'Fair enough. I don't expect you to tell me anything you don't want to.'

'No, and I ain't gonna, neither.' Tommy buried his face in his glass and drank deeply. It was some moments before he spoke again. He fixed Weeks with a stern look, his eyes slightly unfocused, then spoke. 'You said you wouldn't mind being part of something like that van robbery.' Weeks nodded. 'Can you drive?'

'Sure.'

'A lorry?'

'How big?'

'Not very. A three tonner.'

Weeks smiled. 'No problem. Used to drive those in the Army.' Tommy sat up and narrowed his eyes.

'When I did my National Service.' Weeks added quickly.

Atkins sat back smiling. 'Well, Johnny, you might be the bloke I'm looking for.'

'Sounds good to me. How big is the team?'

'Ah, well, that'd be telling.' He took a drink. 'That's something I learned from Billy an' Tel when we did the Eastcastle Street job. You've got to stick to a plan.'

Weeks cocked his head to one side. 'Oh yeah?'

'Yeah... One,' he tapped his thumb, 'keep it simple. Two,' his forefinger was tapped, 'keep it small – that's why I ain't tellin' you how many're on the job. And three...' he sat up straight and held his finger to his lips and lowered his voice, 'keep it quiet.'

'When are you planning to do it?' Weeks asked cautiously.

Tommy drained his glass and smacked his lips. 'I don't know yet an' even if I did I wouldn't tell you...' The look on his face made Weeks wonder if he'd gone too far, but Tommy went on, '...I wouldn't tell you – yet.' With that he got unsteadily to his feet and stood swaying. He put his hands on the table and leaned forward, his face inches away from the other man. 'Meet me here again tomorrow night. I might have something more to tell you then.' Weeks succeeded in remaining still although his instinct was to recoil from the sour stench that came out of Tommy's mouth. 'Six o'clock. Okay?'

'Okay.'

Tommy weaved his way towards the door, fumbled for the handle, then pulled it open. He turned towards Weeks, winked again and in a stage whisper said: 'Mum's the word.' Then he was gone, leaving the door swinging on its hinges, flakes of snow swirling in from the street.

The landlord lifted the counter flap and came out from behind the bar. As he crossed to the door he looked towards

Weeks. 'Don't think much of the company you're keeping,' he muttered. 'I'd be wary of that one if I were you.' He slammed the door shut and walked, heavy-footed, back to the bar. Weeks looked at his half empty glass and decided he didn't want any more to drink. He rose, picked up his paper and made his way out. The snow was still falling but the pavements and road were wet so it wasn't settling – yet.

Russell sat on his cushion in the shrine room. Helen was sitting further along the row of seated figures so he wasn't able to see her. But, he could see Laurie, who was immediately opposite him, looking relaxed, his eyes closed, a serene look on his face. Vidyatara was talking about "being in the moment" and, "living for today". Rather than concentrating on the words of wisdom Russell was more intent on observing the other man. He was curious as to why such a person, especially with his distinctive haircut, would be drawn to a place like this. Perhaps this was just the sort of place distinctive people *were* drawn to. Helen certainly seemed 'different' and, so was he, come to that. A vegetarian policeman, with leanings towards eastern philosophy? He was certainly different. He'd heard the term 'seeker' applied to those, who, dissatisfied with conventional religion, looked elsewhere so perhaps Laurie too was a seeker.

Laurie's eyes weren't completely closed. In fact he was staring straight back through his lashes at Russell. He wondered what the policeman was doing at the retreat centre. He couldn't know about the job, could he? And why was Helen cosying up to him? She was playing a dangerous game, getting so close to a copper. And what on earth was that creep Elsdale doing there? Tommy hadn't mentioned the little snake when he'd asked him and Helen to check out the lie of the land. He'd have words with Tommy when he got back. Meanwhile he'd have to pretend that he was enjoying all this mumbo jumbo nonsense. He closed his eyes and, listening to the monk droning on, drifted into sleep.

He was running down a never-ending street. There were houses, tightly packed on either side. People were hanging out of their bedroom windows laughing and shouting at him. He looked over his shoulder and could see a giant Wolseley police car gaining on him. He tried to run faster but instead his legs grew heavier and heavier and it felt as if he was moving through porridge or thick mud. The police car was gaining rapidly, the bell clanging demonically. He tried even harder to escape, his heart pounding, his breath coming in great gasps. With a start he awoke, shook his head and opened his eyes. The shrine room swung into focus and he was aware that the robed monk was gently banging a small gong. Surreptitiously he peered round, convinced that the others would be staring at him, but no, they were stretching and shifting on their cushions, smiling to themselves, lost in the moment. Shakily he got to his feet and made his way to the vestibule where he had left his coat and shoes. He carefully averted his gaze, not wanting to make eye contact with the others. He took his time, shrugging his shoulders into his overcoat then bending to tie his laces. Soon, the others had left for the main house, a murmur of gentle conversation drifting away with them. Vidyatara was the last to come out of the shrine room. He touched the monk's sleeve and spoke quietly.

'I know we're not supposed to have contact with the outside world while we're here, but I wondered if I might use the telephone.' The monk went to speak but Laurie held up his hand. 'See, I've got this friend and I'm a bit worried about him. He ain't been too well. It'd only be a quick call.'

'Well,' Vidyatara began, he smooth brow furrowing and his dark eyes half-closing, 'I suppose it would be all right – just this once.'

Laurie beamed. 'Thanks ever so. I'm happy to pay for the call.'

The monk waved his hand and shook his head. 'That won't be necessary.' Slipping his feet into his sandals he said: 'I will have to check with the others first. If you go back to the house I will come and find you presently.' They stepped through the outer door and were shrouded in a thick swirl of snow. It looked like winter had returned.

~o~

Weeks sat in the corner of the bar, a pint of bitter on the table in front of him. He was the only customer. It was already a quarter to seven and there had been no sign of Atkins. The barman had been the negative side of surly when he ordered his drink and the miserable coal fire in the corner was doing little to take the chill off the room. He was beginning to wonder if Parker was right, and the 'con' was just stringing him along. He had been sure that he was on to something, despite his superior's disdain and again, he wished Russell was there to counsel him. He sighed. Trust his DI to be away when he really needed him. He decided to leave it another five minutes then give up.

Suddenly the street door burst open. Atkins entered with two men, one built like the side of a house, the other small and furtive. Spotting Weeks he called out. 'Hello, matey. Wanna drink?' Weeks held up his half-full glass and shook his head. Atkins winked and turned back to the bar. 'Three pints landlord, and four whisky chasers.' He took a roll of notes out of his pocket, peeled one off and laid it on the counter. 'And one for you – keep the change.' The barman's mood improved appreciably. It had the makings of a lively evening.

Clutching their drinks the trio made their way over to the table where Weeks was sitting. Atkins upended one of the chasers into Weeks's glass. 'Get that down you!' The big man sat heavily on the banquette causing a cloud of dust to rise and dance around their heads. The smaller man perched on the edge of a wooden chair, his eyes darting furtively from side to side.

'Well, Johnny, how've you been?' Atkins asked.

'Fine thanks.' Weeks took a drink and almost choked on the whisky in it but managed to swallow, hoping his discomfort didn't show.

Atkins seemed not to notice. 'These are my *colleagues*.' He held out his arms. 'Sammy the screwdriver…' he said and pointed to the little man, who nodded briefly then quickly looked away, towards the door. Weeks smiled back and made a quick appraisal. Neatly dressed in a double-breasted blue pinstripe suit he had a beak-like hooked nose and a thin moustache on his upper lip. The way his gaze kept flitting around the room Weeks thought it made him look like a bird. 'And this is Butcher Bates.' The big man proffered his hand. Weeks held his out. Bates smiled and closed his around it. Weeks felt the bones in his hand being crushed. Withdrawing it as soon as he could he held it under the table and nursed it with the other hand.

'Right, mate. Now we've got the intros over, let's get down to business.' Atkins shuffled in his seat and took a deep draught from his glass. 'I've got a couple of my people on site, as it were, checking out the spot where we're gonna do the deed.' He scowled. 'Well they should be, if it wasn't for this bloody weather. Mind you, I expect they'll be cosy enough.' He chuckled and took a drink from his glass.

Weeks took a gamble and asked: 'Why, where have you sent them?'

The big man, Bates, joined in the laughter. 'A bloody Buddhist retreat, whatever that is.'

Weeks was lifting his glass to his lips and only just managed to stop himself from dropping it in surprise. He slowly lowered it to the table. 'Oh?' was all he managed to say, his mouth suddenly dry.

'Yeah,' Atkins said, 'over towards mid-Sussex, somewhere near Uckfield.'

The policeman could hardly believe his ears. It had to be the same place where his DI, Sonny Russell, had gone. He gulped and chanced his arm. 'Why there?'

The little dapper man looked around nervously, his eyes darting, but Atkins was in amiable mood. 'Calm down, Sammy, Johnny's one of us now.' He punched Weeks playfully on the arm. 'I chose it because it's not far from the main Brighton line where I reckon we can do the job. I figured if they were staying in this 'ere retreat place they be able to go out on a walk and find a good spot without raising suspicion. Good cover, eh?' He winked and pinched Weeks's cheek.

'Er, yes. A great idea. Gives them an alibi.'

'Just what I thought.' Atkins sat back, pushed his hands into his jacket pockets and grinned.

Russell kept his head down and his eyes half-closed against the snow as he trotted the short distance from the shrine room back to the house. He stamped his feet on the coconut doormat and shook the snowflakes off his shoulders. Helen had stopped in front of him. 'Brr! I reckon the weather is setting in.'

'I think you're right. I can't see anyone going anywhere for a while if this carries on.'

~o~

'You can use the telephone now.' Vidyatara had come into the warmth of the blue lounge, the snowflakes melting on his bald head causing trickles of moisture to run down his face.

Baker looked up from the book in his lap, open but unread. Helen lifted her head at the same time, a glance passing between them.

'Oh thanks,' he said, closing the book and putting it on the arm of the chair. He stood and followed the monk out of the room.

Although the look had been almost imperceptible Russell had noticed it. He was puzzled but didn't comment. Instead he said, 'I thought we weren't supposed to communicate with the outside world?'

Helen shrugged her shoulders and smiled. 'Who knows?'

~o~

After receiving this unexpected piece of news Weeks had sat quietly listening to the exchange between the men. His eidetic memory was absorbing all the details and he would write up his notes later. He still couldn't believe his luck that Atkins appeared to have accepted him as part of his gang.

Atkins cleared his throat and spoke. 'Anyway, enough banter. We've got a blag to plan.'

He was just about to continue when the landlord called over from the bar: 'Tommy – phone call for you.' He was holding up the black handset. With a 'tut-tut', Atkins got up from his chair and crossed the room.

$\sim$o$\sim$

'Listen Tommy, I want to know what's going on!' Baker barked down the phone, his voice loud in the cramped hall of the monks' accommodation. 'What's that toe-rag Elsdale doing 'ere?!'

'*What*?'

'Dave Elsdale – he's here, large as life and twice as ugly.'

Atkins was taken aback. 'You sure?'

'Course I bloody am. Turned up this morning, bold as brass.'

'Have you spoken to 'im?'

'No, I bloody haven't. Anyway, what's *he* doing here? You never told me you were going to use him. I thought it was just me and Helen out here. What the bloody hell are you playing at?!'

'Now calm down.' Atkins glanced round the bar. His drinking companions were sitting in silence, just Sammy returning his gaze then quickly looking away.

'No, I bloody won't calm down. I want to know what this is all about!'

Atkins furrowed his brow. 'Listen, I'm as much in the dark as you are...'

'You sent him to check up on me.' Baker hissed.

'No, I bloody didn't.'

'Why's he here then?'

Atkins was silent.

'Well?' Baker's indignant voice echoed down the phone. There was a pause while Atkins took a deep breath and collected his thoughts. 'I'm waiting...'

'Honest, Laurie, I've no idea what 'e's doing there.' He paused. 'Let me think for a minute.' The line went quiet.

'You still there?'

'Yeah, give me a moment.' Atkins looked up. The three seated figures were staring expectantly. The barman polished a glass, feigning indifference to the man's obvious confusion.

While Baker waited for a reply, the snow was falling even more heavily outside. With no wind to stir the flakes it was building up rapidly on horizontal surfaces. Down in the valley, below *Shambhala*, the telephone wires sagged under its weight.

The line crackled. 'Listen Laurie. I'm as baffled as you are. I ain't spoken to Elsdale in weeks. I can only think 'e's on some sorta mission of 'is own.'

'What do you want me to do about him?'

The interference on the line increased. 'I think you should take 'im out.....' The rest of the sentence was drowned in static, then the line fell silent. A rotten branch on an overhanging oak had finally given way under the press of snow and fell, causing the telephone wire in the valley to break under the strain.

Baker rattled the rest on the receiver. 'Tommy? Tommy? Are you there?' Silence. 'What's going on?'

Atkins held the phone at arm's length and stared at it. He looked sheepishly at the barman. 'Line's gone dead.'

'Must be the weather.' He pointed the glass he was holding towards the window. Eddies of large white flakes were caught in the orange glow of a streetlamp.

~O~

Baker slowly replaced the handset. He furrowed his brow. Atkins had said "Take him out…" Was that all he meant to say? Or was there more? He knew Tommy was inclined to talk like a gangster but did he really mean do away with Elsdale? It seemed a bit drastic, even for Tommy and his big ideas. He would have to try to get Helen alone and discuss it with her.

# Chapter 3

**Siddhartha** was born into a noble family on the Indian-Nepalese border, 2,500 years ago. As a young man he was supplied with every luxury that wealth could provide but remained dissatisfied. Despite his family's attempts to shield him from the realities of the world outside the walls of his castle he discovered the suffering of old age and sickness and ultimate death. This shocked him and he set out to find the true meaning of life.

He became a wandering aesthete, denying himself the comforts of easy living in order to understand the mystery of birth, life and death and why humans suffer. He tried and mastered many forms of meditation, coming close to death as a result of starving himself, but still he could not fathom the truth.

So, he decided to look inward, to see if the truth lay there. He sat beneath a Bodhi tree for forty days and forty nights, searching his own heart and mind until, on the day of the full moon in May, he attained enlightenment.

From this experience he developed the idea of The Four Noble Truths: That all life is suffering

*That suffering is caused by attachment*
*That we can be freed from this attachment*
*That this can be achieved by following the Eightfold Path,*
*or Middle Way.*

RUSSELL SAT in the green lounge with a handful of the other retreatants. These included Baker, but not Helen, which disappointed him. He'd been enjoying her company until a bell sounded, and they were summoned to their study groups, with Helen staying with the group in the blue lounge.

Their teacher, for this session, was Dharmasiddhi. He was much older than the two Tibetans that Russell had come to know a little, and his grasp of English was far more rudimentary. He smiled sweetly and seemed at ease but his accent made it difficult for Russell to understand what he was trying to put across.

Russell glanced at Baker. The strange man's brow was furrowed. It could have been because he was trying to understand the teaching but somehow he didn't seem to be engaged and Russell wondered if he might be worrying about something else.

Baker *was* worrying. He couldn't give a tinker's cuss what the silly little foreigner was saying – it was all mumbo jumbo anyway. What was bothering him was what Tommy had said: 'Take him out'. He'd heard the expression, probably in some American film he'd seen at the flics, but he didn't think, despite his love of gangsters, that Tommy would use that expression without some further explanation. The trouble was their conversation had been cut off when the line went dead. But what else could he have meant? He hadn't had a chance to discuss it with Helen before they'd been split up. Elsdale hadn't made an appearance since he'd turned up that morning. Baker had seen the look on his face when their eyes met. Not just disbelief but, perhaps, fear? Well, he was right to be frightened if Tommy really did mean what he thought he'd said. The Tibetan's voiced droned on – Baker drifted off.

~o~

Atkins had returned from the bar and, still standing, picked up his glass and downed his drink. He nodded to Weeks, said, 'C'mon' to his two friends and, without a backward glance, walked out of the room and into the snow. Sammy scuttled after him, followed by Bates, his speed belying his bulk. The saloon door slammed behind them leaving Weeks open-mouthed with surprise.

'What was all that about?' he thought. He'd only been privy to one side of the telephone conversation and what he'd heard didn't make much sense. All he really knew was that someone called Dave Elsdale had turned up and Laurie, apparently Atkins's mate, was upset about it. The last command, before the line was cut off, to 'take him outside and give him a good talking to', didn't make a lot of sense. Leaving his drink he got up and headed for the door. The barman shook his head sadly. The prospect of a lively and financially rewarding evening had just disappeared.

Weeks made his way to the police station, the going difficult as the snow was settling in earnest. The desk Sergeant, Wickstead, looked up from the copy of the evening edition, nodded a greeting then went back to reading. Sitting at his desk, Weeks pulled the file on Tommy Atkins towards him and, opening the cover, started looking through the enclosed notes. On the fourth page he found what he was looking for. David Elsdale was a friend of Atkins's from childhood. He continued reading. As boys, they'd had the occasional run-in with the law – nothing serious, well, nothing proven – but as time went by each had acquired a criminal record, both for petty larceny. Atkins has spent three months in Borstal for breaking and entering whereas Elsdale had got off with a fine. In the past year, Atkins had been arrested twice but somehow got away with a caution on both occasions while his school friend appeared to have kept out of trouble, or at least not been caught. There was an address for him but it was too late to do anything about it until the morning. He closed the file and headed back to reception.

'You won't be going anywhere tonight lad,' Wickstead said. 'Take a look out the door.' Weeks walked across and pushed it open. The snow was coming down in a blizzard, an almost solid mass of white. 'I've got a nice comfy cell you can spend the night in,' the Sergeant laughed, his pepper and salt moustache bristling. 'Come round here and you can share my fish and chips first. One of the lads brought them after he'd gone off duty.'

'But….' Weeks began.

Wickstead held up the desk flap and laughed again. 'You'll be doing me a favour. He got them from The Lighthouse, round the corner, and they always give you too much. Then you can give me a chance to win some money off you with a few hands of gin rummy.'

Weeks smiled back and stepped behind the counter. 'Thanks Sarge. I am a bit peckish.'

~o~

'You say we're cut off now?' Russell was talking to Vidyatara. He'd been unable to concentrate on the teaching Dharmasiddhi was giving. With a mumbled excuse he had got up and quietly left the room. He'd found the other Tibetan in the kitchen, washing up.

'That is right. We think the telephone wire must have broken under the weight of the snow. It has happened before.'

Russell frowned. 'So it looks like we're going to be here for longer than just the weekend?'

'It is possible.'

'What about food. Have you sufficient for an extended stay?'

Vidyatara smiled for the first time. 'Yes, we have plenty. There is no need to worry.'

~o~

Baker walked silently, in stockinged feet, to the end of the corridor and tapped lightly on the door. After a few moments with no reaction he knocked again, slightly more forcefully and said, 'Dave, can I have a word?'

The door opened a crack and Elsdale's face appeared round the edge. 'What do you want?' he asked, a slight quaver in his voice.

Baker smiled. 'Just a little chat, Dave... just a little chat.'

# Chapter 4

*Thaw: to become warm enough to melt ice and snow.*

THE FOLLOWING morning things looked very different. The wind had changed in the night, swinging round to the south-west, bringing with it warm air – and rain. By midday the snow on the paths was turning to slush and the steady downpour was dissolving what was left, revealing lawns and flowerbeds. When Sonny Russell had woken he had been surprised to find that Baker, who had shared his room, had already gone downstairs. Stretching, he had looked out of his bedroom window and felt a pang of regret. He had been looking forward to an extended stay but, even at that early time of day, he could see that the snow would soon be gone and he would have to set off back to Collinghurst and routine. He was just about to start gathering his belongs together when there was a light tap on the door. 'Come in,' he said.

The door was pushed open and the face of Vidyatara peered round the edge. 'Mr Russell? There is a phone call for you.'

'Oh? I thought the phone line was down.'

Vidyatara nodded. 'It was, but it has now been fixed. A fallen branch I understand. But come quickly. The man is waiting.'

Russell picked up the handset and spoke. 'Hello?'

'Hello Sonny. John Crooks here.' The booming tones announced the pathologist. 'Have you still got a body for me to see?'

Russell grinned. 'I don't think he's going anywhere – even if he could.'

'Jolly good. The roads are clearing so I'll be setting off shortly. Will you still be there?'

The thought of an extra hour or two at *Shambhala* was not an unpleasant one. 'I'll still be here.'

~o~

Back in Collinghurst, Weeks was cradling a mug of steaming tea in his hands. He'd slept tolerably well, despite the discomfort of the spartan cell, but was looking forward to returning to his home to wash and change his clothes. The snowfall of the previous day had been less heavy in the town and already the gutters were running with melting slush. Weeks was hoping the weather had turned in the west of the county too and was looking forward to the return of his DI. After draining his mug he said goodbye to Sergeant Wickstead, turned up his coat collar and dashed out to his car.

~o~

'I can't believe you did that!' The fury came out in Helen's voice as she turned to face Baker, wrestling with the steering wheel as the car slithered and slid on the slippery road.

He looked sheepish but his voice was defiant. 'I did what Tommy told me to do. He told me to take him out.'

'For heaven's sake! That's all you heard. You said the line

went dead. He could have been going on to say anything, "Take him out for a nice drive in the car – take him out to smell the roses – take him out for…?" I don't know what… but not to do him in.' She shook her head and rubbed her cheeks vigorously with both hands.

'How was I to know?' His voice trailed off.

'So, tell me again what happened.'

Although they had reached the main road, driving was still tricky. He pulled over and stopped the car. 'Look, I did what I thought was best.'

'And that was?'

'I invited him outside. He was reluctant at first but when he saw the gun…'

'*What*? You were tooled up?'

'It wasn't *loaded*, but he didn't know that, so he went out into the garden with me. We walked along the path the monks had cleared. It had stopped snowing; the rain had started and the wind had got up. We went on past the shrine room and the shed, where I think they put the body of that monk that'd died, and into the woods beyond. He stopped and asked me what I was playing at. I told him to keep moving but he began arguing. Then he made a grab for the gun and of course, it didn't go off. We started fighting, more of a grapple really. I shoved him hard and he fell backwards, let out a cry, then went quiet. I waited, but he didn't move. I leaned forward and could see blood running down his front. Somehow he'd fallen on to a bit of broken branch and there was a sharp bit sticking out of his side.' Baker looked crestfallen. 'I didn't mean to hurt him, only put the frighteners on him.'

After a pause, Helen spoke quietly. 'Was he dead?'

'I don't know. I legged it.'

'And you just left him there?'

'What else could I do?' He held his hands out, palms upwards.

Helen put her head in her hands. 'Oh God, what have you done?' Baker reached across and touched her on the arm. She flung out her hand, slapping him away. 'You're a fool!'

'Now hang on! I only pushed him, I didn't *kill* him!'

'Yes, but the body will still be there.'

'But it was an accident.' Baker looked pathetic.

'The police won't think that!' She paused then put her hand to her mouth. 'God! That policeman – Russell.'

'What?'

'He's still there. What will he do when they find Elsdale?'

~o~

'I reckon you were right in your analysis, Sonny'. The pathologist arched his back, pushing out his ample belly and exhaling noisily, his breath condensing in a cloud in front of him. 'Blimey, it's chilly in here!' They were standing in the outhouse where the other monks had reverently placed the body of their colleague.

'You said to keep him somewhere cold,' Russell replied.

'Quite right, quite right. Anyway, I'm pretty certain there has been no foul play. As you said, it was an unfortunate accident. Look here.' He handed Russell a magnifying glass.

Taking it, the DI peered closely at the neck of the monk, lying on the rough wooden bench. He could see a definite incision where the glass shard had entered the flesh. 'And you're sure that's what killed him?'

'As sure as I can be. Talking to the other monks it seems he was healthy, with no apparent ailments. I could arrange a post mortem, but I don't think it's really necessary. I understand they have their ways of dealing with the dead so I suggest I sign the death certificate and let them get on with it – if that's okay with you?' He looked quizzically at Russell.

'I guess so.'

'Right. I'd best go back to Collinghurst. Where can I wash up?'

~o~

Russell returned to the warmth of the dining room in *Shambhala* while his colleague went to the bathroom. Sanghaketu had prepared a hearty vegetable soup and there were chunks of freshly baked bread to go with it. Although some had already left there was still a handful of retreatants sitting down to eat. Russell was hoping he'd see Helen but she was not around. When Vidyatara came into the room he asked if he'd seen her.

'Ah. She left early, as soon as the road was clear enough.'

'I didn't know she had a car.'

'She went off with Mr Baker. The one who was sharing your room.'

Russell was puzzled. 'Oh, I didn't realise they were friends…'

The monk shrugged, his face impassive.

'What about the man who turned up on Saturday, Elsdale, wasn't it?'

'He's gone too. He must have left early.' Giving a little bow, he turned, went into the kitchen and was soon deep in conversation with Sanghaketu.

Although he had barely touched his soup, Russell slid the bowl away and sat back in his chair, frowning. This turn of events had come as something of a surprise. He thought that he had developed a rapport with Helen and was upset that she had left without a goodbye. Then he remembered something. The previous evening, when Vidyatara had told Baker that he could use the telephone, a look passed between the man and Helen, fleeting, but definite. He thought hard, trying to recall if there had been anything else but that seemed to be all. Perhaps he had been mistaken. He sighed and pulled the bowl back towards him. He was just about to take a mouthful of the steaming broth when he stopped, the spoon poised. He realised he wasn't hungry any more. The events of the past couple of days were jumbled in his mind and he needed some air.

Russell shrugged his arms into the sleeves of his overcoat and pulled his hat firmly on to his head. Opening the back door he could see that the rain was easing so he set off down the path, passing the shrine room and the outhouse where the body of the monk lay. With no clear plan he headed towards the woods, at the back of the garden, his mind churning and his feet on autopilot. Turning right, he made his way down a flight of wooden edged steps, holding the handrail and being careful not to fall on the slippery surface. He continued on through the woods, his mind turning over the events of the past few days; his feet finding their way along the winding path. The fresh air was clearing his head and he felt something was coming forward, from the back of his mind when suddenly, he tripped over a branch, stumbled and almost fell onto Elsdale's prone body. Regaining his balance he let out a gasp as he saw the jagged branch sticking out of his side. Immediately he knelt, regardless of the melted snow seeping through the knee of his trousers, and pressed his fingers against the prone man's neck. After a moment he could feel a faint fluttering. He was still alive. Quickly rising he turned and ran back to the house. Not waiting to speak to anyone he ran to the front door and out into the car park, just in time to see the pathologist manoeuvring his car. He wrenched open the driver's door.

'What the…?!' Crooks began.

'Sorry, but this is an emergency. Quick, follow me!'

Crooks stopped the car, heaved his bulk out of the seat and followed Russell as he disappeared back through the house.

'You're right. He is still alive – just. Amazing as it looks like he's been here for some time.' They were leaning over Elsdale, with three of the monks hovering behind them. 'We've got to get him indoors before hypothermia sets in – if it hasn't already.'

'But what about that wood splinter?' Russell said, pointing to the bloody protrusion.

'We'll just have to take the chance. It must have missed his heart but God knows what other damage it could have done.' He turned to the monks. 'One of you fetch towels. I think there could be a lot of blood.' Dhamasiddhi turned and ran back to the house. 'And you two,' he gestured at Sanghaketu and Vidyatara, 'you'll have to help me lift him.'

As they bent and gently eased the unconscious man away from the fallen branch, Dharmasiddhi returned with a bundle of towels. Crooks pressed one against the front of the man's side, where fresh blood had started oozing out of the wound and, as the man was lifted, he did the same at his back.

Crooks held the towels in place, cradling the man in an embrace. 'Sonny, clear a table in the kitchen, there's no time to take him upstairs.'

Russell trotted ahead and into the dining room where the remaining retreatants were standing around, looking baffled. 'Quick! Move this stuff!' The tone in his voice galvanised them into action and within seconds there was a clear surface. As the two monks gently laid Elsdale on the table, Crooks slid his arm out from beneath him and leant forward, his ear to the man's mouth. 'He's breathing – but we need to get him to hospital. Can someone ring for an ambulance?'

Karunavadra strode into the room. 'I have already done it. They are on their way.'

Amazingly, considering the weather conditions, the ambulance arrived in less than 20 minutes. The ambulance men worked efficiently and quickly had Elsdale bandaged and laid on a stretcher. The consensus was that he was lucky and the splinter of wood may have missed his organs. However, his breathing was very shallow and they were anxious to get him to the hospital in Uckfield.

$\sim$O$\sim$

Russell and Crooks sat in the *Shambhala* dining room, cradling mugs of tea. 'What do think, Sonny?' Crooks asked.

Russell leaned back, a puzzled look on his face. After a pause he spoke, 'I'm not sure. He may have tripped and fallen. But somehow I don't think so.'

Crooks cocked his head to one side and stroked his chin. 'Really?'

'In order to fall heavily enough he would have had to have been running, and in that case, would most likely have fallen *forward*.'

'Yes, I see what you mean.'

'I think it's more likely that he was pushed – hard, and fell backwards, bashing his head at the same time.'

'Hence the contusion on his skull.'

'Quite.'

'So the question is: who pushed him?'

'I've got an idea.'

'Oh yes?'

Mmm. I think so. I'll need to talk to the monks.'

'Do you need me anymore?'

'No, that's fine, John. You get back off to Collinghurst. I'll join you later.'

# Chapter 5

*The **London, Brighton and South Coast Railway** (**LB&SCR**) known as "the Brighton line", was a railway company in the United Kingdom from 1846 to 1922. Its territory formed a rough triangle, with London at its apex, practically the whole coastline of Sussex as its base, and a large part of Surrey.*

'I'VE CHECKED those addresses, Sir, and they don't appear to exist.' DC Weeks looked baffled, his mop of dark curly hair, flopping over a furrowed brow.

Russell was leaning back in his chair, hands clasped behind his head, and whistling a snatch of Junior Parker's *Mystery Train*. He sat forward. 'I'm not surprised. I wondered about that Laurie Baker when I first set eyes on him. He seemed such a strange little man with that odd haircut.'

Russell had returned to the police station at Collinghurst after a slow but uneventful journey along the slippery roads. The monks at Shambhala had furnished him with the address for Baker but Week's search had thrown up a blank – the place didn't exist. He'd also got Helen's address and was rather upset to find that it was also false. He had wondered about her since he heard she'd left early with Baker. He was reluctant to admit that he might have misjudged her. He put the notion out of his mind.

'Anyway, tell me about your new career as a getaway driver.' Russell's eyes sparkled with mischief.

Weeks all but blushed. 'W-what do you mean?' he stammered.

The DI chuckled. 'Just pulling your leg, son. I think you did well to get into Atkins's confidence. When do you think you'll be seeing him again?'

'I don't know. He left the pub in such a hurry after the phone call; he didn't say anything about another meeting.'

'Tell me again what you heard.' Russell knew that the younger man would have perfect recall of what was said.

'Well, although I only heard one side of the conversation – Atkins's – it sounded pretty heated. It seemed that Laurie…'

'Ah, Laurie Baker…'

'Yes, Laurie Baker. He was concerned because Elsdale had suddenly appeared and he couldn't understand why he was there.'

Russell scowled. 'I can quite understand that. Elsdale turned up unannounced on Saturday morning. We had a chat and he said his train had stopped at Buxted because the line was blocked.'

'But why did he make his way to *Shambhala*?' Weeks asked.

'He said he'd seen a notice saying there was a retreat and he assumed that the monks would give him shelter. Anyway, go on.'

'Atkins said he thought Elsdale was on some sort of mission on his own. Then he said,' – Weeks looked at his notes – '"Take him outside and give him a good talking to". The trouble is, I think the line went dead before Elsdale heard the whole sentence.'

Russell let out a snort. 'That explains it. Apparently a branch fell on the telephone line – presumably just at the critical moment.'

'How much of the sentence do you think he *did* hear?'

There was a pause, then, 'I wouldn't be surprised if all he heard was "Take him out",' Russell said, in his best James Cagney impersonation.

Weeks grinned. 'That was rather good, Sir.'

'Thank you. Anyway, I reckon Baker got the wrong end of the stick…'

'…And Elsdale ended up on it.'

Russell raised his eyebrows. 'Quite. Going back a bit, when I was away, did you say you told DI Parker about your meeting with Atkins?'

'That's right, Sir. As usual, he dismissed it. Talked about being conned by a con.'

'Typical. Anyway, *I* think you're on to something, and you have my full backing.'

'But what about the Super?'

'You leave Superintendent Stout to me. Now, you might have been lucky so far in gaining Atkins's trust but have you considered what you'll say if he asks what you do for a living?'

Weeks looked thoughtful. 'Only vaguely. Do you have any suggestions, Sir?'

'Actually, yes. I've given it some thought and come up with an idea. How about you say you worked for a family firm?'

'Ye-es.'

'You had a falling out with, say, your father, and you started filching money from the company. How does that sound?'

'I like the idea of that.'

'Then you got found out.'

'But wouldn't it have to go to court, then get in the papers?'

'Not necessarily. It's quite possible they'd want it hushed up – wouldn't want the publicity.'

'Yes, I see.'

'Then you could tell Tommy you were between jobs.'

'D'you think he'd buy it, Sir?' Weeks still looked doubtful.

'I don't see why not. If he started digging I'm sure we could provide some evidence. But, to be honest, I don't think he will. He's taken quite a shine to you. But just in case, you'd better come up with a name and a place, far enough away that he's unlikely to have heard of it.' Russell gave a big smile. He pulled back his sleeve and looked at his watch. 'Meanwhile, the sun's nearly over the yardarm. I think it's time you took your crossword off to the Queen's Head. I've a feeling that our friend Tommy Atkins is likely to turn up there before too long.'

~O~

Sure enough, Weeks had taken only a few sips from his pint and filled in a couple of clues in his crossword when the door of the saloon bar opened and a smiling Atkins breezed in, on his own this time.

''Ello cocker,' he said, smiling at Weeks. 'Ready for another?' Weeks gave him the thumbs up. Atkins marched up to the bar. 'Two pints and two chasers please landlord.' He carried the drinks over to the corner table on a tin tray. The tray was printed with a picture of a toucan balancing a pint of stout on its beak. Atkins sat down and punched Weeks playfully on the arm. 'Good to see you, mate. What you been up to?'

Weeks was taken aback. 'Me? Oh, you know, this and that, ducking and diving.'

Atkins's manner changed. He looked directly at Weeks. 'What *is* it that you actually do?' he asked.

'Er, I'm between jobs at the moment.' He was glad that he'd had that talk with his boss.

'Oh yeah? Well, what was the last one?'

Weeks lowered his voice. 'It's a bit awkward really. I don't like to talk about it.'

Atkins leaned towards Weeks until his face was only inches away. 'Listen chum. I've invited you to take part in somethin' that's gonna earn you a lot of money for very little effort. I don't want no nasty surprises so you'd better tell me about it – *awkward* or not.'

'Yes of course, Tommy.'

'So spill the beans.' Atkins sat back and took a drink.

'We-ell, it was like this. When I left school my dad wanted me to work for the family firm.'

Atkins cut in. 'An' what was that?'

'Stockbrokers.'

'Blimey! I thought you was bright.'

'It was only a small firm, Holloway and Son.'

'But still…'

'Anyway, I wasn't keen but he insisted, so I gave in and joined the firm.' Weeks was starting to enjoy his new fictitious life and was getting into his stride. 'I stuck it out for a while, but just couldn't get enthusiastic about it. I was dead relieved when I got called up to do my National Service.'

'Yeah, you said you'd been in the Army.' This part at least was true.

'I enjoyed my time and was sad to leave.'

'Didn't you want to join up as a regular?'

'No, I'd had enough. But also, I didn't want to go back to the firm.'

'What did you do?'

'I had to go back.'

'But why?'

'Oh you know, family pressures…'

'What a bugger.'

'Right.'

''Ow come you ain't there no more?'

Weeks took a deep draught from his glass, then put it down carefully on a beermat, bearing the phrase, *Guinness is good for you!* 'I just didn't want to be there. Didn't know how I was going to stick it out.'

Atkins leaned forward, totally absorbed by the story. 'How did you?'

'Embezzlement.'

'You what?'

Weeks realised he might have gone too far. 'Oh you know, started filching money.'

'Really?' Atkins beamed his amusement.

Weeks relaxed into his chair, his arm thrown casually over the back. 'It was easy really. Because I was a member of the family I handled quite large sums of cash. I found I could siphon some off without it being noticed, small amounts at first, gradually getting bigger.'

'What happened?'

'I got found out. Probably because I got too greedy.'

Atkins whistled. 'Christ!' He paused, looking thoughtful. 'Why ain't you inside?'

'I should be but the family didn't want it to go to court. Made me pay back the money, then booted me out.'

'Shit! No wonder you could do with some dosh.' Weeks gave his best cheeky puppy grin and inwardly breathed a sigh of relief. He reckoned he'd got away with it. Atkins took a swig from his glass then grinned. 'You old dog.' He had obviously accepted the yarn. 'Anyway,' he said, 'sorry about running out on you last night. I 'eard something that gave me a bit of a shock. Think it's sorted now.'

'Really?' Weeks said mildly.

'Yeah, I reckon. Anyway, you still up for the job?'

Weeks was about to reply when the door swung open and a little man with a distinctive haircut bustled in. He looked round, and spotting Atkins, made straight for their table. Seeing Weeks he scowled. 'Who's this?'

Atkins grinned. 'Laurie mate. Relax. Meet Johnny.' He lowered his voice. 'He's gonna 'elp us with the job.'

The other man sat down slowly but looked suspiciously at Weeks: 'All right?' Weeks nodded in return. 'Tommy. Can I have a word – in private?'

'Nah, don't worry about Johnny.' He put his arm round Weeks's shoulders and grinned. 'It's okay, 'e's one of us. He won't say nuffink, will yer?'

'Course not.' Weeks tapped the side of his nose with his forefinger. 'Mum's the word.' Inside he was quaking but he couldn't believe his luck. This must be the very man who had been at the retreat with his DI.

Atkins spoke again: 'What's so important then, Laurie? Did you suss out the railway?'

'Afraid not, the line was blocked by snow when I was there. I'll have to go back once it's cleared.' He paused, and then with some reluctance went on: 'I think we might have a bit of a problem.'

Atkins stiffened. 'What's that then?'

'You know I told you on the phone that Elsdale had turned up?'

'Yeah.'

'And you told me to "Take him out"?'

'*What*?'

'You told me to…'

'Yes I 'eard what you said!' Atkins said sharply. 'Except I said, "take 'im outside and give 'im a good talking to".'

Baker blanched. 'Oh God! I didn't hear all of that. The line went dead.'

Atkins leaned forward and grabbed the other man by his shirt front. 'What 'ave you done?' he growled.

'I think I killed him.' Baker had turned white.

Weeks gazed from one to the other in horrified fascination.

'*What*?!' Atkins barked, through gritted teeth. Baker then described the tussle in the woods behind *Shambhala* and how Elsdale had fallen on the branch. 'And you left him?'

'What else could I do?'

'And you're sure he was dead?'

'I don't know,' Baker said, wretchedly.

'That's just bleedin' wonderful. What the 'ell are we gonna do now?'

There was silence for a few moments then Weeks spoke, 'Er, do you know what hospital they're likely to have taken him to?'

Baker turned quickly towards him. 'Why?' he spat.

Weeks thought rapidly. 'Oh, er, I might know a nurse who works over in mid-Sussex.'

Baker's eyes narrowed. 'Who said it was over in mid-Sussex?'

'Er, you did. You said it happened at *Shambhala*, near Buxted.' Weeks was sweating but trying hard not to show it.

Baker relaxed and sat back in his chair. 'Mm. Yes, so I did.' A pause. 'Do yer think yer might be able to find out if 'e's, you know, dead, then?'

'I can give it a try.'

Atkins slapped Weeks on the back. 'I told you 'e was one of us.'

~O~

'So they bought your line about knowing a nurse?' Russell asked.

'They seemed to, Sir.' The two detectives were back in Russell's office. 'Have we heard how Elsdale is doing?'

'He's still alive – just. He'd lost a lot of blood and lying there, in the cold and wet, for so long had made him very weak. If he does survive, he won't be the same.'

'Are we going to bring Baker in?'

'No, I don't think so, not just yet.'

'Is that because we don't have enough evidence?'

'Partly that, but mainly I don't want to rattle Atkins and his cohorts. From what we know and, thanks to you what we've found out, they seem to be planning a big job. But, if Elsdale doesn't make it, I reckon the Super will demand we make an arrest and charge somebody with murder. So let's hope he does survive.'

# Chapter 6

*An Oast House or hop kiln is a building, often cylindrical,
designed for drying hops as part of the process in
brewing beer.*

RUSSELL RUBBED at the condensation on the small windowpane and peered out. The heavy grey skies of the past few days had been replaced with lighter cloud and glimpses of blue; not enough to "patch a sailor's trousers" but a sign that the freak winter conditions were gone and spring had returned.

He lived in a converted railway carriage, called *Shinglesea*, which was grounded just inland from the beach, behind a shingle ridge. The Victorian coach had been there since the 1920s, made redundant when superseded by a more modern design. There were several such dwellings lining the track, along with other unique cottages. A second carriage sat close behind his with a lean-to extension on the back, together providing compact but adequate accommodation. The DI shared it with his rough-coated Jack Russell terrier, Aggie, who accompanied him nearly everywhere. He had missed her while he was at *Shambhala* and suspected that Weeks had been over-generous with treats while looking after her. 'Come on Ag, time for a blow on the beach before we head off to work. You need to run off some of that podge.' The small dog cocked her head to one side and looked at him expectantly.

The two crossed the strip of pasture, close-cropped by rabbits, and climbed up on to the ridge. As they crested the top the fresh breeze caused Russell's hair to swirl round his head like a dervish and ruffled the dog's shaggy coat. The tide was out and they made their way down towards the sea, crunching across the shingle and on to the sand left smooth by the receding water. Aggie loved being there and ran in huge circles, ears flat against her head, tail straight out behind and going like the wind. 'Mad dog!' Russell chuckled. They set off east for half a mile before Russell whistled to the dog and they turned back, heading into the stiff westerly. The walk had cleared Russell's head and he felt ready to face another day. As they climbed back over the ridge he could see a car making its way gingerly along the rutted track. He waved as it stopped outside his home. Weeks had come to pick him up.

As the car bumped slowly around the potholes the detectives discussed the case. 'When's your next meeting with our felon?'

'Atkins?'

'Yes, him.'

'He said he'd be in the pub again this evening.'

'Jolly good. I suppose I should let the Super know what's been going on – how you've managed to gain their confidence and be accepted as one of the gang.'

The car jerked as a wheel dropped into a particularly deep rut and Weeks wrestled with the steering. 'Haven't you told him, Sir?'

'Mmm, not yet. I thought I'd leave it for a while, see how we progressed. But, I suppose if I don't tell him he might find out anyway.'

'Yes, Bonnie and Clyde might tell him.'

Russell chuckled. 'Detective Inspector Parker and Detective Constable Barrow to you, Constable.'

'Sorry, Sir.'

'That's okay. But you're quite right. They're more than likely to tell him – if only to get one over on me. I'll go and see Superintendent Stout when we get in.'

~o~

'So DC Weeks has gained the confidence of this Atkins fellow?' Russell nodded. 'How come I haven't heard about it before? Oh yes, you've been away.' Stout grinned.

'That right, Sir. On retreat.'

'But surely he could have told DI Parker?'

'He did try to tell him, Sir, but Bonnie – I mean Parker – suggested that Atkins was conning him.'

'And you don't agree?'

'No, Sir. I trust Weeks's judgement implicitly. He has a photographic memory and everything he's told me about the meetings rings true.'

'How do you suggest we proceed?'

Russell smiled inwardly. He was pleased to see that the Super was taking it seriously. 'I think Weeks should be allowed to continue with the meetings and find out exactly when and where this job is planned before we do anything else.'

'But what about this unfortunate...' Stout looked down at his notes, 'this Elsdale fellow? Do we have an update on his condition?'

'I've been on to the hospital in Uckfield this morning and he's off the critical list but is still very poorly.'

'Is he going to die do you reckon?'

'Hard to say, Sir. They wouldn't commit, but reading between the lines it seems like he might pull through.'

Stout harrumphed. 'Let's hope he does or a murder investigation would put an end to your clandestine operation. Now, before you go, do you think Weeks is safe, meeting these people, or should we put some sort of surveillance in place?' Russell paused for a moment. Stout was impatient. 'Well?'

'No, I don't think we should, Sir. It's amazing that Atkins has accepted Weeks so readily. If there is even a suggestion that he is connected with the police…'

'Point taken. Very well, tell Weeks to continue but for goodness sake, tell him to be careful.

'You can be sure I will, Sir.'

~O~

'Right, Stout says you can carry on with your meetings with Atkins.' Weeks tossed back his mop of hair and grinned. 'But for heaven's sake, *be careful!* I don't want anything happening to you. Don't forget that business with Wolfgang Müller last year.'

A shadow passed across Weeks's face. He well remembered the little German with the withered leg and how he'd been forced to sail to France with him. Then the show-down in the barn in St-Valery-sur-Somme, when he'd just managed to stop Wolfgang from committing another murder and had almost lost his own life. 'Don't worry, Sir. I'll be careful.'

'You'd better be. I don't want to have to start training up another DC.' He pulled back his sleeve and looked at his watch. 'Right. Time for a cuppa. Then you'd better write down what's happened up to now, so I've got something on paper to show the Super.'

When Weeks had gone, Russell leaned back in his chair and linked his fingers behind his head. Quietly he whistled Rodgers and Hart's, *Bewitched, Bothered and Bewildered*. He was glad that Stout had given the go-ahead for Weeks to continue with his meetings. He'd stuck his neck out, suggesting that there shouldn't be any surveillance, but what if Atkins turned nasty? It was a dilemma, as he was pretty sure the man would quickly smell a rat if Russell put anyone in to watch him, but what if he didn't? He had full confidence in Weeks's abilities but couldn't help having a worry, niggling at the back of his mind.

~o~

Weeks was sitting in his usual corner of the Queen's Head when the street door swung open and Atkins swanned in with Sammy and Butcher Bates in tow. They collected drinks from the bar and made their way over to the table.

'Well? Did you speak to your nursey friend? Is 'e dead?' Atkins took a deep draught from his pint glass and waited.

'Yes. I spoke to her. Looks like he's going to pull through.'

Atkins banged his glass down on the table and clapped his hands together. 'Hooray! Fan-bloody-tastic! I might've fallen out wiv 'im but I don't want 'im dead.'

'I thought you'd be pleased,' Weeks smiled.

Bates spoke, 'You were right, Tommy.'

'Course I was. I knew 'e'd be okay. That's why I've sent Laurie down to Uckfield again to check out the lie of the land. No bloody snow this time.'

Sammy looked round furtively. 'Did Helen go with him?'

'Nah. She's busy elsewhere.' He looked pointedly at Weeks.

'And don't ask. Helen's nuffink to do with you.' Weeks remained silent.

Sammy took a sip of his drink, wiped his mouth with the back of his hand then asked: 'Have you decided on a date for the job, Tommy?'

This time Atkins looked round the bar. The handful of regulars were intent on their drinks and the barman was studiously polishing a glass. Atkins lowered his voice. 'I ain't quite made up me mind yet. It'll 'ave to be a Tuesday, cos that's when the banks send the cash up from Brighton. But until Laurie comes back with the info I don't know which Tuesday it will be. Soon though.' He let the words hang in the air for a few moments, then spoke again, louder this time. 'So, you'll just 'ave to wait.'

~o~

Laurie Baker sat by the window on the train to Brighton, a copy of the *Daily Sketch* open in his lap. He had the compartment to himself and the paper remained unread as he stared out of the window at the scenery passing by. The snow had all but gone and there were signs of spring: buds on the trees and the occasional new-born lamb with its mother. They passed a farmstead with the distinctive conical shape of an oast house, topped with a white-painted wooden cowl in the yard and a Ferguson tractor trundling off to the fields. He found it hard to believe that only a few days before he'd been snowed in at that blasted retreat centre. He shuddered as he remembered the struggle in the grounds and Elsdale falling on the wooden spike. Tommy had assured him that the man was going to be okay, that he'd pull through, but he still felt sick when he thought about it. Ah well, what would be would be. He just hoped Tommy was right. Meanwhile he had a job to do.

As the train approached Buxted Baker pulled the blinds down on the corridor side. He wanted the compartment to himself. The train drew into the station. Doors slammed. He heard voices outside and slumped in the corner of the compartment, feigning sleep. The door slid open and through half-closed eyes he saw a woman lean in. 'Oh, sorry,' she said and slid the door closed again. He smiled as the engine whistled and the carriage jerked as they set off again.

Now he sat up, alert, as the train passed through the landscape. He knew it wouldn't be long before they approached Uckfield. He looked at his wristwatch. Five minutes, and they should be there. Sure enough, just as Tommy had said, the train slowed to a walking pace and as he peered through the grimy, soot-speckled window, he heard a blast on the locomotive's whistle and saw the gated crossing over a rough track. He sat back and waited for the train to pull into the station.

Baker slung the strap of his khaki haversack over his shoulder, got off the train and loitered until the few passengers had left, the train had departed and the porter had disappeared into his office. He made his way to the end of the platform and, looking back to check he hadn't been observed, walked down the slope and along the side of the railway track. He had consulted the timetable before he had left and he knew there wasn't another train due for a while so he was quite safe. He walked along by the side of the evenly spaced sleepers, stumbling over lumps of ballast but even so, it took barely 10 minutes to reach the crossing.

A single track was bisected by the railway line. This was Hempstead Lane. To the west it turned into a metalled road which eventually led to a residential area backing on to the High Street. But in the eastern direction a rutted track, bordered by grass and weeds, went into Hempstead Forest. Then it meandered through a series of narrow byways until finally reaching the B2102 near the small village of Framfield. This was of great interest. Tommy had said that was the direction in which they would make their getaway after robbing the train.

Baker lifted the latch on the gate and pushed it open, the bottom scraping on the long grass. There was a sign on the inside of the gate, he smiled. Leaving the gate open would be the least of

> **LBSC Rly**
> PENALTY
> FOR LEAVING THIS GATE OPEN
> 40 SHILLINGS

the authority's worries, after they had carried out the job. But for now, he pushed the gate closed, latched it securely and set off along the track. The surface was uneven, made up of compacted soil, rubble and pieces of broken brick. The track climbed steadily causing Baker to lean forward and breathe more laboriously. After a while he stopped and took a piece of paper out of the pocket of his jacket. Unfolding it he studied the neat map that Billy had drawn on it. It showed the railway line and the crossing, a spidery network of lanes that ran through the forest and a boldly drawn cross. This marked an isolated farmhouse that Tommy had found, which was where Baker was heading.

The forest was thickly wooded, stark twisted branches pointing skywards like witches' fingers. Even without a full covering of leaves, the trunks and crooked limbs of the beech and chestnut trees still made it quite gloomy. Baker shuddered. He was a townie and he did not like the countryside. Plus it was quiet – hardly a bird had made itself heard. He preferred pavements and streetlights, not rutted tracks and trees. Still, he knew that this isolated spot was perfect for what Tommy was planning and, boy, had he planned it well. He might seem naïve and a bit cocky, especially when he'd had a few. But he had learned his lessons from Billy and Tel when he worked with them on the Eastcastle Street robbery: plan everything meticulously, and stick to that plan. The blasted freak weather had set the timetable back by a few days but that could not be helped. At least the snow had not lasted and now he could get on with looking over the area. The lane levelled out and 10 minutes after leaving the level crossing he came to a gate, closing off the end of the track and opening on to the junction with a slightly less weedy road. He consulted the map. Right would take him along Sandy Lane, which soon joined the B2102 at Framfield and then back into Uckfield. But pushing the gate open he turned left along Spurlings Lane, and after a few hundred yards, left again on to Etchingwood Lane. He passed the entrance to a substantial house; the lane curved round to the right then there was a sharp bend to the left. Just after this he found what he was looking for.

Set well back from the road, down a long stony drive was a small, run-down farmhouse with a group of outbuildings. These included a large and a smaller barn, all well-screened by thick conifers. It had seen better days and was just as Billy had described it. No one had lived there for years, apparently – some dispute over ownership – which meant no one was likely to be interested in it either. How Atkins had found this out, he had not let on to Baker, but he assured him that it would be the perfect hideout.

The farmhouse was four square; two first-floor windows and two windows either side of the porch. The walls were rendered, coloured bilious brown, the paint peeling in places. A rickety five-bar gate, between straggly hedges, barred the way, a rusty chain and padlock keeping trespassers out. This was no obstacle to Baker. From his jacket pocket he produced a bunch of skeleton keys. Carefully selecting one, he inserted it in the slot in the padlock and twisted it a few times until the lock clicked open. He removed the chain and pushed the gate wide enough to slip through then pushed the gate shut again, securing it with the chain and the padlock. He didn't close it fully this time but it would look locked to the casual observer.

He walked up the stony track to the house then climbed the single step to the front door. Again, expertly selecting a key he put it in the lock. The lock was a little stiff, but with a bit of persuasion, the key turned and, with an eerie creak, the door swung open. The room was sparsely furnished with a sagging sofa and a pair of armchairs of indeterminate colour, a wonky table and four battered wooden chairs. Dust motes danced in the shafts of light from the low sun that filtered in through the grimy window. Opposite was a fireplace with an ornate tiled surround, the grate filled with a jumble of sticks, probably from a last year's rook's nest on the chimney pot. Dumping his haversack on the table he set off to explore. An open doorway from the main room led to the kitchen. Beneath the window looking over the yard at the back of the house was a deep Belfast sink. A single cold tap dripped rhythmically, leaving an orange stain on the sink where the water fell. On the opposite wall was a rusty range, which had probably been black at one time. It had an open grate to one side, an oven door and single square hotplate. Baker rubbed his hands. At least he'd be able to have a brew and a hot meal. Next to it was another door. Turning the handle he pushed it open, revealing a flight of stone steps descending into the gloom. A damp, musty odour rose from a cellar. He shuddered and quickly closed it. Wandering across to the other side of the kitchen he unlocked the back door and wandered out into the yard in search of firewood.

# Chapter 7

## The previous year

*Newhaven is a town in the Lewes district of East Sussex.*
*It lies at the mouth of the River Ouse and is a port*
*for ferries to Dieppe.*

WOLFGANG MÜLLER sat disconsolately on the helmsman's seat in the wheelhouse of *Moonshine*. Well, although he still thought of it as *Moonshine*, the name painted on the stern now read *Cormorant* and the boat had been given a complete repaint from white to dull black.

When he had escaped capture by disappearing into the fog outside Saint Valery the previous year, he had set off blindly in *Moonshine*, out to sea, and then turned south-west, heading vaguely towards Dieppe and, more by luck than judgement, had stumbled upon a narrow creek. As the fog gradually thinned he nosed the boat between the muddy reed-topped banks and found a perfect berth, away from prying eyes. He had lain low, constantly on the alert, looking out for the French police who were undoubtedly seeking him. After several days, when he had seen no one and his supplies were running low, he climbed over the gunwale of the craft, stepped on to the springy marram grass and set off to explore his surroundings.

Dragging his withered leg, he found it hard going but gritted his teeth and pressed on. In a short time a collection of cottages came into view either side of a narrow, metalled road. He walked more easily now and he could see at the far end a *bar-tabac*. He pushed the door open and made his way inside. A solitary figure sat on a stool at the zinc topped bar, with the patron standing behind, polishing a glass with a tea towel. The man on the stool turned his head and they both looked towards the stranger. Wolfgang was prepared to be recognised but was relieved to find that neither displayed more than idle curiosity.

'*Bojour, Monsieur. Que voulez-vous boire*?' the barman asked.

Wolfgang thought quickly. 'Ah, I'll have a beer, please.' His French, though accented, was good enough to pass muster. The barman nodded and turned to the shelf behind him. Adeptly he flicked the top off a bottle and placed it next to a glass on the counter. Wolfgang slid awkwardly on to a bar stool, the other customer coughed and turned back to reading a week-old copy of *L'Equipe*, opened out in front of him. The barman went back to his polishing.

Wolfgang had almost drained his glass before the barman spoke again. 'Are you staying nearby?'

He thought quickly. 'Quite close.' Not wanting to admit where he had actually come from he said, 'I've just brought my boat up from Cherbourg. I need to do some work on it.'

His neighbour looked up from the newspaper and moved the smoldering *Gitanes Maïs* to the corner of his mouth. 'Oh yes? What are you planning to do?'

Wolfgang felt a little uncomfortable but replied, 'She needs a repaint.'

'Why didn't you get it done while you were in Cherbourg?'

'Er, the yard wanted too much to do it.' He made a rubbing gesture, between thumb and forefinger. 'I thought I'd paint her myself.'

'I might be able to help you there,' the man said. 'What colour were you thinking of?'

'Er, black.'

The man grinned. 'You're in luck. I've got several cans of black. Do you need a hand doing it?'

Wolfgang was sweating but tried not to show his discomfort. 'That would be helpful.'

The man grinned even more widely. 'Good. There's not much work around here. I could do with earning a bit of money.'

~o~

His name was Marcel, an odd-job man, simple, but steady and apparently without curiosity. Wolfgang knew that the *gendarmerie* would be on the lookout for him but whether the hamlet was too remote, or somehow they had missed it, for several days no one came seeking him. Gradually he relaxed in Marcel's company. The man was a good, neat worker and knew what he was doing. After a day busying themselves on the boat, they would make their way to the *bar-tabac* where the owner would happily supply them with a meal and Wolfgang started to feel secure. After a few days the boat had gone from white to black and Marcel, showing surprising artistic talent, had painted the legend, *Cormorant* on the transom. When the project was completed, Wolfgang paid him off, giving him a little more than he'd asked for but not so much as to appear suspiciously over-generous.

As had become his custom, Wolfgang made his way to the hamlet that evening to have a meal. He had just stepped off the sandy path between the reeds, relieved to be walking on the easier tarmac of the road. He had his head down, concentrating on dragging his foot but when he looked up he saw the unmistakable shape of a police Citroën parked outside the bar. His stomach lurched and he stumbled, just saving himself from falling. Turning on his heel, he made his way back to the boat as quickly as he was able.

Wolfgang spent nerve-racking minutes with the engine ticking over until the tide lifted the boat off the bottom. To save time he sawed through the mooring line with his knife then clambered back into the wheelhouse. He banged the gear lever into reverse and opened the throttle wide; the propeller churned up mud and silt, causing whirlpools and eddies on the surface of the water. The boat sat vibrating then suddenly came unstuck from the mud and slowly started to move out of the berth. As it speeded up he turned the craft round and headed into the Channel. Again he'd made a lucky escape. Setting a course for England he studied the chart. He needed somewhere on the south coast, preferably towards the east, where he could hole up. Then he would be in a better position to plan the liberation of his brother, Ludwig, who was in prison on a murder charge. He needed to steer clear of the area around Compass Point and Nottery Quay, where, even with the changes to the boat, she might still be recognised. With his finger he traced the coastline, further along to the west, and was drawn to the river Ouse at Newhaven. He hoped that he would be able to find a small boatyard where he could pay cash, no questions would be asked and, most importantly, the boat would not be recognised. With the decision made, he plotted the course and swung the helm heading north-west by west.

~o~

'Describe this man to me.' Inspecteur Guillaume Bruissement stood in the doorway to the bar, his bulk filling the frame and his luxuriant moustache bristling as he spoke. Marcel was just about to open his mouth when Bruissement held up his finger. 'No, let me tell you. A little man, probably speaking good, but accented French. He has a withered leg, with an iron brace which makes walking difficult. Am I right?'

The man nodded, dumbounded. After a moment he spoke. 'But how did you know?'

'He's wanted for murder – not for one but for three.' Marcel looked about to pass out. 'His brother, his accomplice, is in custody in England, but we have been seeking Wolfgang Müller for several days now. We thought the trail had gone cold but it looks like we've caught up with him.' He looked towards the patron. 'So he comes in here for his meals? Were you not suspicious?'

The barman looked down and mumbled, 'He seemed so pleasant. Always polite – and generous.'

'Pfff! It was just an act. Where is he now?'

'Probably on his boat.'

'When did you last see him?'

'He came for a meal yesterday. I was expecting him again this evening.'

Bruissement turned to Marcel. 'And you. When did you see him?'

'We finished painting earlier today. He paid me off this afternoon and I came here. He said he would join me later.'

'You'd better show me where this boat is – and quickly. I don't want him to give us the slip again.'

Marcel led the way out of the bar and along the village street. They hurried between the houses then, at the end of the tarmac, on to the sandy path between the reeds, Bruissement following with two gendarmes close behind. After a few minutes they reached the edge of the land where the water gently lapped. Marcel stopped and threw up his hands. 'He's gone!'

'What?!'

'He was here. I swear it!' He crouched and held up a length of rope, its cut end frayed. 'Look!'

The Inspecteur snatched it from him, his face contorted with anger. 'I don't believe it!' he bellowed. 'He's done it again!'

~O~

Since then, Wolfgang had indeed found a quiet boatyard, tucked away upriver from Newhaven. It was the sort of establishment that had never seen better times, with rotting hulks sitting in the mud, piles of split and mouldering timber and tangles of rope and chain lying around, ready to trip the unwary. But it suited Wolfgang perfectly. The owner, Paddy Dickens, was more than happy to accept ready cash, giving him a snug berth for his boat and not enquiring why he needed it. Nor did he ask why the little man with the withered leg and unnaturally precise way of speaking was apparently happy to spend long periods hunkered down in his black boat, then disappear for several days before returning and doing the same again.

What Wolfgang had been doing was getting himself in a fit state to prepare to spring his brother from jail. He knew that his disability would make it much more likely that he would be recognised and apprehended. He'd contracted polio as a boy which had left him with a withered leg, much weaker and shorter than the other, which necessitated wearing a built-up boot and caused him trouble when walking, especially over uneven or rough surfaces. He was aware that it was too late for the treatment that Jonas Salk had developed in the States but he was determined to discover anything that would help with his mobility. Money was not a problem – his late parents had left him well-provided for so he decided to seek help in the best possible area – Harley Street.

The first thing he did when the boat was secured at its berth was to rummage around in the stern locker and find a tin of leftover black paint and a brush. Then, carefully leaning over the transom, he obliterated Marcel's handiwork, rendering the boat nameless and thus less recognisable. This anonymity was further enhanced by the berth he had secured. It was simply an indentation in the soft, loamy soil of the bank. So after a very few ebbs and flows of the tide, the sides of the boat had become streaked with mud and thus less black and more subfusc. Wolfgang also realised that his name, Müller, would immediately mark him out, so he needed a new identity. He reckoned that his French was pretty good – he'd had no problems in the *bar-tabac* – so perhaps pretending to be French might be the answer. If necessary he could explain his accent by saying that he came from the Alsace, which bordered Germany. As for a name, Müller translated into French as *meunier*, so he would become Monsieur Meunier. Also, he would make sure that the leg iron he wore would be concealed as far as possible. He bought a stout stick to give him something to lean on and help with walking. The top terminated in a small V. He understood this was a thumb stick. He found it comfortable to use and was pleased with the purchase. A pair of dark glasses and a wide-brimmed hat bought in a local shop changed his appearance considerably. He was satisfied with what he saw when he examined himself in a mirror in the cabin of *Cormorant*. Suitably prepared, he set off for the railway station.

He had no trouble purchasing a ticket – the clerk showed little interest in him – and he easily found an empty compartment on the train standing at the platform. However, things were different when he got to Lewes, where he had to change trains. The station was busy, and there was quite a crowd waiting for the London train. But, to his amazement, his apparent disability, and, possibly, the dark glasses, seemed to make him appear vulnerable and needing assistance. Two kindly souls not only helped him on to the train but made sure he had a seat. He thanked them in, what he hoped, was English heavily accented with French, and received just smiles and encouragement in return. Thus prepared, he set off for his first visit to the capital.

Arriving at Victoria station, he gave up his ticket at the barrier and made his way out on to the station forecourt where a row of taxis stood. As he leaned into the window of the first one a gruff voice asked: 'Where to, guv?'

'Harley Street, please.'

'In you get then.' Herr Müller/Monsieur Meunier climbed into the taxi; the driver waited until he had settled back into his seat, and then headed off.

# Chapter 8

*Sir Giles Gilbert Scott was an English architect known for his work on Battersea Power Station, Cambridge University Library, Liverpool Cathedral and Waterloo Bridge and for designing the iconic red telephone box.*

RUSSELL GENTLY replaced the receiver on the handset. He sat back in his chair and rubbed his face with both hands then let out a heartfelt sigh. He whistled a snatch of Frankie Laine's *Answer Me*. He had just had a long telephone conversation with his French opposite number, Bruissement. Under normal circumstances he would have welcomed a chance to chat with his friend. The previous year they had greatly enjoyed each other's company, succeeding in preventing a cruel murder and bringing Ludwig Müller to justice but now, several months on, there was little to celebrate. The shame was that the German's brother, Wolfgang, had evaded capture not once, but twice. Bruissement had rung with the disappointing news that his superiors were going to review the case against the absent Müller brother. They hinted that if no further progress was made it would be shelved. There was a knock on Russell's door. Aggie, sitting under the desk, pricked up her ears.

'Come in,' Russell said wearily. Superintendent Stout's pudgy face appeared around the door. Russell quickly got to his feet.

'Sorry, Sir. I didn't realise it was you.' He couldn't remember the last time Stout had come to see him. Almost without exception he was summoned to the boss's office. The dog was about to growl but fell silent when Russell nudged her with his foot.

'Sit down, man. Don't stand on ceremony.' Surprised, Russell sat down again, Stout taking the chair opposite him.

'What can I do for you, Sir?'

'I've been thinking about this business at that place you went to.'

'*Shambhala*?'

'That's it. The Buddhist place over near Uckfield.' Stout wriggled in the chair, trying to make his bulk more comfortable. He reached into his inside pocket and took out a slim cheroot. He waved it at Russell. 'D'you mind?'

Russell wasn't keen but Stout was the boss. 'Of course not, Sir,' he said, opening a drawer and taking out an ashtray. 'Go ahead.' Stout nodded, put the small cigar between his lips and, from a side pocket, produced a Zippo lighter.

Russell had often wondered why his boss had a Zippo instead of a Ronson lighter, which seemed more fitting to his position. Then he found out. Stout had served in the Royal Air Force during the war. He had been stationed at an airfield in Norfolk used by American bomber crews and had become friendly with them. Hence his preference for the US-designed Zippo.

Stout thumbed the flint wheel several times before the lighter produced a bluish flame. Holding it to the end of the cheroot he sucked greedily until the end glowed orange. Then, taking it out of his mouth, he tipped his head back and sent a stream of smoke towards the ceiling. Russell put his fist up to his mouth and tried not to cough. As a non-smoker his sinuses were easily affected by tobacco smoke although he didn't find cigars too objectionable, unlike 'Bonnie' Parker's foul Capstan Full Strength. The terrier lay down, her chin resting on her paws, and gave a long sigh.

'Now, Russell.'

'Sir?'

'About this business at Shamb-whatsit…'

'*Shambhala*, Sir.'

Stout waved his hand, scattering ash across the desk. 'Yes, whatever.'

'Do you mean the monk who died?'

'Of course not.' he said impatiently. 'Crooks established that was death from natural causes, didn't he?' Russell nodded. Stout went on: 'I meant this Elsdale fellow. The one who got impaled on the branch.'

'Oh, right.'

'Did you interview the monks about those two who went off early?'

'Well, I got addresses for them.'

'Yes, yes, but they didn't exist, did they?'

'Er no, Sir.'

'No.' Stout took a long drag on his cigar. 'Did you find out anything else about them?'

Russell could have kicked himself. 'I'm afraid not, Sir. I didn't think of it at the time. I assumed we'd be able to track them down easily.'

'And of course, you couldn't.' Stout's face had reddened. 'I expected better of you, Inspector.'

Russell spoke quietly. 'Yes, Sir.'

'I think you'd better go back and do the job properly. And take Weeks with you. Hopefully *he* won't miss anything.' Stout ground the cigar butt into the ashtray, heaved himself out of the chair and left the room, without another word.

Russell rose and went to the door, Aggie at his heel. Peering round the frame he called: 'Weeks?' The tousled head of his DC appeared above a teetering stack of files. 'We're off to Uckfield. Get your coat.'

When they arrived at *Shambhala* the car park was empty and there was no reply when Russell knocked on the front door. 'Strange,' he said, 'I was sure there would be someone here.' He scratched his head. Aggie, who had been sitting patiently at his feet, suddenly took off, round the side of the house. 'Aggie!' he called. But she was gone.

'Should we follow, Sir?' Weeks asked.

'I guess so,' Russell answered. 'C'mon.' The two officers set off after the dog and made their way round to the back of the house but there was no sign of the monks. They continued on to the shrine room. The terrier was standing by the door, wagging her tail. Weeks was just about to knock when Russell placed a hand on his arm. 'No wait, lad. They could be meditating.' Walking along the side of the building, he came to a window, the sill low enough to see in. Shielding his eyes from the reflected light, Russell peered through the glass. Sure enough, four figures, swaddled in blankets, sat motionless. 'Ah, I was right.' He stepped away from the window. 'Let's go and have a cuppa while we wait.' They went into the house through the back door and Russell led the way to the dining room.

Once they were settled at a table with two mugs of tea, Aggie, lying on the floor under the table, Weeks spoke: 'What is this meditation business all about, Sir?'

Russell took a draught from his mug, sat back in his chair and thought, his brow furrowed. 'Well,' he began, 'essentially, the idea is to clear the mind, let go of random thoughts and try to achieve a state of higher consciousness.'

It was Week's turn to look baffled. 'But how do you do that?'

'The idea is pretty straightforward, but the practice is a little more difficult.'

'How's that, Sir?'

'Well it sounds simple but it's amazing how many random and unconnected thoughts seem to clog up the mind.'

'What do you actually do?'

'We-ell,' Russell said slowly, 'you have to get yourself comfortable first. It's best to sit cross-legged on a low cushion, with extra support under your knees, if necessary.' He grinned. 'We Europeans aren't quite as flexible as our Asian cousins.'

Weeks was intrigued. 'And then what?'

'When you get comfortable – if you can – you concentrate on emptying your mind.' Russell was about to continue when the door opened and Sanghaketu and Vidyatara entered. The policemen stood up.

Sanghaketu stepped forward. 'Hello, Mr Russell, and…?' he looked towards the other policeman.

'This is Detective Constable Weeks. I hope you didn't mind us helping ourselves to some tea – we didn't want to disturb you. I'm afraid we need to ask you a few more questions. Please, sit down.' The four of them sat round the table. 'We need to ask you about the two who left early, Laurie Baker and Helen.'

'What do you wish to know?' Sanghaketu asked.

'Anything you can tell us really.'

'Like what?'

'Where they had come from, for instance.'

'I'm afraid I cannot tell you any more than I already have. I did give you their addresses, did I not?'

'Yes you did, but both addresses were false.'

Vidyatara held up a finger. 'I think I may be able to help you.'

'Oh yes?' Russell cocked his head on one side.

'I remembered that the woman…'

'Helen.'

'Yes, Helen, she has been here before.' Russell sat up straight. 'I remember her. She was very good at meditating. What you would call a natural. I looked back through our records and found the dates.'

'And?'

'There was an address, and it was different from the one she gave this time.'

Russell was visibly excited. 'Do you still have it?'

'Of course, I will get it for you.'

'Did she tell you anything about herself?' Weeks asked Sanghaketu when the other man had left.

The monk seemed lost in thought. Russell was just about to prompt him when he spoke. His words were slow and measured. 'She told me that she lived on the other side of the county. Somewhere near a place called…' He thought again. '…something Quay, I think.'

The policemen looked at each other. 'Nottery Quay?' Weeks asked.

'Yes, I think that was the place.' Sanghaketu said slowly.

'Did she say what she did for a living?'

'Not really. Something in an office perhaps?'

'And did she mention any friends?'

'No.'

'What about Baker, the man who was here at the same time.'

Again a long pause. 'No. They did not appear to be friends.'

'But they left together – early.' The monk just shrugged.

Any further questions were halted as Vidyatara came into the room. 'Here.' He held out a sheet of notepaper.

Russell took it from him. *Helen McDermott, The Old Storehouse, Watchbell Street,* he read.

Weeks smiled. 'That's definitely different from the other address we had. That was somewhere in the north of the county – if it had existed.'

~O~

Back in the car Weeks sat in the driving seat but did not start the engine. 'Come on lad, what are you waiting for?' Russell asked.

'I was thinking about Helen, Sir.'

'What about her?'

'Something that Tommy Atkins said.'

'And that was?'

'Let me think…' Weeks paused. '…Sammy screwdriver asked if Helen had gone with Baker to Uckfield.'

'What did Atkins say?'

'He said she was busy elsewhere, and then he looked my way and said she was nothing to do with me. It was rather strange.'

Russell wasn't sure how to respond. Despite what he had heard about her he found it hard to believe that she was in any way involved with Atkins and his cronies. He didn't like to think that he had been taken in by her, she seemed so warm and genuine. Admittedly he had been on his own for a long time – except for his little terrier – and, by his own admission, wedded to the job. For the first time in as long as he could remember he had entertained an idea of a liaison, and he was reluctant to let this idea go. He shook his head sadly.

'Are you all right, Sir?'

Russell turned to see a look of concern on the DC's face. He grinned. 'I'm fine, son.' Then, smoothly changing the subject, 'Hey, aren't we somewhere near where they plan to rob the train?'

'Very close, I think.'

'Let's go and take a look then.'

Baker had found plenty of kindling wood around the yard behind the farmhouse and had the stove burning merrily. He put some larger pieces in, shut down the damper and set off to find a phone box. He assumed there would be one in Framfield so headed in the direction of the village. He passed the gate leading down to the level crossing then continued along the lane. After another 10 minutes he reached the outskirts of the village and soon spied the distinctive red form of the Gilbert Scott-designed call box. The street was deserted and he scuttled inside, the door slowly closing behind him. It had the usual smell of stale tobacco smoke and urine. He inserted four pennies in the slot and dialled the number for the pub in Collinghurst, as Tommy had said he would be waiting for his call at that time.

'Hello? Queen's Head,' a male voice said.

He pressed button A. The coins clattered into the box. 'Oh, hello, is Tommy there?'

'Hang on.' The line crackled. He could hear the landlord shouting, 'Tommy! Call for you.'

There was a pause, the line crackled, then, ''Ello? Who's that?'

'It's me – Laurie.'

''Ello mate. 'Ow you doin'?'

'I'm alright thanks.'

''Ave you been to the farm'ouse?' Waddyer think?'

'Yes, it's fine. Just as you described.'

'Told you it would be alright.' Baker could picture Tommy smiling. 'Where are you now?'

'Call box in Framfield.'

Atkin's tone changed. 'Anybody see yer?' he growled.

'No mate. It's all quiet here.'

'Make sure it stays that way. Don't want nobody gettin' suspicious.'

Baker was a bit peeved. 'Here, hang on…'

Atkins relented. 'It's all right. Keep yer 'air on. Just need to stick to the plan. You stay put and I'll come and find yer.'

'When are you coming, Tommy?'

'I'll be over in a day or two. Got enough grub to keep you goin'?'

'Enough for a day or two I guess.' Baker sounded unsure.

'Don't worry cocker, you could always go and snare a rabbit,' Atkins chuckled.

'Or pop into the village shop?' Baker said hesitantly.

'Don't you bloody dare!' Atkins sounded murderous, his mood changing like the wind. '*I'll* bring the food.'

'All right, Tommy. Don't worry, I won't. Just don't leave me on my own for too long. You know I hate the countryside.' The pips sounded on the line. 'I'll put some more money in,' Baker said, panic in his voice.

'Don't bother mate, ring me tomo…..' Atkins's voice was cut off as the money ran out.

Baker put the receiver down gently. The man had the ability to boost your ego or leave you deflated and Atkins's words had left him feeling hollow. He pushed the heavy door open and set off back to the farmhouse.

Weeks had parked the car by the gate at the end of Hempstead Lane and he and Russell had walked down to the level crossing over the Uckfield line. Aggie dashed in and out of the trees, either side of track, excitedly picking up the scent of woodland creatures.

'Is this where the deed is to be done?' the DI asked, leaning on the crossing gate.

'I think so – I'm pretty sure it is.'

'Your pal Tommy Atkins has picked a good spot,' Russell said, with a twinkle in his eye. Weeks grinned back. They stood for a while without speaking. Although cool, it was a calm evening. The rain had held off. The only sound was the wind, soughing in the trees and the songs of birds. Russell could identify some: robin, great tit, wren and a couple of others he wasn't sure about. Suddenly there was the distant sound of a whistle and within a few minutes, a locomotive came into sight. It was pulling a pair of work-worn carriages that rattled and clattered slowly over the crossing as the train climbed the slight gradient and disappeared out of view, round the bend.

After it had gone Russell stood upright and brushed dust off the sleeves of his coat. He looked towards the darkening sky. 'C'mon lad, time to head back.' They made their way up the rutted track between the beech trees as the night closed in, the terrier still frantically seeking rabbits. It was beginning to get dark by the time they reached the car. Weeks started the engine and switched on the headlights, lighting up the trees, standing like silent sentinels.

They had just set off towards Framfield, the car gathering pace, when suddenly he flung the steering-wheel over and the car swerved violently. Russell was thrown sideways, his cheek pressed against the glass of the window. 'What the…!'

'Didn't you see him?!' Weeks wrestled the car back in a straight line.

'I just saw a figure. Bloody fool out walking at this time of night…'

'But Sir. It was him!'

'Who?'

'Baker!'

'What?!'

'Laurie Baker, Sir.'

'Oh no! Do you think he saw us?'

'I doubt it. It's too dark now.'

'But what about the car?'

'It's not as if it's marked, is it.'

'I just hope he's not suspicious.'

~O~

Baker stood by the side of the lane, dazed and shaking, as the tail lights of the car dwindled into the distance and finally disappeared out of view; the fading rumble of the engine the only sign it had been there. If the driver hadn't swerved he might not be here. His mind had been on Atkins and he hadn't expected to see a car. And *bloody hell*! So close to Hempstead Lane. *Jesus*! What if someone had found out that was where they planned to do the job? And the car – the shape looked familiar. Then it came to him, it was a Wolseley. The police use those! Replaying the last few seconds in his mind he suddenly felt icy fingers squeeze his guts. 'Oh, my *God*!' he said out loud, as he realised the face pressed against the car window was familiar. It was that copper, Russell! The one at that blasted Buddhist retreat. Helen had told him he was a detective. What the hell was he doing here? 'I've got to tell Tommy!' He started running back towards the village, all thoughts of discretion flying from his mind.

~o~

'What the hell are you doing ringing me again?' Atkins's anger was unconcealed.

'Now calm down, Tommy…'

'Don't you tell me to calm down, you bloody idiot! I told you not to ring 'til tomorrow!'

'But something's happened,' Baker pleaded.

'What? It better be good!'

Baker explained about the brush with death and how he thought it might have been Russell in the passenger seat.

'Oh *Christ*!' Atkins exploded. 'Did you see who was driving?'

'No, it was too dark.'

'Did the bloke in the passenger seat see you?'

'I don't think so. The car swerved so hard the side of his face was pushed up against the window.'

'And they didn't stop.'

'No.'

Atkins let out a sharp breath. 'It weren't the rozzers then. They would 'ave stopped to see if you was alright – or would 'ave done you for bein' out at night,' he chuckled. 'Anyway, don't worry. It's just a coincidence. Nobody, except the chosen few, knows about our little plan.'

Baker was silent for a moment, thinking. Then: 'Tommy…?'

'Yeah? What is it?'

'Weeks.'

'What?'

'Johnny Weeks.'

'Yeah… What about him?'

'How well do you know him?'

'How well do I know him?'

'That's right.'

'Umm, a bit…'

'But can we trust him?'

There was a pause.

'Sure we can. He's sound as a pound.' There was laughter in his voice.

'Are you sure?'

'You doubtin' my judgement?' Atkins growled. Again, the instant mood change.

'Of course not. I was just wondering…'

'Well don't! 'E's alright. I just know 'e is.'

'If you say so…'

'I do. An' if that's all, I've got a pint to get back to.'

'Fair enough. I just don't want this to go wrong.'

'It won't, trust me. Okay?'

'Okay, Tommy.'

'Right, now scuttle back to the farmhouse. And stop worrying. I'll see you soon.'

# Chapter 9

## The previous year

*Harley Street, in Marylebone, central London, has been noted
for its large number of private clinics. It was named after
Thomas Harley, who was Lord Mayor of London in 1767.*

AFTER PAYING the fare, Wolfgang Müller got out of the taxi
and found himself at the junction of Wigmore Street and Harley
Street. He pulled his hat down firmly – there was quite a breeze
whistling round the buildings – and leant on his stick. He had
no idea where to start. He could see houses with grand facades
stretching along each side of the street, the weak sun glinting on
brass plaques. He stood for a moment, and then made a decision.
He would go into the first clinic and ask.

He walked a few yards along the street then, using his stick
for support, he climbed the two steps and pushed open the heavy,
panelled door. A uniformed receptionist sat behind a desk in
the foyer. It was a grand room, high-ceilinged with decorative
cornicing.

'Can I help you, Sir?' she asked, smiling.

'Ah, yes,' he said, hesitation in his voice. 'I am looking for a
specialist who can help me with this.' He tapped his leg with his
stick.

'I see,' the woman said, her smile appearing to be fixed. 'I'm afraid you've come to the wrong place. We deal with burns and skin complaints here.'

'Oh.' He affected a crestfallen look.

Her smile broadened further. 'But don't worry. I'm sure we can point you in the right direction.' She started to get up. 'Please take a seat and I'll go and ask.' She went out through a door behind the desk and quietly closed it after her. Wolfgang was happy to sit and had to wait only a few minutes before she returned. 'I thought someone would know.' She sat at the desk and, pulling a pad towards her, wrote down an address.' She tore off a sheet and held it out. 'There you are, Mr…?

'Meunier, Monsieur Meunier.' He got up from the seat, crossed to the desk and took it from her. 'Thank you. You have been most kind.'

The smile stayed fixed. 'That's perfectly all right. Will you be okay? It's not far.'

'I will be fine. Thank you once again.'

After walking for a short time, and looking at the numbers on the buildings, he found the one that the receptionist had written down. This time the room he found himself in was not so opulent. The ceiling was lower and the décor dingier. In addition, the person behind the desk was a youngish man. He was dressed in a sharp, double-breasted suit, dark blue with a narrow white pinstripe. He had a thin strip of a moustache across his top lip and severely Brylcreemed hair, swept back off his high forehead. A cigarette burned in an ashtray on the desk. He gave a smile that wouldn't have disgraced a shark. 'Good morning, Sir. What can I do for you?'

'I believe you may be able to do something with this.' He looked down and touched his leg.

'I'm sure we can, Mr...?'

'Monsieur Meunier.'

'Ah – a French gentleman.' He showed his small, pointed teeth. 'Take a seat.' Getting to his feet he ran his hands down the front of his jacket, smoothing non-existent creases. 'Won't be a mo.' He walked down a corridor and disappeared from view. Wolfgang sat on the edge of the chair, his stick between his knees. It was more than five minutes before the man returned. He was accompanied by another man, dressed in an almost identical fashion, rounder and wearing a pair of wire-rimmed spectacles. His hair was thin and sandy, his face pasty.

He held out his hand. 'Monsieur Meunier?'

Wolfgang took the hand in his. It was soft and limp.' Yes, that is correct.'

'I am Dr Nathan Baxter. How can I help you?' The smile he gave was as weak as the handshake.

'It is my leg. Poliomyelitis.'

'Ah, I see. Perhaps I could take a look?' He cocked his head to one side, reminding Wolfgang of a small chubby bird. 'Would you care to follow me?' He made a sweeping gesture with his arm, finishing with a finger pointing along the corridor.

Wolfgang found himself in a small, cream-painted room. A desk stood to one side and against the other wall was a raised couch with a large lamp hanging over it. 'Please would you go behind the screen and take your trousers off, then lie down on the bed. I will join you in a moment.' Doctor Baxter turned and left the room, shutting the door behind him. Wolfgang did as he was asked and, with some difficulty, climbed on to the high bed. He lay down and shivered. There didn't appear to be any heating in the room and the sheet was icy cold. After a few moments the doctor returned.

'Ah good.' His voice was low, almost a hiss. 'Now let me see.' He put his hand on the withered flesh of Wolfgang's leg. His hand was a cold as the sheet and Wolfgang shivered again. The doctor responded with a thin smile. 'Good. I see that you have feeling in the limb. Tell me, how long have you been like this?'

'Since I was a boy.'

'I see. And do you always wear this?' He tapped the iron brace.

'Yes. It gives me support. Without it I struggle to stand up, let alone walk.'

'Have you considered a wheelchair?'

'Not really. It would not be suitable for, er, where I live. And besides, I do not think my arms would be strong enough to propel it.'

The doctor's face brightened and his smile was almost genuine. 'Ah, there is a company called Ernest and Jennings who have developed a power wheelchair. It is not cheap but I understand it is very manoeuvrable.'

Wolfgang smiled back. 'That is not the solution I was looking for. I would just like to be able to get about a little more easily and...' He sought for the best way to phrase what he wanted to say. '...and be less – conspicuous.'

Again the wan smile. 'Have you thought of surgery?'

Wolfgang, shivering on the bed said, 'I did not know that it was possible.'

'Oh, anything's possible – but it could be expensive.'

# Chapter 10

*The Bedford QL was a 3 ton, 4 x 4 general service truck, manufactured by Bedford for use by the British Armed forces from 1941 to 1945.*

RUSSELL AND WEEKS drove back to Collinghurst, not saying much, each lost in his own thoughts. As they approached the town Russell said: 'Drop me at the station, lad. I can get a lift from there. You go on to the Queen's Head and see if your mate Atkins is around. Best you show your face – don't want him to get suspicious.'

'Righto, Sir.'

'Let me know how you get on. And take care! I've a feeling his mood can change like the wind, so be vigilant.'

'I will, don't worry.'

'Oh, and another thing…'

'Yes, Sir?'

At some time you need to ask how much you're getting for taking part. It'll look more than suspicious if you appear to be doing it for nothing.'

As soon as Weeks walked into the pub there was a loud shout, 'Watcher Johnny! Where've you been?' Before he could answer, Atkins continued. 'You've turned up just it time – it's your round!'

Weeks ordered the drinks and carried them over to the table. Only the big man, Bates, was there. In his crumpled suit, he sat like a partially deflated balloon. Weeks nodded a greeting then turned to Atkins. 'How's tricks?' he asked.

'Not bad me old mucker, not bad. 'Ere, you would've laughed earlier.' Atkins paused, looked around and lowered his voice. 'I spoke to Laurie. 'E rang from near the farmhouse where we're going to 'ide out when we've done the job. 'E'd been out walking when this car nearly flattened 'im.' Atkins chuckled, the sound deep in his throat. 'He reckoned that copper, Russell – the bloke from that Buddhist place – was in the car.'

'No!' Weeks had little trouble feigning surprise.

'Told him it couldn't be. If it was the law they would 'ave 'ad 'im for jaywalking!' Atkins guffawed. Weeks quickly joined in the laughter. Almost instantly, Atkins was suddenly serious. He leaned forward. 'We need to get a lorry.'

'Why, are we doing the job soon?'

'That's right.' He tapped the side of his nose in a familiar gesture. 'Yeah, I reckon we're good and ready.'

'Right.'

'Now I thought I knew where to get one, but the bloke who was getting it for me 'as let me down.'

'Oh, that's a nuisance.'

'It's more than that – it's a bugger. I won't be forgetting that in an 'urry. An' I don't just mean 'e'll be off me Christmas card list, neither, if you get me drift.' Again the tap on the nose.

'So, have you got another plan?' Weeks asked innocently.

A grin spread across Atkins's face. Butcher Bates, who had remained impassive during the exchange, smiled too, his piggy eyes all but disappearing in the soft folds of his fleshy face. 'It's about time you proved that you're genuinely part of the gang.' Atkins prodded Weeks's chest with his finger. 'You're gonna find a lorry.' He sat back in his seat, picked up his glass and took a large swig. He put the glass down and belched. 'Ooh, *pardon*!' he said, with mock politeness.

Weeks, momentarily stunned, said: '*Me*?'

'Yes, you. Didn't you say you drove one in the Army?'

Weeks was surprised he'd remembered. 'Yes, but...'

'No buts, mate. Would've thought you still 'ad some contacts.'

Weeks thought fast. 'We-ell, I might have...'

'Good. Then you get it sorted. If you don't, we'll just 'ave to look for one ourselves – and for another driver. Get my drift? I ain't got room for no baggage. An' I tend to dispose of me bags when they're no use to me any more...' Atkins's smile didn't reach his eyes this time.

The heat from the coal stove was warming the room nicely and Russell was happily dozing in his armchair, the little terrier lying across his lap. Rubenstein's version of the Chopin preludes was playing quietly on the radiogram. Suddenly the peace was interrupted by a loud knocking on the front door. Immediately Aggie pricked up her ears then leapt to the floor, letting out a single bark. 'Quiet!' Russell commanded, rising stiffly from his chair and walking across the room. He opened the door to find Weeks, who appeared even more dishevelled than usual, a look of panic on his face. Russell stood back and held the door open. 'Come in, lad. You look like you've seen a ghost.'

'You'll never believe it, Sir...'

'Try me. Oh, and sit down. I'll get you a drink. Looks like you need one.' He went to the cupboard and took out a bottle of Jameson Irish Whiskey and two glasses. Pouring a generous measure into each, he passed one to the DC who drank half of his in one gulp. His face turned puce and he had a coughing fit.

'Calm down, lad. You've obviously had a shock.'

Eventually Weeks stopped coughing and as the whiskey worked its magic he seemed calmer. The dog jumped on to his lap and settled down. That seemed to help. 'You can say that again, Sir. Not only did Baker think that he'd seen you but Atkins has asked me to find a lorry!' He went on to explain what had passed between them in the pub.

Russell sat quietly for a few moments, sipping at his drink. 'Mmm. I can see why you were surprised. Why did he think you'd be able to get hold of one?'

'Some time ago I'd told him that I'd driven a three-tonner when I did my National Service and he assumed I'd still know people in the Army.' Weeks drained his glass.

'And don't you?'

'No. All the fellas I was in with have gone on to do other things. I don't know anyone who stayed on as a regular.'

'But you do know someone in the Army now.' Russell smiled and got up to refill their glasses.

'I do?'

'I'm surprised you don't remember. I thought you were the one with the photographic memory – never forget a thing.' Russell sat down again.

Week hit his forehead with the heel of his hand. 'Of course! Must've been the shock that made me forget. Captain Valiant.'

The previous year, Captain Valiant, of the local bomb disposal unit, had become embroiled in the case involving the two Germans and the grisly murders. It turned out that his number two, Private Rankin, had been even more heavily involved and subsequently had served a term in prison.

'He owes us quite a big favour.' Russell said. 'I would imagine he can find a lorry for you. We'll pay him a visit tomorrow.' He stifled a yawn. 'Unless you'd like another…' He held up his empty glass.'

Weeks looked sheepish. 'Sorry, Sir' I've disturbed your evening.'

'That's all right lad. I'm just feeling a bit weary. Come and get me in the morning.'

~o~

Weeks drove the Wolseley up to the barrier in front of the barracks. A uniformed soldier, holding a Lee-Enfield rifle loosely across his body, strolled up to the car. Weeks wound the window down and the soldier leaned towards the opening. Russell reached across, holding out his warrant card. 'We're here to see Captain Valiant.'

'Is he expecting you, Sir?'

'No, but I'm sure he'll see us.'

'I'll just have to check. Won't be a moment.' He stood up and walked over to a small guardhouse. The policemen could see him making a telephone call. In a couple of minutes, the soldier came out and crossed to the red and white striped barrier, pushed down on the weighted end and waved them through. They motored along the tarmac roadway between the neat barracks and Weeks brought the car to a halt outside the last building. Walking up to the door Russell knocked on the plain wood panelling.

'Enter,' a voice called from inside. Russell turned the handle and they walked in. 'How nice see you both.' Valiant stood up from behind his desk and held out his hand. 'Please, sit down.' Although in his late 30s, Valiant had the build of an athlete and looked younger. He'd been a bomb disposal officer for some time and was reckoned to be one of the best. He had an easy manner and liked things ship-shape, as his almost bare desk showed, the few objects neatly lined up.

The two policemen sat opposite him. 'I understand that Rankin is back with you,' Russell said.

'That's correct.' Valiant looked serious. 'It took a lot of string-pulling, I can assure you.'

'He was charged with aiding and abetting, wasn't he?'

'Yes. Luckily the CO spoke up for him in court – talked about his good character and how he was an invaluable asset when dealing with UXBs. That got his sentence reduced to 18 months. He was released after nine for good behaviour. Not surprising really. He said that prison wasn't so much different from the Army – just without the uniform.'

'And is he a reformed character?' Russell asked.

Valiant guffawed. 'I should say so! That brush with death, when he went into the harbour at Nottery Quay with Ludwig Müller, scared the living daylights out of him. He always was good at his job, but now he's excellent.' The Captain sat back and smiled. 'Anyway, enough banter, what can I do for you? I'm rather intrigued as I can't think of any reason for you to be here.'

Now Russell smiled. 'We've come to ask a favour of you.'

'Ask away. I'm sure I owe you one or two.'

'We need a lorry, preferably unmarked.'

Valiant looked surprised. 'Something wrong with the Wolseley?' he asked.

'No, it's just fine. This is a little delicate. The purpose we need it for is not strictly legal.' Weeks looked quizzically at his boss. Russell looked back then nodded. 'In fact, it's not legal at all.'

'I'm even more intrigued now.' Valiant leaned forward, an eager look on his face.

'I trust I can rely on your discretion?'

'Absolutely. What is said in here, stays in here.' He got up, walked to the door and turned the key on the lock. 'Just in the unlikely event that someone walks in unannounced,' he said, as he made his way back to his seat.

'Right, I won't give you all the details – it's as well that you don't know everything. Suffice to say that Weeks here,' he nodded towards the DC, 'has been asked to acquire a three-tonner for a certain job.'

'And this job is, how shall I say, not within the law?'

'Quite.'

'Hmm.' Valiant was momentarily lost in thought. 'After a few moments he spoke again. 'Getting a lorry won't be a problem, but explaining its disappearance may well be.'

'Oh, you'll get it back,' Weeks said.

'That's as maybe, but if it's going to be used for some sort of nefarious purpose, I can't just *lend* it to you, can I?'

'I suppose not.'

'What if it appeared to have been stolen?' Russell asked.

'Yes, I suppose that's a possibility,' Valiant said slowly.

'Look, if all goes to plan, the lorry will come back unscathed after a few days. Could you cover for that long?'

'For a few days, yes, but any longer… I don't know.'

'But are you willing to take the risk?'

Valiant pause again, and then appeared to make up his mind. 'Yes of course. I'm sure I can trust you.'

'Thank you,' Russell said, rising from his chair. 'We'll be in touch.'

$\sim$O$\sim$

'So, matey, 'ave you sorted out a lorry?' Atkins and Weeks were alone in their usual corner in the Queen's Head. It was quiet, just how Atkins liked it. The early evening drinkers consisted of a pair of old chaps playing dominos and a travelling salesman sitting on a stool at the bar. He looked miserable. Business must be bad.

'I have,' Weeks said, lifting his glass to his lips.

Atkins slapped him on the back, just as the DC was taking a drink. He sprayed beer across the table, making Atkins roar with laughter. The two old codgers barely glanced up, more intent on their game. The salesman didn't even react, just stared into the middle distance, his hands cupping his glass.

'Well done! I knew you wouldn't let me down. Now I can tell you a bit more about the job.' He took a neatly folded piece of paper out of his inside jacket pocket and opened it on the table, smoothing out the creases. It was similar to the map that he had given to Baker, just as carefully drawn but without the cross marking the farmhouse. 'Right, this is the plan. You drive the lorry to Uckfield and park up here, in Hempstead Lane.' He pointed to the location. 'Then, just before the 10.15 train from Uckfield to Buxted is due, you open the gate and park the lorry on the level crossing.' A horrified expression crossed Weeks's face. Atkins patted him on the arm. 'Don't worry, the train ain't movin' very fast by then, just a walking pace, an' anyhow, you're gonna stop it.'

'B-but how?' Weeks stammered.

'You're gonna run down the track, wavin' a lantern. I'll make sure you have one.'

Weeks relaxed enough to say: 'Like in *The Railway Children*?'

Atkins frowned. 'You what?'

'It's a book by Edith Nesbit.' Atkins looked blank. 'She's buried at the churchyard in St Mary in the Marsh, the other side of Compass Point.'

'Nah, still don't get it.'

Weeks was getting quite excited. It was one of his favourite childhood reads. 'There's a landslip in a cutting and the children run up the track and stop the train…'

Atkins shook his head sadly. 'Don't mean a thing to me. You know your trouble? You read too much.' He sighed. 'Anyway, that's what you do.'

'O – kay,' Weeks said slowly. 'What then?'

'The rest of us will be 'iding along the side of the track. We come out as soon as the train 'as stopped. Two of us deal with the driver an' the fireman, another sorts out the guard. The two crewmen from the engine are asked politely…' He chuckled. '…They're asked politely to make their way to the guards van, where we lock the three of them up. Then Sammy – 'e's not called Screwdriver for nuffink – picks the lock on the wagon holding the money.' He paused and took a drink from his glass. 'Meanwhile, you go back to the lorry and move it off the crossing and wait for us to load it up. Then you drive it to our hideout.'

'Which is where?' Weeks asked.

'Now, now. You don't think I'm gonna tell you that, do you?' Atkins raised his eyebrows and pursed his lips.

Weeks shook his head. 'No, I guess not.'

Atkins punched him on the arm. 'Don't worry, you'll find out soon enough.'

'When are you going to do the job?'

Atkins frowned. 'Don't you mean when are *we* going to do the job?'

'Sorry, yes, that's what I meant,' Weeks said quickly.

'Hmm. You're part of this now, and don't you forget it.'

'No, of course not, I just wasn't thinking.'

'Not like you. It's seems you're always thinking!'

Weeks responded with a weak smile. 'When is this going to happen?'

'Next Tuesday.' Atkins said smugly.

'What?! So soon?'

'Is it a problem? You *said* you could get a lorry.'

'Er, yeah. Yes I did.'

'And can you get it for Tuesday?'

Weeks quickly recovered. 'Yes of course I can. No problem.'

'That's all right then. Now, this is our last meeting before the job. I'm off to get things sorted out down at the site.' He pointed vaguely at the map. 'There's still quite a few loose ends to tidy up.'

'How will I know if the job is definitely on?'

'You make sure that you're in 'ere on Sunday at seven. I'll ring you – let you know if there are any last minute changes. Oh, and by the way…' he leaned in conspiratorially. '…just before I ring there'll be a call from another party. You take the message and pass it on to me. Okay?'

Weeks nodded, then said, 'There's only one thing.'

'Yes?'

You haven't told me how much I'm getting.'

Atkins smiled. 'I wondered when you'd get round to askin' about that.'

Weeks felt it was time to be a little bolder. 'I'm taking quite a risk, running up the track with a hulking great steam train bearing down on me...'

''Ere, I told you it'll only be goin' slow.'

'That's as maybe. It's still a risk *and* I've got to supply the lorry.'

'Fair enough. 'Ow does 10 grand sound?'

Weeks was stunned, but managed to keep his cool. 'Is that what everyone else is getting?'

Atkins smiled again. 'Somethin' like that.'

'So the total haul is in the region of £50,000?' Atkins nodded. 'How can you be certain?'

The other man's mood changed. 'Now look 'ere,' he growled, 'you're bleedin' lucky to get that. I've taken you on face value right from the start. I've defended you when the others have started questioning me about using you – an outsider. An'... I've never checked up on what you've said you've done.'

Weeks held up his hands. 'Fair enough Tommy, I was only asking.'

'That's all right then. Jus' don't get above yourself. Now, are we going to 'ave another pint or what?'

# Chapter 11

## The previous year

*Poliomyelitis, usually known as polio or infantile paralysis, is an infectious disease caused by the poliovirus. It can result in muscle weakness, most often involving the legs.*

'NOW I think we'll just take this off,' Doctor Baxter said. 'I presume I have to undo these buckles?'

'Yes, it's quite simple.' Wolfgang said. 'Would you like me to help?'

'No,' Baxter said sharply. 'I think it best that you stay lying still.' The doctor fumbled with the straps, eliciting a painful gasp from Wolfgang, which he ignored. 'There, done. Now let's see how much movement you have in the leg.' He bent the withered limb at the knee and Wolfgang cried out. Baxter lowered the leg again. 'Ah, it seems there is very little natural articulation. I'm not sure if we can easily do anything about that. But let's not dismiss it just yet. First off we'll take measurements and do some calculations.'

He turned to his desk and, opening a drawer, produced a steel tape measure. Turning back to his patient he extended it and measured Wolfgang's leg from hip to foot. When the cold metal touched his already chilled flesh he flinched. Again the doctor seemed oblivious to his discomfort. After repeating the exercise on the sound leg he went back to the desk and wrote down some figures on a pad.

'I think we may be able to something about the difference in length with surgery.'

'What does that entail?' Wolfgang asked.

'It is quite simple. Effectively we break the bones then extend them using steel pins.'

'Is it safe?'

'It is at the forefront of this type of procedure but I believe the results have been encouraging. You may get dressed again. Oh, and put your brace back on too.'

'How many such operations have you carried out?'

'Me? Oh, I don't think that is relevant.' He waved a hand dismissively. 'But I know that it has been successful in a number of cases.' Before Wolfgang could question him further he went on quickly: 'But you must understand, it will be quite expensive.'

'Money is not a consideration,' the little man said as he sat up. 'I would just like to have more mobility.'

'I think we can be sure you will notice a big difference.'

Wolfgang struggled to get off the couch. 'When will you be able to do it?'

Baxter offered no help but sat at his desk writing. 'Quite soon, I would think,' he said, without looking up. 'If you leave your details at reception, I will be in touch when we have a slot.'

'How long will the recuperation take?' Wolfgang asked from behind the screen as he struggled to put his trousers back on.

'Oh, that depends on a number of factors,' Baxter replied casually.

'Can you say if it will be days, weeks, months?'

'Hard to say. But let's not worry about that now.' He looked up, a reptilian smile on his face. 'Let's just get the operation done first, shall we?' He tore a sheet off the pad in front of him and held it out as Wolfgang appeared around the screen. 'Here's my fee for the initial consultation. Please pay the receptionist before you leave. And I prefer cash. Good day.' With that, the little man was dismissed.

The receptionist was still sitting behind his desk and a cigarette was still smouldering in the ashtray. He gave Wolfgang another cold smile. 'Ah, you have come to pay. I trust everything was satisfactory?' Wolfgang, rather shaken and taken aback by the experience, just nodded and reached into his jacket for his wallet. The man took the proffered notes. 'Now your details please.' Wolfgang gave him the address at the boatyard, and reminded himself to tell the yard owner that a letter would be coming for Monsieur Meunier.

# Chapter 12

*An Escritoire* or Secretary Desk is made of a base of wide
drawers topped by a desk with a hinged surface.

THEY HAD driven down in Bates's bottle green Morris J type
van, Atkins riding in the passenger seat. Sammy was sitting on
a pile of blankets in the back, wedged uncomfortably between
boxes and tins. The three-speed gearbox, the noise from the
straining engine and the weight in the van had made the journey
long and tedious and they had arrived tired and scratchy. Even
so, Atkins had insisted that they hide the van in the smaller of the
two barns. So, with much grumbling, they had moved assorted
junk and a couple of lumpy pieces of rusty farm machinery out of
the way, making enough space for Bates to back the van in. Then
closed the doors.

Baker had done his best to make the farmhouse comfortable.
He had found some hessian hop pockets in one of the
outbuildings and stuffed them with straw that was just on the
dry side of mouldy. With the blankets they had brought with
them they made up beds that were acceptable although Sammy,
who had shared a room with Bates, had complained about
his snoring. In the morning they had a fry up with sausage,
egg, bacon and tomatoes and were all feeling much more
settled.

They had brought enough supplies in the van to last for several days: tins of corned beef, Spam, mushy peas, baked beans, and for dessert, peaches and mandarins; a sack of potatoes; tea, milk and sugar; a couple of loaves of bread, rashers of bacon, eggs, tomatoes, marge, jam and lard; plates, mugs, saucepans and cutlery. And of course, four crates of bottled beer and six bottles of whisky. 'That should keep us going,' Atkins had said, when they'd unloaded it.

Even though the house was well back from the road he had insisted that the windows at the front of the house were covered, so an inquisitive passer-by wouldn't see that anyone was inside. Bates and Sammy had been dispatched to search in the outbuildings and had come back with some dirty, frayed cloth and more sacks. With a hammer and nails from the van they had fixed them roughly in place. Although it made the rooms gloomy, Atkins was satisfied that it would shield them from prying eyes.

'Well, this is a bit of all right,' he said, cup in hand, looking round. A fire was lit in the grate and it was burning merrily, cheering the room. Baker smiled his appreciation. Butcher Bates and Sammy the Screwdriver sat either side of the table, each with a chipped mug of tea. The empty plates had been cleared away and were piled in the sink. Atkins walked across to the table. 'C'mon Butch, budge over. Yer takin' up two seats.' The big man shifted his bulk, the wooden chair creaking ominously. Baker joined them on the last vacant chair. 'Right, lads,' Atkins began, spreading a map out on the table. 'This is the plan.'

~O~

The Wolseley bumped along the cobbled street and Russell had to reach up and hold on to the grab handle to stop his head connecting with the roof of the car. After an uncomfortable few minutes Weeks brought the vehicle to a halt outside The Old Storehouse in Watchbell Street. They got out and walked up the flagstone pathway to the front door. Russell lifted the dolphin-shaped brass knocker and rapped three times. Silence. He tried again. Still nothing.

'Can I help you?' The policemen looked round. A small neat woman in her late sixties with a pair of wire-rimmed spectacles perched on her nose was peering through the gateway. 'She's not there you know,' she said sharply.

Russell walked towards her. 'Who's that, madam?'

The woman looked him up and down and frowned. 'And you are?'

'I'm Detective Inspector Russell...' he held out his warrant card, '...and this is Detective Constable Weeks. Are you talking about Helen McDermott?'

'That's her name – yes.'

'And you say she's not at home? How can you be so sure?'

'Because I'm feeding her cat whilst she's away.'

'Oh, I see. So when did she go?'

'Yesterday morning.'

'And do you know where she's gone?'

'What's it to you?' the woman said suspiciously.

'Madam,' Russell began, keeping his voice even, 'I am afraid I can't divulge any information of that nature. Let's just say it would be a great help if you would tell us as much as you know.'

The little woman visibly relaxed. 'In that case, do you want to take a look inside? I'm sure Helen wouldn't mind.'

The policemen glanced at each other. This was unexpected but most welcome. The woman introduced herself as Mrs Denise Major, and produced a key from the pocket of her floral housecoat.

She put it in the lock and opened the door. 'You stay here,' she instructed, holding up an admonishing finger, 'while I make sure Cleopatra is shut away. She doesn't like strangers, you know.' With that she disappeared inside and closed the door, leaving Russell and Weeks standing in the porch. After a few minutes she returned. 'You can come in now; just don't open the kitchen door. I don't want the puss getting out. There would be a terrible to-do if she escaped.' The policemen stepped inside the hall. The floor was covered with encaustic tiles, in terracotta, cream and blue and a small table, with just a Bakelite telephone on its surface, stood between two doorways. Weeks politely wiped his feet on the doormat. 'This is the lounge.' Mrs Major said expansively, opening the first door. She reminded Russell of an estate agent. They entered a small neat room.

Several watercolours of local views hung on the walls. He peered at the nearest. It showed the windmill at Nottery Quay, silhouetted against the sunset with the outline of boats, sitting on the mud alongside the wharf, in the foreground. The painting was well-executed although he didn't recognise the signature. 'Very nice,' he muttered. There was little furniture; just a pair of armchairs, covered in a dark fabric with an understated pattern, and what appeared to be an escritoire against the wall, with the hinged flap, which served as a writing surface, closed shut.

After giving them a few moments to look round, Mrs Major bustled out of the lounge. 'Come along now, here's the dining room.' It was again small, and tastefully decorated. A dark, polished wood table stood in the centre with four matching chairs.

Russell slid one out and held the back. 'Would you sit down please Mrs Major, then perhaps we can ask you a few questions?' The woman sat meekly, although she folded her arms defensively across her bosom. Russell remained standing but motioned for his DC to sit. 'Would you get Mrs Major to give us some information about Helen McDermott. I'm just going to have another look at that painting. I'm sure I recognise the artist,' he said, and left the room before the woman could protest.

Mrs Major hugged herself tighter. 'What do you want to know, young man?'

Weeks took out his notebook. 'How long have you known Mrs McDermott?'

'Oh no!' she said sharply, unfolding her arms and leaning forwards. 'She's not Mrs, she's Miss!'

'Oh, I see.' Weeks made a note on his pad. 'How long have you known Miss...'

'Just over a year,' she cut in. 'Ever since she moved here.'

'Do you know where she moved from?'

The woman furrowed her brow. 'Not exactly, she never said, but I think it was London somewhere.'

'Oh, right.' He wrote that down. 'And do you know if she works; what she does for a living?'

'Not really. She doesn't do anything regular, like.' Mrs Major frowned again. 'She does go off for a few days at a time though – leaves me to look after Cleo.' Weeks looked up. 'Oh, I don't mind. I'm happy to do it. It's no trouble.' The words tumbled out in a staccato rush. 'Besides, she always makes sure I'm not out of pocket.' Seeing the policeman's questioning look she quickly added, 'I buy fresh fish and milk you know. Cleo is a very particular cat.'

While this exchange was taking place Russell had gone into the lounge and, ignoring the watercolour, went straight over to the escritoire. Carefully pulling out the two wooden supports he lowered the flap until it was resting on them in a horizontal position. Like the room, the interior of the desk was tidy; just a fountain pen, a dark blue bottle of Quink, some plain envelopes and a blotter. There was no notepad and Russell did not think he had enough time to open any drawers to look for one – he was concerned that Mrs Major would suddenly appear and he was sure her co-operative mood would quickly vanish. Then he spotted some faint writing on the corner of the blotter. Written in blue, in a neat hand, he could just make out:

*Meet SH*
*Victoria Station*
*6.45 Sunday*
*by the clock?*

He made a mental note, quickly closed the lid and joined the others in the dining room. Weeks was putting his notebook away and rising from his chair. 'Thank you, Mrs Major,' he said, 'you've been most helpful.'

Just as they were leaving Russell turned. 'By the way, when is Miss McDermott due back?'

'Didn't I say?'

'No, you didn't.'

Mrs Major pulled back the cuff of her pale pink cardigan, revealing a small, octagonal gold wristwatch. 'Any time now.'

Russell started. '*Really*?'

'Oh yes. She never goes away for long.'

'We'll say goodbye then.'

Russell was just walking along the hall wondering what to do when the front door swung open and there stood Helen McDermott. It was difficult to say who was the most surprised. They stood in silence for several seconds then Helen spoke. 'Sonny! What on earth are you doing here – in my house?'

Russell actually blushed, then stammered, 'Er, Mrs Major let us in.'

'Yes, but why are you here?'

Weeks peered round his boss and took the initiative. 'It's just routine, Miss McDermott. We're following up enquiries.'

'Enquiries into what?'

Russell regained his composure. 'There was an unpleasant accident at the Buddhist retreat you attended. A man was seriously injured. We'd like to know if you can help in any way.'

Helen looked baffled. 'Really? What happened?'

'Perhaps we'd better go and sit down,' Russell said, holding his arm out to her. They made their way back along the hall. As they re-entered the dining room he realised that the neighbour was still with them. He turned to her. 'Thank you for your help Mrs Major, you can leave us now'. The woman sniffed; her pursed lips made her look as if she had sucked a lemon. Turning on her heel she left without a word.

They sat round the table and Weeks opened his notebook. He started the questioning. 'We understand you left the retreat early. Why was that?'

'I wanted to get home – to my cat.' She peered round, a concerned look on her face. 'Where is Cleo?'

She was starting to rise from her chair when Russell put his hand on her arm. 'Don't worry, your neighbour shut her in the kitchen. She'll be fine.' Helen relaxed and sat back down. 'You left with another person from the retreat, Laurie Baker. I presume he's a friend of yours?'

'What? No, he's not.'

'Then why did you go with him?'

'Why, oh, he heard me enquiring about a taxi to the station and offered me a lift, that's all.'

'And what about the injured man – Elsdale?'

'Who?' Her face gave nothing away.

'Dave Elsdale. He wasn't part of the retreat. He turned up on the Saturday morning.'

Helen's expression turned to one of uncertainty, then recognition dawned. 'Oh him. I saw him briefly – in the dining room. What happened to him?'

'He sustained a nasty injury.'

Her hand flew to her mouth. 'Oh! What happened?'

'I'm sorry. I can't go into details.'

'Is he all right?' The hand had come down and there was a look of genuine concern on her face. Russell was struggling to keep his composure.

Weeks spoke. 'He's off the critical list but is still gravely ill.'

'I'm sorry to hear that. But I don't know how I can help you.' She held her hands out, palms uppermost.

Russell couldn't understand the effect this woman was having on him but with an effort he managed to keep a grip on his feelings. 'You've been most helpful, Miss McDermott,' he said formally. 'That will be all for now but we may need to talk to you again.'

She smiled. 'That's fine. Any time.'

The two policemen got up from their chairs. As she was showing them out of the house she turned to the younger man and said: 'By the way, we haven't been introduced.'

'It's Detective Constable Weeks, Ma'm,' and he held out his warrant card.

She peered at it and noted the initial 'J'.

~O~

As soon as the policemen had gone Helen turned the key in the lock on the front door and started pacing the small hallway. She was furious with Mrs Major for letting them in. She had no right to do so. But… she didn't want to upset the woman as she was useful when she had to go away. And she might be gone for some time – soon. But what was more troubling was the younger policeman, Weeks. Something didn't feel right. Something about him was nagging at the back of her mind. As she paced an idea came to her.

She had felt a little uneasy when Tommy had told her he'd found a getaway driver, even though no one knew him or had come across him before. Tommy had assured her that he was kosher. She remembered that he had told her about the man embezzling money from the family firm. She had a friend who worked in the Stock Exchange who might be able to help. Now what was the name of the firm? She stopped pacing and leant against the wall, thinking hard. Hardcastle? Holborn? Headingly? What was it? She resumed pacing, thinking back to the conversation she'd had with Atkins a few days earlier. Before he'd gone off to the hide-out. Then it came to her. Holloway! That was it, Holloway and Son. She pulled open a drawer under the table and took out a small address book. Flicking through it she found the entry she was after. She put the book down on the table and smoothed the pages flat. Picking up the receiver she dialled a London number. The call was answered on the third ring.

'Yes,' she said, 'can you put me through to Dennis Smart?' She waited a few moments until he picked up. 'Hello Dennis. How are you?' After the pleasantries were over she asked about Holloway and Son and the supposed embezzlement. He said he'd look into it and would ring her back. After thanking him she was unable to relax so opened the door into the kitchen so she could make some tea. Thoughts of the Siamese cat had gone out of her head and she almost tripped over her.

'Oh Cleo!' she cried. 'I'm so sorry, I'd clean forgotten all about you. Let me get you some cream.'

~o~

They bumped back along the cobbles, the interior of the car too noisy to make conversation easy, so Russell didn't speak until they reached the smooth metalled surface of the main road and the atmosphere quietened. However, he used the time to meditate on what they had learned. He was still struggling to admit that Helen wasn't what she had at first appeared and part of him didn't want to believe it. But, he thought, sighing inwardly, he needed to put emotion aside and let the policeman in him come to the fore.

'What do you think, Sir?' There was no response. 'Sir? Are you all right?'

He realised that Weeks was speaking to him. 'Sorry! What did you say? I was miles away.'

'I said, what are your thoughts about this meeting at Victoria station? And who is SH, do you think?'

They were now on the road back to Collinghurst. 'I've no idea. But there is something that did occur to me...'

'What's that, Sir?'

'Aren't you supposed to be in the Queen's, waiting for a call from Atkins at seven on Sunday?'

'That's right.'

'That's just after this meeting with SH.'

'True.'

'What if the two things are connected?'

Weeks concentrated on the road for a while and then spoke. 'Do you think Miss McDermott – Helen – is involved somehow?'

Russell sighed. 'Yes, I suppose I do.'

'Is there something you're not telling me, Sir?' Weeks could be surprisingly insightful. Normally Russell welcomed this ability but he found it rankled in this case.

'Certainly not!' he said more sharply than he'd intended. 'No, of course not,' he said, in a gentler tone, 'it's just that I'm struggling to see how she can be involved. She seemed so... *nice*.'

'Appearances can be deceptive, Sir.' Again, that insight.

The sigh this time was more heartfelt. 'Yes, of course you're right. Anyway, let's suppose this meeting in London has some bearing on Atkins's plan. What should we do about it?'

'I can't go. I need to be in the pub, near the telephone.'

'And it'll be difficult for me to go. After all, she knows what I look like.'

'But what's the alternative? Send Bonnie or Clyde?'

'Weeks...'

The DC smiled. 'Sorry, Sir, Parker or Barrow...'

'I don't think so. Not only would it be an uphill struggle to persuade them of its importance but I doubt they'd handle it with the necessary sensitivity.'

'What can we do?'

'There's no other way. I'll have to do it.'

'But Sir, surely she'll recognise you?'

'I guess that's a risk worth taking. I'll just have to think up a convincing disguise.'

~o~

Sammy screwdriver, Butcher Bates and Laurie Baker leaned in as Atkins smoothed the creases out of the map laid out on the table. He pointed and said: 'Here's the level crossing where Johnny will park the lorry.'

Bates, normally taciturn, spoke up, his voice hushed. 'Are you sure about him, Tommy?'

It was out of character for the man to question anything and Atkins bristled. 'Of course I am! D'you think I'd use someone I wasn't sure of?'

But the big man pressed on. 'You say that, Tommy, but how do we know we can trust him? None of us has come across him before, after all.'

Atkins didn't like his authority being challenged but the fact it was the usually reserved Bates who had questioned him gave him cause for doubt. But he quickly dismissed this and thumped the table. 'If I say we can trust 'im then you'd better believe me. Right?'

Bates looked a little shame-faced. 'Sure, boss. If you say so.'

'I do, so let's 'ear no more about it.'

~o~

After an agonising half hour, when Helen had made two pots of tea and drunk both of them, the phone finally rang. She dashed into the hall almost falling over the cat again and picked up the handset. 'Hello? Dennis. Thanks for getting back to me. What did you find out? What? There's no such firm? Are you sure? No, I'm not doubting you, it's just that… Oh never mind. Thanks anyway, I owe you.' She laughed. 'Okay, next time I come up to town. Bye.' She slowly put the down the receiver, a frown on her face.

So if the company didn't exist, Johnny was shooting Atkins a line. Johnny? She thought back to her last conversation with Laurie Baker. How had he described him? "Like an overgrown schoolboy with a mop of dark curly hair." Hmm. Detective Constable J. Weeks. What if it was…? Atkins was due to ring her later. She'd put it to him then.

~o~

On their return to the station Russell and Weeks had been summoned to Superintendent Vic Stout's office. They were sitting expectantly opposite his vacant chair, on the other side of the imposing, highly polished desk. The room was spacious, with a large window overlooking the park, next to the Collinghurst police headquarters. Even though he was absent, the distinctive odour of Stout's habitual cheroots hung, like a pall, over the room. They had to wait for several minutes until he finally bustled in. As they rose from their seats he said: 'Sit down – sit down. No need to stand on ceremony,' and lowered his bulk, the chair groaning as it took his weight.

'Right, now, I want a progress report. And it had better be good. I've got the Chief Constable on my back. He's on the warpath, for some reason, and is demanding answers.'

'Well, Sir,' began Russell, as his superior lit up a cigar, 'it sounds like the job is definitely on for next Tuesday. And…' he paused. 'There's been something of a turn of events.'

Stout blew out a column of smoke. 'Oh yes?'

'Yes. Weeks,' Russell looked towards to his companion, 'has been asked to get hold of a lorry.'

'I see. And how do you plan to do that, Constable?'

'Um,' he mumbled, 'Captain Valiant is going to lend me one.'

'Who? Oh yes, that wallah from the barracks. The bomb disposal chappy.'

'That's him,' Russell said.

'How is he going to *lend* you a lorry?'

'We've yet to work out the details, but he was happy to help. He does owe us after all.'

'Quite. But I don't think I want to hear any more. This is your show and the less I know about it the better.... especially if it all goes badly wrong.' He put the cigar in his mouth and stared pointedly at the DI.

Russell sat up and coughed, holding his hand over his mouth. 'I'll make sure it doesn't, Sir,' he said quietly.

'Hmm, it had better not. Anyway, what else has happened?'

Weeks spoke up. 'We got the correct address of that woman who was at the Buddhist retreat. The one who went off early with Baker.'

'He's part of Atkins's gang, isn't he?'

'That's right. Also we're pretty sure he had something to do with the man, Elsdale, who was badly injured.'

'He's still alive then?'

'Yes. He's off the critical list but it will be some time before he's out of hospital.'

'Did you go and see this woman?'

'We did.'

'And?'

Weeks took the lead again. 'She claims she doesn't know Baker – he just gave her a lift to the station. Nor does she know anything about what happened to Elsdale.'

'But I did find something that might link her to them.' Russell said, then explained about the note he had found on the blotter.

The Superintendent violently stubbed out his cigar. 'But that could mean anything!' he said, angrily. 'Who the hell is SH? Could be anybody!'

'I'm aware of that, Sir. I just have a feeling that it's critical to this case.'

'You've got a *feeling*!' Stout thundered. 'Oh, for heaven's sake!' He put his head in his hands and groaned. Then, after a moment he looked up and spoke quietly. 'I don't really care about your *feelings*. What I want is some solid evidence. This whole case is turning into a right old mare's nest. Do I make myself clear?'

'Perfectly, Sir.'

'Right. Then come back with some answers, not just *feelings*.'

The two detectives left the room and walked down the corridor to Russell's office. 'That went well,' he said, a sardonic smile playing around his lips.

They sat down and Weeks spoke, 'Sir.'

'Yes, lad?'

'We didn't mention seeing Baker when we went to Uckfield.'

Russell settled in his chair, hands clasped behind his head. 'I think that was just as well. The Super may have made us bring him in for questioning over the Elsdale business. That would be bound to put Atkins and co' on their guard and they be would more than likely to call the job off. Which is *not* what we want.'

'So what now, Sir?'

'Let's see.' He held up his hand and starting ticking items off on his fingers. 'One: I'm going to have to put together a plan for Tuesday. We'll need a few bodies to stake out that level crossing and I've got to persuade the Super that it's worthwhile. Two: We have to arrange with Valiant where he's going to leave the lorry so you can *borrow* it. Three: You need to be ready for instructions from Atkins when he rings the Queen's Head. And four: I've got to work out how I can observe Helen's meeting with SH, without being noticed.'

# Chapter 13

## The previous year

*The Lee-Enfield is a bolt action, magazine-fed, repeating rifle that was the main firearm used by the British Army during the first half of the 20th century.*

WOLFGANG TOOK a taxi from the station to the boatyard after his visit to Harley Street. He paid off the cab and started making his way back to the boat. He was feeling particularly weary after his trip and was looking forward to having a lie-down and taking the weight off his leg. After the manipulation by Doctor Baxter and the extra distance he had walked he knew he had overdone it. He just had to rest. So he made slow progress, being careful not to trip on ropes, chains and lengths of wood that littered the untidy yard. He had to stop several times. About halfway to his berth, he perched on a convenient barrel while he regained enough strength to carry on. He had been sitting for several minutes when he became aware of noises coming from one of Dickens's tumbledown sheds. This particular structure was especially rickety and looked as if a moderately strong gust of wind would flatten it. How it remained standing was one of life's mysteries.

The sounds he heard were the scraping and screeching of

heavy objects being moved, along with an occasional human oath. After catching his breath he was curious enough to lever himself off the barrel and move slowly towards the partly open door. Cautiously, he peered inside. Dickens, with his back to him, was just sliding the lid back on to a long, flat, rectangular crate, placed on a stack of similar wooden ones. Just before the lid was fully home, Wolfgang glimpsed the dull sheen of oiled metal. Dickens picked up a hammer, banged half a dozen nails home and pulled a ragged tarpaulin over the stack. Wolfgang had just enough time to turn and start back along the path towards his boat before Dickens came out. With a grunt he forced the door shut, its uneven bottom scraping on the weeds growing round the shed. He turned and saw Wolfgang.

'Ah, Monsieur Meunier. Back from your trip I see. Did you have a good time?' Dickens was small and wizened, of indeterminate age, wearing old grubby clothes and a ragged beret. His skin too looked grubby, his face was lined, his small, dark eyes deep set. He had a wispy pepper and salt beard, which he stroked continually as he spoke.

Wolfgang stopped and faced him. 'Yes, Mr Dickens. Very satisfactory, thank you.'

'Oh, please call me Paddy.' His voice had the gentle lilt of an Irish brogue. He pushed his beret up with a stained hand and scratched his forehead. He grinned, showing broken stumps with large gaps between. 'I feel like we're old mates now.'

Wolfgang shuddered inwardly. He was keen to get away from this creepy little man. 'Thank you... Paddy.'

Dickens moved closer and Wolfgang could smell the mixed odours of pitch and paint, alcohol and sweat. 'And what about you, *Monsieur* Meunier? Do you have a first name?'

Er, *oui*, it is Marcel,' he said, the name of the man who helped him paint the boat the first thing to come into his head.

'That's nice, *Marcel.*' He held out his hand and Wolfgang was forced to grasp and shake it. 'Anything I can do for you, just ask.' With that, he gave a small bow, turned and walked towards the entrance to the yard where another ramshackle building contained his home and his office.

~O~

Back in the relative security of his boat, Wolfgang sat on the bunk in the cabin cradling a generous measure of brandy against his chest, trying to stop the glass from shaking in his hands. It wasn't so much the boatyard owner's supercilious attempt to be friendly, more, what he had seen in the shed. He was pretty sure what the crates contained but curiosity made him want to have a closer look to check. He determined to wait until after dark and go back. Trembling, he lifted the glass to his lips and drank until it was empty. Then he lay down on the bunk and drifted into an exhausted sleep.

~O~

When he woke it was dark outside. Slowly, as his eyes became accustomed to the gloom, he could distinguish the regular flashing of the red and green navigation lights marking the channel in the estuary and the steady soft glow of gas lamps on the opposite bank. He sat up shakily; the brandy had left his brain a little fuddled and his mouth dry. Holding on to the edge of the bunk to steady himself, he stepped into the small galley where he knew there was a bottle of clean water. He drank deeply, slaking his thirst and clearing his head. Feeling a little better, he struck a match and lit the oil lamp, fixed by a bracket to the bulkhead. The lamp cast a warm light over the cabin.

*Cormorant*, or rather, *Moonshine*, was a 30-foot, former fishing boat. When Wolfgang and his brother had bought it, they needed none of the trawling gear that came with it, just wanting a reasonably fast, comfortable craft that could cross the Channel with ease. And she had proved perfect for their needs. Forward was a small wheelhouse with good visibility on three sides. Aft of this was a raised coach-house roof. A companionway led down to a cosy cabin with a bunk-cum-settee either side of a mahogany table with a brass fiddle rail round the edge. A doorway in the forrard bulkhead led to a compact galley. Above and below the bunks were shelves and storage lockers and Wolfgang liked to keep everything neat and tidy. He took a slim torch off one of the shelves and clicked the switch on to ensure the batteries were good. The torch sent out a narrow, bright beam and, satisfied, he switched it off again. Bending, he opened a locker beneath the starboard bunk and took out a claw hammer. He made his way up on to the deck and could see from the light reflected on the water that the tide was full. This made disembarking easier as the rough wooden jetty was almost level with the deck of the boat. He slipped the shaft of the hammer into the side pocket of his jacket and climbed ashore. Switching on the torch he shielded the beam with his hand, providing just enough illumination to see his way.

When he reached the shed, Wolfgang had to put the torch down so he could force the door open. It seemed to make a horrendous amount of noise as it scraped along the ground. When there was a big enough gap for him to get through he stood still, holding his breath and listening. All was quiet. He picked up the torch, slipped inside and played the beam over the interior. After pulling back the tarpaulin he managed to wedge the torch so the beam shone on the uppermost crate. He took the hammer out of his pocket and, using the claw, started levering the lid up. As the nails were pulled they made a screeching sound that he was sure would be heard but, after a pause to listen, it was still silent outside. Finally, the cover was free and he slid it to one side. His hand shaking, he shone the torch on the contents. It was as he had suspected. *Rifles*! British Army-issue Lee-Enfields…

Wolfgang looked at the number of similar crates and took a sharp inward breath. This looked like gun-running on quite a scale. He pushed the lid back into place on the box he had opened and, deciding that hammering the nails back in would be just too noisy, he levered them out, one by one, with the claw. As he slipped the canvas sheet back over the pile he hoped that Dickens would have forgotten that he'd nailed it down and blame it on the booze.

# Chapter 14

*The crown cork, or cap, patented in 1892, had 24 teeth and a cork seal with a paper backing to prevent contact between the contents and the metal cap.*

HELEN COULDN'T face any more tea; instead she had poured herself a large glass of dry sherry. Tommy had been due to ring at six-thirty but he was late. It was nearly seven o'clock. She didn't like being kept waiting at the best of times and was growing agitated.

On top of that she had become more convinced that Atkins's new mate, Johnny was, in actual fact, DC Weeks. If this was the case it would jeopardise the whole project. She knew she would have an uphill struggle trying to convince him – he had become very protective of his new pal – but she had to find out if he was the policeman and get Atkins to deal with it. At long last the phone rang. She snatched up the receiver before it could ring a second time. 'Hello? Tommy?'

She heard the coins drop into the box. ''Ello darlin',' came the smooth reply, ''ow are you?'

'I'm fine Tommy,' she gushed. 'Just pleased to hear your voice. I thought you weren't going to ring.'

'That's nice,' he went on, 'course I was gonna ring. Wouldn't let yer down, now would I?'

'I should hope not,' she laughed. 'Anyway, a lot's been happening here.' She went on to explain about coming home and finding the policemen in her house.

'Strewth! That must have been a bloody shock!'

'You can say that again.' She was about to continue when the pips went.

''Ere darlin', can you ring me back? I ain't got many coins left.'

'Quick, give me your number.' He recited it off the front of the receiver in the call box and she scribbled it down, just before the line went dead. She dialled the number and waited until she heard him pick up the handset. 'Tommy?'

'Yeah, me again. Now carry on wiv what you were sayin'.'

She decided to plunge straight in. ''It's about Johnny...'

'Not you as well?' he said gruffly. 'I've been gettin' grief from all quarters. First of all Laurie 'avin' a go then Butcher bangin' on about 'im. I'll tell you the same as I told them. Johnny's as sound as a pound, straight as a die, one 'undred percent copper-bottomed. 'E's a good lad an' I won't 'ave nuffink said against 'im. All right?'

'No Tommy. It is not all right. Your friend Johnny has been shooting you a line.' Before Atkins could interrupt she continued. 'That supposed family firm he was meant to have embezzled money from doesn't exist'.

'*What*?' Atkins was incredulous.

'I spoke to an old friend who works on the Stock Exchange. He checked quite a long way back through the records and there never has been a Holloway and Son.'

'Well I'll be...'

'And there's something else.'

'There can't be.'

'There is.'

'Go on. What is it?'

'You're not going to believe it.'

'Try me.'

'I think your precious getaway driver is a copper.'

'*What*? You're bloody 'avin' me on!'

Atkins had yelled so loudly, Helen had to hold the phone away from her ear. 'I'm afraid he may well be, Tommy,' she said, her quiet voice contrasting with his. 'Tell me again what he looks like.'

Atkins sighed. 'About my height – 5' 8"; a load of dark curly hair. Keeps flopping over his eyes.'

'Looks a bit like an overgrown schoolboy?'

'Yeah,' he said, resignedly. 'You think I've been 'ad?'

'Afraid so, Tommy. I guess he must have been convincing.'

''E certainly was. What am I gonna do Helen? Help me out here.'

~o~

'You know the bombed-out warehouses, behind the old hospital?' Captain Valiant had telephoned Russell in his office.

Russell was leaning back in his chair, Weeks across from him, Aggie snoozing under the desk. 'I think so,' he said slowly, 'just a moment…' He held his hand over the mouthpiece and sat up. 'D'you know the derelict warehouses, lad?'

'The ones in Stone Street, Sir?' the DC answered.

Russell nodded and took his hand away. 'Yes, we know them, in Stone Street.'

'That's the place. I'll drop the three-tonner off at the crack of dawn on Sunday morning.'

'How long before its absence will be noticed?'

'She's one of our older lorries – not much used; so two days – three at the outside, I should think.'

'Hopefully we'll return her before then.'

'That's fine. I should be able to cover for that long.'

Weeks coughed and said quietly, 'What about the key?'

Russell held up his finger. 'Good point. Valiant?'

'Yes, Inspector?'

'Weeks has just asked about the key.'

The Captain chuckled. 'No problem. Old army trick. The key will be on top of the nearside front tyre, tucked towards the back. You'll have to feel for it.'

'That's fine. We're very grateful to you. We'll let you know how we get on.' He put the phone down and turned to Weeks. 'Right, lad, that's arranged. Now what about my disguise?'

'I've been giving that some thought, Sir.'

Russell placed an elbow on the desk, rested his chin in his hand and cocked his head to one side. 'Oh, yes?'

'Yes, Sir. Although Helen knows what you look like, she probably won't notice you if you blend in with your surroundings.'

'Go on…'

'Who are the most numerous, but also inconspicuous people on a station platform?'

'Passengers?'

'True, but I was thinking of station staff…'

Russell frowned, and then his face lit up. 'Porters – *of course*!'

'That's right. Everyone knows they are there, but no one takes any notice of them…'

'Unless they want them to carry their bags.'

'Exactly! All you need is a waistcoat and a peaked cap. Dressed like that, you'll be able to get close without being noticed.'

'Brilliant! Just one thing – where can I get the cap and waistcoat?'

'Easy, Sir. I'm sure they'll have a spare set at Collinghurst railway station you could borrow.'

'Of course. Could you pop over and see?'

'I could…' Weeks said hesitantly. 'But it might be better if you went, Sir. Make sure you get a good fit, if you know what I mean…'

Russell chuckled. 'Fair point, lad. I'll go over now. See if they've got something in *my* size.'

~o~

Bates, Sammy and Baker were again sitting round the table in the farmhouse. The mood was sombre and little had been said for some time. Empty mugs, beer bottles, a couple of candle stubs and an overflowing ashtray littered the surface. They heard a noise from the road. Sammy looked round nervously, Baker got up and crossed to the window. Cautiously lifting the corner of the ragged sacking he peered out. 'Thank Christ for that!' he said. 'It's just Tommy coming back.' He dropped the cloth again and slumped in his seat.

The front door eventually opened and Tommy walked in. He didn't look too happy. 'I've got some bad news for you, lads.'

'What is it, Tommy?' Bates asked, concern on his pudgy face.

'It's Johnny – or should I say, Detective Constable Weeks. I hold my hands up – you were right and I was wrong.'

'*What?!*' Baker roared, jumping to his feet. His chair crashed to the floor.

''E's a copper,' Atkins stated simply.

'But *how*?' Sammy said, fear in his eyes. 'You said he was "sound as a pound".'

'Yes I did. An' I was wrong. I was proper shafted by the bastard.' Atkins shook his head dazedly and kicked the leg of a chair before sagging on to the seat. 'Gimme a drink.' Bates leant over and took a bottle of Courage beer out of the crate on the floor. He rested the cap on the edge of the table and thumped down on it with his fist. The cap flew in the air and he handed the bottle, creamy foam running down its neck, to Atkins who tipped the bottle to his lips, his Adam's apple bobbing furiously as he guzzled the contents. When he'd drained the last drop he banged the bottle down on the table, belched and wiped the back of his hand across his mouth.

'We've been 'ad, good and proper. Stitched up like a bleedin' kipper.'

Bates coughed, softly. ''Er, we did warn you Tommy.'

'Yes, yes, I know,' he said, shaking his head. 'But what's done is done. How're we gonna get out of this one? I ain't gonna let this job go; it's too good to lose.' He had a wild look in his eyes.

'C'mon, calm down Tommy. First of all, tell us how you found out,' Baker said.

~o~

Atkins went on to explain his conversation with Helen and how she'd discovered who Weeks really was.

'What did she suggest we do?' Baker asked. 'She usually comes up with a good idea.'

'It all depends on whether 'e'll manage to get 'old of the lorry by Sunday.'

'Oh, yeah?'

'Yeah. Assumin' 'e 'as, she reckons I shouldn't wait to speak to 'im on Sunday evenin'.'

'Then what should you do?' Sammy asked, his eyes slightly less panic-stricken.

'She reckons I should show up at the Queen's an' face 'im.'

We should *all* go up and sort him out!' Baker said angrily, his fists clenched.

'No, no.' Atkins held his hands up. 'The last thing we want is a fuss. Helen reckons, if we're careful, we can carry on as planned.'

'How?'

'This is the way she sees it. Gimme another beer an' I'll tell you what she said.' Bates popped the cap on a bottle and handed it to Atkins. He took a deep draught, and then spoke. 'Now what she reckons is that, as long as 'e *as* got the transport, we can still use 'im as a driver.'

'I don't see how that's going to work,' Bates said.

'Now 'ang on, I ain't finished. What she's suggested is that I sit all peaceful like with 'im in the pub until she rings from Victoria station – and we 'ave the final details we need from 'er contact. She's got a feeling that the day may be changed, but we won't know 'til then. After she's rung, me and Johnny – Weeks – quietly leave the pub and go an' get the lorry. That means 'e won't 'ave time to tell nobody about exactly what's 'appenin'. 'Specially that bloody Russell bloke. Together, we drive down 'ere, but stop at Buxted and wait for Helen who's comin' down by train.'

'That sounds all well and good, Tommy, but what's going to happen on the actual day of the job? Johnny – Weeks that is – is more than likely going to skedaddle in the lorry.'

Tommy tapped the side of his nose. 'Ah – well, that's where Helen comes into 'er own.'

'How so?'

'She's gonna be in the Bedford with 'im – make sure 'e don't do anythin' stupid.'

'That's fine, as far as it goes Tommy,' Bates said thoughtfully, 'but what happens after? You're not going to give him his cut, pat him on the head and send him on his merry way – are you?'

'Of course I bloody ain't!' Atkins said forcefully.

'What *are* you going to do?' The big man looked puzzled.

'Don't you worry. I've already warned 'im I ain't got room for baggage – and *you* know 'ow I deal with any unwanted bags.' Atkins accompanied this statement with a wink which was more of a leer.

'Here. You don't mean what I think you mean?' said Sammy, alarmed.

'Just wait and see. I don't take kindly to bein' duped so he's deserves what 'es got comin' to 'im. Right. Now who's turn is it to get the grub ready?'

~o~

'Right, Sonny. Let's see what we've got.' The dapper form of Captain Salt, retired, rummaged around in a cupboard in his office at the Collinghurst terminus of the three foot gauge railway to Compass Point. Russell had decided not to enquire about a uniform at the mainline railway station. He reckoned that, as Salt was an old friend, he would have what was needed and that possible gossip would not be spread. 'Ah, this looks promising.' Salt said. He held out a dark blue serge waistcoat, with brass buttons. 'I don't think this will be too much different from what they're wearing nowadays at Victoria.'

Russell shrugged his arms out of his jacket and laid it over the back of a chair. He sported a crisp white shirt, the sleeves shortened with expanding metal armbands, and a dark navy tie. Salt helped him on with the waistcoat then passed him a peaked cap.

Russell put it on his head then fastened the buttons on the waistcoat. He stood back. 'How do I look?'

Salt smiled, his blue eyes twinkling. 'Excellent. You'll blend in perfectly.' He cocked his head to one side and squinted. 'Just a minute,' he said. 'Give me the cap.'

Russell took it off and handed it over. 'Why? What's wrong?'

'This is,' said Salt, unpinning the badge. 'Bit of a giveaway.'

'Why's that?'

Salt chuckled. 'It says 'WVR' – Wichmere Valley Railway. That won't do if you're supposed to work for British Railways! You'll just have to wear it without a badge – nobody will notice.' He handed the cap back. 'I suppose you can't tell me why you need the uniform?'

'I'm afraid not. Best if I don't say any more for now. I'm sure you'll hear about it in the fullness of time.'

# Chapter 15

## The previous year

*Courvoisier launched the Josephine bottle in 1951,
to honour Napoleon's first wife. The shape of the bottle,
with a thin neck and wide base, may possibly mimic
Josephine's love of corsets.*

SOMETIME AFTER his discovery of the gun shipment Wolfgang was lying on his bunk, staring at the ceiling. He'd been thinking about what he'd found but had come to no conclusions about it. He felt he may be able to turn it to his advantage, but wasn't sure how to. There was a step on the deck, the boat swayed slightly, then a rap on the roof. The little German started. He never had visitors. Peering out of the window in the side of the coachhouse he could see a pair of legs encased in grubby trousers. Dickens. What on earth did he want? He never came to the boat. The only time Wolfgang normally saw him was when he visited his office to pay his mooring dues. He slipped off the bunk, stepped on to the companionway and pushed open the doors. Dickens's sideways face appeared in the doorway.

'Can I come aboard, shipmate?' he asked, jovially.

'I suppose so.' Wolfgang stepped back while the Irishman descended into the cabin.

'Well, this is very nice,' he said, looking round. 'You've made yourself very cosy I see. Mind if I sit down?' Wolfgang shrugged. Dickens sat on the bunk, smiling and stroking his beard.

Wolfgang resented the intrusion but was determined to be polite. 'Would you like coffee – or something stronger?'

'Ooh, thanks a million. A drop of grog would go down a treat.'

Wolfgang made his way into the galley and came back with a bottle of Courvoisier and two glasses. Dickens smacked his lips. This was a rare treat. When the drink had been poured and he had taken a good mouthful he stared pointedly at Wolfgang. 'I'm wondering if you can do me a bit of a favour.'

'Oh, yes?'

'Dickens scanned the cabin. 'You've got a very nice craft here. I bet it's a good sea boat.'

'Yes, it is actually.'

'Perfect for making a long passage.'

'Yes it is.'

'So I'm wondering if you'd be prepared to do a little delivery for me.'

Wolfgang felt a cold chill run through his body. 'I am not sure.'

'You haven't got anything to keep you here, have you?'

'I have actually,' Wolfgang said, remembering the appointment in Harley Street. 'I'm waiting for an important letter.'

'Oh yes? And when you are expecting this letter?'

'Anytime soon, I should think.'

'Well the trip I have planned for you probably won't take too long – a week at the most, I would imagine. Surely you can spare that for an old mate?' He held out his glass for a refill.

'Hmm. I really am not sure. Why exactly are you asking me? Are there no other *old mates* you could ask?'

'To be sure, but I think this is something you'd be glad to do for me.' His raisin-brown eyes twinkled.

Wolfgang was baffled. 'And why would I be glad to do it for you?'

'Ah, well, perhaps it's because you'd like me to keep a little secret.' Dickens winked.

Despite the warmth of the brandy, Wolfgang felt unnaturally cold and the cabin had lost its cosiness. 'I do not understand.'

'Let me put it this way.' Dickens settled back on the bunk, wriggling until he was comfortable. 'A little bird has told me that you're not all you seem, Monsieur *Meunier.*'

Wolfgang's blood had turned to ice. He had trouble speaking but just managed to blurt out: 'I – I do not know what you mean.'

'What if I tell you that I'm aware that your rather fine craft,' he threw his arm out, encompassing the cabin, 'is actually called *Moonshine.*' Wolfgang was stunned, and it showed. 'Isn't it?'

'B – but how do you know?'

Dickens pursed his lips. 'Let me just say that I have my sources.'

'But how?'

'A little bird told me,' he said again and tapped his nose. 'I also heard that you might have had a bit of a run-in with the not so local constabulary of late,' Dickens smirked. 'To be more precise, there's something of a price on your head, isn't there… *Herr Müller?*' Wolfgang was speechless. Dickens leaned forward and placed a non-too clean hand on the German's knee and leered up into his face. 'Not to put too finer a point on it, you're wanted for murder.' He leaned back against the side of the boat and folded his arms across his chest.

They sat in silence for some minutes while Wolfgang gathered his thoughts. Finally he spoke, his voice croaky. 'So, tell me what you know.'

'Well, *Herr Müller*, it seems you're on the run, not only from the British police but also the French gendarmes, and probably Interpol too, I wouldn't be surprised. It seems that you've been party to the death of three Nazis and almost bumped off a fourth. You're something of celebrity – a rather infamous one, but a celebrity, none the less.' He paused. 'You look like you need a drink. Here.' He reached across, picked up the brandy bottle and poured a good measure into Wolfgang's glass.

'Is that all?' Wolfgang said, and took a good swig.

'Holy Mother of God! Isn't that enough?'

Wolfgang put the glass down carefully. 'Well...'

'What I don't understand, is why you fetched up here, rather than going to ground on the Continent.' Dickens rested his chin on his upturned finger and frowned. 'Oh yes,' he said, 'Ludwig.'

'How dare you!' the German hissed.

Dickens was unruffled. 'Oh, I dare all right.' He leaned forward and grasped Wolfgang's wrist. 'I think I'm holding all the trump cards – don't you?' He let go of the man's wrist and pushed it aside, as if it was diseased. 'You're only here because your brother is banged up in prison and you can't cope without him. Am I right?'

Wolfgang looked deflated. His beloved brother, Ludwig, was his Achilles heel. Ever since the arrest he had struggled to cope without his reassuring presence. He was close to breaking down.

Dickens sensed his distress and his manner softened. 'You help me and I may be able to help you. Now, can we talk about this little job you're *happily* going to do for me?'

The two men sat quietly for some time, sipping their drinks and eyeing each other over the rims of their glasses. Wolfgang spoke. 'You want me to smuggle your guns.'

It was Dickens's turn to look surprised. 'What? How?' Then he chuckled. 'I knew I'd nailed that lid down.' He held his glass up in salute. 'Very clever.'

Wolfgang, feeling he had scored a minor point, went on, 'Where I am supposed to be going?'

'Ireland… Cork to be exact.'

'*Ireland*? But that's miles!' He'd just lost his point.

'About 500, give or take.'

'But that will take weeks!'

'I don't think so,' Dickens mused. 'In this fine craft, I reckon you'll be able to average about 10 knots, so it shouldn't take longer than a couple of days, three at the most. Then about the same for the return journey – *if* you decide to come back.'

Wolfgang was desperate to regain some control. 'Are you not forgetting something?'

'Oh yes? And what could that be?'

'Fuel.'

'Come again?'

'*Moonshine* might be a *fine craft*, but she does not run on air…'

Realisation dawned. 'Ah, I see what you're getting at. You think we'll have to stop to refuel.' He grinned. '*And*, maybe you'd be able jump ship?' The grin spread and he waggled his index finger from side to side. 'Naughty…' Wolfgang thought he'd scored another point but the next statement took the wind out of his sails. 'We'll take it with us. I've got plenty of oil drums. We can lash a couple of them on the deck.'

Wolfgang tried one more gambit. 'You've forgotten something else. I'll need to sleep.'

Dickens was still grinning, his mouth a dark maw. 'Ah, well, I've got a solution for that.'

'What?'

'You won't be on your own.' The grin grew wider, the shadows in his mouth, deeper. 'I'm coming with you!'

# Chapter 16

*__Little Ben__ is a cast-iron miniature clock tower,*
*situated at the intersection of Vauxhall Bridge Road and*
*Victoria Street, in Westminster, close to the approach*
*to Victoria station. Its design mimics Big Ben, at the*
*other end of Victoria Street.*

SUNDAY WAS a busy day for travelling. Helen, dressed for a day out, and Russell, with his disguise carried in a valise, both headed for London, albeit on different trains. Bates took Atkins to the station at Buxted in his Morris van, dropping him off and skedaddling back to the farm where the others helped him reverse it back into the secrecy of the barn.

There was a palpable air of tension in the farmhouse. Despite Atkins's reassurances, they were rattled by Weeks's unmasking.

'I just knew he was a wrong'un, the moment I clapped eyes on him,' Laurie Baker said, looking out moodily from under his low fringe.

'Me, too.' Bates added. 'I dunno what came over Tommy – he's usually so careful.'

Sammy spoke. 'I know what it was.' They looked at the little man but couldn't hold his gaze. His eyes were everywhere, avoiding contact.

'Go on then, tell us.'

'It was either women or booze.' His eyes continued searching the corners of the room. 'You know how he gets when he's had one too many. Everyone's his friend.'

'True,' Baker said.

'And I seem to remember him saying that first night he met *Johnny* he'd had a run in with some tart and *Johnny* was nice to him – listened to his problems.'

'I bet he bleedin' did,' Bates added, and went on, 'What d'you think Tommy plans on doing with him, Laurie? You know him better than the rest of us.'

Baker cupped his chin and rubbed his hand on the bristles. 'I shudder to think. You know what Tommy's like – one minute all sweetness and light, the next…'

'Yeah, he can certainly be a moody bugger,' Bates said.

Sammy stopped looking round the room for a moment, his eyes fixed on Baker. 'Worse than moody, he can be downright dangerous.'

Helen had some time to kill so she went to the WH Smiths bookstall and perused the magazines. She was delighted to find the latest copy of *Harper's Bazaar*. With Audrey Hepburn on the cover, she knew she was in for a treat and was happy to pay the price for the American import. The day was mild so she took it outside and sat on a bench to read. From this position, she could clearly see the clock face on *Little Ben* and keep an eye on the time: Six-thirty-five. She didn't want to miss her rendezvous.

Earlier, Russell had arrived at Charing Cross Station. He was in plenty of time and as it was a pleasant afternoon he decided to walk. Once through Admiralty Arch he turned into Saint James's

Park, passing nannies pushing their charges in Silver Cross prams and gentlemen in their weekend lounge suits taking the air. He picked up Buckingham Palace Road and was at Victoria station in less than half an hour.

Once inside he went down into the gents, so he could effect a change. The dapper man in a trim navy suit who had entered the cubicle, emerged, still smart, in a porter's garb. He had put his jacket and homburg hat in the valise and when he regained the station concourse he found the left-luggage lockers and deposited the bag, locking the door and tucking the key in his pocket. Looking round, he soon spotted a porter's barrow near the entrance to the platforms. He stood nearby for a while, thumbs hooked in the waistcoat's pockets, but nobody claimed it. So, whistling a snatch of Mack Gordon's *Chatanooga Choo Choo* he walked up to it, grasped the handles and wheeled it along the station concourse.

There was a tricky moment when a porter came towards him, struggling with a trolley, laden with cases, but the man just nodded and passed by. Emboldened, Russell continued outside the station building, into the gathering gloom. Pushing his barrow he saw a woman sitting on a bench, with a magazine on her lap, and almost started when he thought it was Helen. But, as he drew closer, he realised he had been mistaken; the woman was older and coarser. He kept away from the rank where a row of Austin FX3 cabs stood – he didn't want anyone actually to employ his services. He just stood whistling nonchalantly and staring into space. He hoped it looked as if he was waiting for a particular fare.

Then, further along, he saw her. Russell's heart skipped a beat, whether from emotion or tension he couldn't say. She was sitting on a bench near the clock. He needed to get closer but not too close, so that he remained unobtrusive. Pulling his cap further down over his eyes, he began to push the barrow in a wide circle behind where she was sitting. He settled on the other side of a large iron pillar where he gauged he was in a good position to observe her and any companion she might meet, and also hopefully to hear what was being said between them. He settled down to wait. But just then he felt a sharp, painful tap on his shoulder and smelt a waft of 4711 *eau de cologne.*

'My man, my man!' Russell's heart sank into his boots as he turned reluctantly to face a large, imposing woman, the spitting image of Margaret Rutherford. 'My man!' the piercing voice rang out again. Russell wondered if his cover was blown but daren't look round to see.

'Madam,' he said at last, somehow managing to sound relatively cheerful, 'how can I help?'

'I need to catch a train of course,' the woman boomed as if she was talking to a fool. 'Take this and this while I carry my little *Bobo* and be quick. Platform 10 – *now!*' *Bobo*, a small, brown, bad-tempered Yorkshire terrier, bared its tiny teeth and snarled at him.

The woman had only one bag and two small packages wrapped in brown paper and was quite capable of transporting them herself. But she was obviously used to being waited upon and having her orders obeyed. So, rather than make a fuss and draw any more attention to himself, Russell touched his cap and put the luggage, such as it was, on to his barrow. He followed in her wake to the platform she had indicated. Once he had decanted her and her property into a first-class carriage, he hurried back towards the bench where Helen was, much to his relief, still sitting engrossed in her magazine. He hadn't received a tip from the woman – or a thank you, and had narrowly avoided being nipped by the repulsive Bobo. He continued past Helen, back to his position behind the pillar, but she took no notice of him. His disguise was working.

He hadn't been standing back there for long when, from the corner of his eye, he saw a man, dressed in what he initially thought were standard British Railways clothes. Coming out of the station, he walked past Helen, then stopped and sat on the bench next to her. Russell sneaked a sideways glance. He could see the man was actually wearing drainpipe trousers and sported a bootlace tie. His hair was elaborately styled with a sculpted quiff and the sides combed back to form what was known as a duck's arse at the neck. They made an unlikely pair – the elegant lady about town and the BR Teddy boy.

As soon as he had sat down Helen threw her arms round the man's neck and kissed him full on the mouth. Then, just as quickly, she took her arms away and glanced round, embarrassed in case anyone should have witnessed her impetuous show of affection. Russell didn't count, he was an anonymous railway servant. But Russell was embarrassed by what he had witnessed – and more than a little confused. But still he stood there, secretly observing.

The pair sat without speaking for some time then Helen looked at the man. 'Are you okay, Simon?' she asked.

He nodded and replied. His back was towards Russell so, frustratingly, all he heard was a mumble.

'Is it still okay?' Russell could hear Helen clearly.

The man spoke again.

Suddenly she sat bolt up right. '*What*?' she exclaimed.

The man held his hands out in submission and appeared to say something placatory.

Helen visibly relaxed. 'It's still on?'

The man nodded.

'And the train leaves Brighton at 9.30?'

Again he nodded.

'Still a goods train?'

Russell caught a few words in reply. Something about 'overcrowding' and the 'need to reschedule'.

Helen put her head in her hands and he heard her mumble: 'Oh, *God*.'

The man took her hands down, held them in his and said something.

'So it shouldn't make any difference?' she asked.

He shook his head and began to stand.

She reached up and held his arm. 'Are you sure?'

He nodded. She stood up and kissed him on the cheek. He smiled and squeezed her hand and Russell heard him say, 'See you soon.' Russell looked into the distance as Simon passed by in front of him.

# Chapter 17

## The previous year

*Slough of Despond: described by Bunyan as: 'A place that cannot be mended where, as the sinner is awakened about his lost condition, there ariseth in his soul many fears and doubts and discouraging apprehensions'.*

WOLFGANG WAS on tenterhooks. For several days, since the uncomfortable, not to say nerve-racking, hour or so he had spent in the company of the creepy Dickens, he had been waiting. Not only for a return visit but for a letter from the equally creepy Doctor Baxter. Neither had turned up so far. He was getting low on food and had been drinking tea and coffee without milk. He didn't want to leave the boat yard to go to the local shop, in case he bumped into the yard owner.

He was very tempted to slip his moorings in the night and just disappear. But to where? His options were pretty limited. He couldn't head east along the coast, as that would bring him too close to Nottery Quay, where the boat was known. And, even more dangerous, Compass Point, where he had bought her, so that direction was out. And west? That would take him to the more populous waters of Chichester, Portsmouth and the Solent. Also not a good idea. France? After his near miss with

Inspecteur Bruissement in the *bar-tabac*, France didn't seem a very wise choice either. If it wasn't for the fact that his brother, Ludwig, was locked up in prison and he had a determination to get him released, he would happily have ended it all. Without that burning desire, there didn't seem much point in carrying on, especially as Dickens now had such a vice-like hold over him. Not for the first time he felt totally helpless, if not hopeless.

He was starting to spiral down into what Bunyan had described as a *Slough of Despond*. He knew he didn't want to go to that dark place, but seemed to have no will to stop himself. He was just reaching for the brandy bottle when there was a step on the deck. The boat lurched and so did his stomach. It could only be Dickens. Sure enough, the cabin doors opened and the man's grimy face appeared, grinning as he descended the steps. Noticing Wolfgang holding the bottle, his eyes lit up.

'Good man! What a great idea.' Reluctantly Wolfgang picked up two glasses and poured a measure into each. Dickens grabbed his and toasted Wolfgang. '*Sláinte*,' he said, then drained the glass, immediately holding it out for a refill. After Wolfgang had topped him up he sat back and relaxed, his hand going automatically to the scrubby beard. The less than companionable silence stretched for a while until he said: 'Oh, I almost forgot, this came for you.' He reached into his jacket and withdrew a crumpled envelope. 'Sorry, it's a bit battered. Oh, and I opened it by mistake – couldn't read the name on the front properly. Thought it might be meant for me.' He gave a toothless grin.

Wolfgang, almost speechless with fury, snatched it from him and was just able to grunt, 'thanks.'

'Aren't you going to open it then? Might be important.' Dickens feigned surprise. 'Oh, it is important, isn't it? 'Cause I've seen it already.' He cackled and had another drink. Wolfgang's hands were shaking as he took a single sheet of paper out of the envelope and read:

Dear M. Meunier,

I am writing following your visit to my clinic last week. After assessing the results of my thorough examination of your diseased limb and consulting with my medical colleagues, I have come to a number of conclusions.

1. This infliction, visited upon your person in childhood, has caused you great distress and discomfort and inconvenience, as well as actual pain.

2. If this infliction had received adequate treatment earlier in your life the spread of its debilitating effects may have been mitigated.

3. But, as the continuing onset has not been checked, you find yourself in this unfortunate state.

4. However, I believe that with the correct surgery, we can not only halt the progress of this debilitating affliction but actually reverse its progress.

In consequence, I urge you to accept my offer of surgery. This would require a general anaesthetic, to render you incapacitated. But, in this unconscious state we will be able to operate on you. As explained, I intend to break then lengthen the bones of the leg.

The operation will take several hours and I will need a competent team around me — anaesthetist, two assistants and two nurses. As a consequence, this procedure will not be inexpensive. In addition you will need several weeks, if not months convalescence in a suitable location with nursing staff on hand. I can organise such a facility if you so wish, and I urge you to take advantage of my knowledge in this area.

My fee for undertaking the operation and providing convalescent after care facilities for a minimum of four weeks comes to a total *of six hundred guineas. Further convalescent care will be on a pro rata basis.*

*In order to show your good will, I ask that you pay a security deposit – in advance – amounting to one third of the total. That is two hundred guineas – in cash. I suggest you send the money by registered delivery.*

*On receipt of the said deposit, I will inform you of the date of the proposed procedure.*

*Yours, Nathan Baxter*
*Doctor Nathan Baxter, FRCS.*

Wolfgang read the letter twice. The first time he scanned it quickly, the second he took his time to absorb the details. When he had finished he sat back, non-plussed.

'Thought that would give you a bit of surprise.' Wolfgang looked up. He had forgotten that Dickens was still there. The man was grinning at him, all stumps and gaps. 'You want my advice?' Wolfgang just stared. 'I wouldn't touch it with a bargepole.' He leaned forward. 'You don't know this man, do you?' The German shook his head. 'He might have letters after his name, but anyone can do that. It seems a whole heap of money, doesn't it?' Wolfgang nodded solemnly. 'And, to put it frankly, it sounds awfully bloody risky. Are you sure you want it done?'

Wolfgang felt wretched. The letter had just piled more misery on to his already depressed mood. He felt helpless and, however distasteful he found the man, he was the nearest thing to a friend he now had. 'What do you think I should do?' He looked imploringly at Dickens, whose smile widened.

'First of all, I think you should top up our drinks.' He held out his glass. When it was filled to his satisfaction he continued:

'Then you should consider very carefully if you want to go through all that pain and distress, not to mention the length of time you'll be out of action.' He paused. 'And of course, the cost. Do you have that sort of money?'

'I do have funds, but it might be a little difficult to gain access to that amount of cash.'

'Mmm. That's what I thought.' Dickens was quiet for a moment. 'Now listen…' Wolfgang looked up, a hopeless expression on his face. '… I didn't intend that you undertook our little *voyage* without some sort of pay-off. That would be just cruel. I'm not saying that the amount you'd get would cover what you need but it might go some way towards it.'

Wolfgang nodded slowly. He was still deeply depressed but perhaps there was a glimmer of light at the end of a very long tunnel. He knew that what Dickens wanted him to do was highly dangerous. But with the life he'd led and the risks he'd taken over the past few months, it couldn't be any worse than what he'd been through. If it all went according to plan and he could free himself from the burden of Dickens's hold over him, he would be able to continue his quest to have his brother released from prison. His mind was clearing and he was able to think ahead – beyond the present. He put his thoughts into words. 'You might be able to do something else for me.'

'Ah, well, that depends what it is.'

Wolfgang seemed to rally slightly. He decided to appeal to the man's vanity. 'You appear to be a man of many abilities.'

Dickens smirked. 'I suppose you could say that.'

'And you have contacts in many areas?'

'That's true, I do.'

'Are you able to get hold of papers?'

'What sort of papers exactly?' His expression had changed to one of suspicion.

Wolfgang pressed on, feeling he might have gained a slight advantage. 'Identity papers – passports.'

Dickens's smirk returned. 'Oh, I see. You'd like to change your identity – properly.'

'It could be advantageous to you too...'

'How so?'

'If I was actually able to become Monsieur Meunier and anything untoward occurred on our *voyage*, it might be better if my real identity was hidden.'

'That's true,' Dickens said thoughtfully, his hand on his beard. 'The Irish do have certain sympathies for Germans, but they probably wouldn't for you!' His laugh was more like a cackle and ended in a fit of coughing.

Wolfgang sat and watched until the man had regained control. 'So, can you do it? Do you know the right people?'

'I'll think about it.' Dickens stood up, put his empty glass down on the table and looked sternly at him, the laughter now gone. 'Yes, I'll think about it. Meanwhile, you'd better hurry up and decide what you're going to do about this letter. I've got a cargo that needs shifting – and I want it moved soon.' The smile returned to his lips but the look in his eyes remained hard. 'You do realise that I could just take your boat, if I wanted to? I don't think you'd be inclined to report it stolen to the police. Would you now?' He gave a little bow. 'Anyway, I'll leave you to decide – for the time being. I'll pop by to see you tomorrow. Oh, and by the way. You can go out to the shop now. I know you've been avoiding me.' He winked, and made his way out of the cabin.

# Chapter 18

*The London Underground, also known by its nickname the Tube, is a public rapid transit system serving London and some parts of the adjacent counties of Buckinghamshire, Essex and Hertfordshire.*

AS SOON as Helen had started moving back towards the station entrance, Russell followed, at a suitable distance. She had made straight for a red telephone box, pulled the door open and let it close behind her. Russell knew it was so well built that he wouldn't be able to hear anything. He just hoped that Weeks would be able to fill him in when he got back.

The DC had been sitting in the Queen's Head since it opened and was nervously sipping from his drink. The landlord had shown little surprise at seeing him standing on the doorstep when he opened at seven o'clock and was happy to pull him a pint. Weeks kept checking his watch, concerned that he'd missed the phone call. Now that the day of the job was getting closer he was starting to wonder if he'd made a massive mistake, getting in so deep. He knew he was a good copper but didn't think he was a particularly brave man. His run-in with

Wolfgang Müller the previous year, when he had come close to dying, had shaken him more than he cared to admit. He didn't relish getting into a similar situation with Atkins and his gang.

However carefully the robbery had been planned, there was always room for error with so many unknowns. What if there were security guards on the train or the locomotive crew proved stubborn? He didn't think that Atkins planned any violence but Weeks was well aware of how quickly his mood could change. What the consequences would be if he grew really angry just didn't bear thinking about…

At seven-fifteen the phone rang. Weeks was just was rising to his feet when the door was flung open and Atkins marched in. Weeks stood rooted to the spot – stunned. 'T – Tommy!' he stammered.

Atkins flung his arm out, his finger pointing at Weeks. 'You just sit there and don't move,' he snapped. Weeks slumped back into his seat, his mouth gaping while Atkins took the telephone from the barman. 'Helen,' he said, smiling, 'good to 'ear from you. How did the meetin' go?'

A pause.

'Did he give you the details?'

'Good.'

'So it's still on for this week?'

Another pause.

Then, loudly:,'What?! Why's that then?'

'Oh, I see.'

He was silent for a few moments, listening. Then he laughed, not a cheerful, musical laugh but an unpleasant one. The sort that a pantomime villain would adopt to frighten children in the audience.

'No, that's not a problem. Everything's in place and that will act in our favour. Can't say more at the mo,' he looked across at Weeks, who was still dumb-founded, 'our *driver* is sittin' just over there.'

Atkins listened again, then:

'Great. What time you gettin' in? Okay, see you in a couple of hours. Ta-ta for now. Bye.' He handed the phone back to the barman and nodded at the beer pump. 'Yes, please.'

'And one for your friend?' he said, hopefully.

'Nah. Not for 'im. 'E's drivin'.' He paid the barman, picked up his drink and walked across to where Weeks was sitting. ''Ello me old cocker. 'Ow's it going?' He punched the other man on the arm, non too gently and took a deep draught of his drink.

Weeks had gained a modicum of composure. 'But Tommy, you were supposed to ring me. What are you doing here?'

Atkins pulled a face, half-way between a grin and a grimace. 'I thought you'd like some company.'

'Yes, of course, but wasn't I going to meet you...' he looked round but the barman was nowhere to be seen, '...down in Uckfield?'

'Change of plan, mate.'

'But I thought you'd worked it all out meticulously – you said once the job was planned you had to stick to it.'

Atkins grabbed his lapel and leaned in close to Weeks's face. 'Are you questionin' my judgement?'

'No, of course not, Tommy. It's just that...'

'Listen. You're *only* the driver, and don't you forget it.' He pushed Weeks back against his seat and pointed his thumb at his own chest. 'I'm the mastermind behind this job.' His face was like thunder as he took another drink. Then he relaxed a little. 'Now, finish your pint and let's go and get the truck.'

'But…'

'No buts. As I said, change of plan. We're takin' it down tonight. Is that a problem? I presume you've got the lorry?'

Weeks was panicking. He needed to let his boss know what was going on. 'Of course, Tommy. It's just…'

'Listen, I ain't going to say it again. Drink your pint – or leave it. Whichever. We're off – now.'

The landlord came back behind the bar in time to see the street door swinging closed. He looked across towards the table where an empty glass stood next to one that was half-full.

~o~

Outside the pub Atkins had his hand gripped tightly round Weeks's elbow. 'Right, where's this bleeding three-tonner?'

Weeks couldn't understand what was happening. Atkins had never acted quite like this, particularly for such a long period. Normally his mood lightened quickly. 'It's over by those bombed-out warehouses – in Stone Street.'

Atkins grip lessened, but he didn't let go. 'Ah, bombed-out buildings.' He smiled at the memory. 'I used to love 'em as a kid. Amazing what you could find. Doubt there's anythin' worth 'aving there now – except our transport, of course.'

While they were walking Weeks had been wondering if he could make a run for it, but the grip on his arm was still tight, so he just carried on, thinking furiously but making no sense of the situation. What was Tommy up to? He didn't mind going down to the location of the job early but he just couldn't understand why. Plus, how was he going to let DI Russell know about the change of plans?

''Penny for your thoughts mate?… Mate?'

Weeks realised that Atkins was talking to him. 'Sorry? What?'

Atkins grinned. 'You was miles away. Somethin' Important?

'No, no. Nothing in particular.' He shrugged though he was starting to feel uncomfortably out of his depth.

'That's all right then. C'mon, we're nearly there.'

They turned the corner into Stone Street and approached the derelict warehouses. Half-way along the tumbledown row, a pair of wooden doors stood slightly ajar. Weeks peered through the gap. 'Here it is.'

Finally Atkins let go of the other man's arm. 'You grab that side. Let's get these doors open.'

~O~

Russell retrieved his valise from the left-luggage locker. He was in too much of a hurry to change so he just stuffed the cap in the top of the bag and hurried to the Underground station. It was just three stops on the Circle and District line to Embankment. He bought a ticket, made his way to the platform and stood near the edge, waiting impatiently. After a few minutes, the air began to stir and there was a murmur in the distance that gradually became louder. The murmur turned into a roar and the familiar shape of the aluminium Tube rushed along the line and shuddered to a halt at the platform edge. The doors opened and Russell bustled inside.

As it was Sunday, there was no crush of bodies, just a few people; well-dressed couples mainly, on their way out to dinner perhaps, Russell thought. Although agitated he took a seat, but only perched on the edge of it, staring up at the network diagram while willing the train to get a move on. Taking a deep, calming breath he looked down. The gaps between the hardwood slats that made up the floor were packed with cigarette ends, discarded tickets and other scraps of rubbish.

St. James's Park followed by Westminster were quickly passed until finally the train was braking as it approached Embankment station. Once the door had opened Russell hurried out and made his way up the escalator, taking the moving stairs at a run. He handed his ticket over to the collector at the barrier and virtually trotted along Villiers Street; up the steps and into Charing Cross Station. Panting, he stared up at the board, as the lettered panels revolved and clattered. He saw that his train was leaving in two minutes so he dashed to the platform, presented his ticket and got on board, slamming the door behind him. As he slumped into a seat, he heard the guard blow his whistle, the locomotive respond with an echoing *toot!* and the train pulled away. It was now too dark to see anything but lights that flashed past the window, diminishing as the train left the capital. He wished he'd brought something to read.

Weeks felt across the nearside front tyre of the lorry and, as Valiant had promised, there was the key. Taking it, he walked round to the driver's door, opened the lock and climbed into the cab. He reached across, unlocked the passenger door and Atkins climbed in. Weeks pressed the starter; the engine turned over, coughed, and burst into life. Just as he was putting it into gear, Atkins leaned across and said, pointedly: 'And no funny business please, Johnny. You just drive. I'll tell you where to go.'

They headed west, and apart from the noise of the engine and occasional directions from Atkins, travelled in silence. As they approached Buxted, he said: 'Take the next right. The train's not due for half an hour. We need to hole up for a while.' As Weeks turned the heavy steering wheel he saw a sign – Spotted Cow Lane. After a few hundred yards Atkins said: 'This'll do. Pull over.' Weeks slowed and they bumped off the road and on to a patch of rough ground. He switched the engine off. After the noise of travelling the silence was almost deafening, leavened with the metallic pinking of the engine as it cooled.

Weeks turned to his companion. 'What train are we waiting for?'

Atkins tapped his nose. 'Just you wait and see. I'm gonna 'ave a snooze. Wake me up in 20 minutes.'

~O~

Russell's train pulled into Collinghurst. He hurried quickly to the police station. The desk Sergeant, Wickstead, looked up from the paper he was reading. 'Evening, Sonny. Didn't expect to see you here today.'

'No,' he laughed. 'I wasn't planning on coming in. Have you seen Johnny Weeks?'

'Funny you should say that...' He folded his arms and frowned. 'He was in here...let me see... about half past six, then went off. Hasn't been back since.'

'Do you know where he went?'

'He didn't say. Left his car though. It's out the back.' He pointed over his shoulder with His thumb.'

'Mmm. Strange. I suppose he didn't mention the Queen's Head?'

'Do you think he might have gone there to drown his sorrows?' Wickstead's moustache bristled as he grinned.

'Why do you say that?'

'We-ell. He wasn't exactly miserable, but he seemed agitated. Sort of… wound up.'

'I see. I don't suppose he left his keys?'

Wickstead reached under the counter. 'He did. Do you want to take them?'

'Thanks,' Russell said, 'I will. If he comes back, tell him I've got the car.'

First he drove towards the Queen's Head but parked a couple of streets away. Locking the car, he walked to the pub and entered the bar. Sundays were usually quiet and there were just the customary two old chaps, playing yet another game of dominoes; a middle-aged couple sitting in silence at one of the tables, he staring into his beer and she, tight-lipped, clutching her capacious handbag to her ample bosom, an almost untouched gin and bitter lemon on the table in front of her; he in a flat cap and she in a black felt hat, a faded flower in the brim – not the cheeriest of sights. Russell made his way to the bar.

'Yes, Sir, what can I get you?' the barman asked.

'I'll have a Jameson's please.'

'A double?'

'No, just a single, thanks.'

'Fair enough.' The man turned, took a glass off the shelf and pushed it up under an optic. The measure of amber liquid tumbled into the glass. Turning back he asked: 'Anything else, Sir?'

'That's all thanks. How much do I owe you?' He counted out the coins. 'I don't suppose a friend of mine was in here earlier?' he then asked.

'What did he look like?'

'My sort of height, younger, with a shock of black curly hair.'

'Oh, Johnny. Yes he was here. Went off in hurry – left half his pint behind.'

'I see. Did he leave a message?'

'Afraid not.'

Russell was baffled. He would have thought that Weeks would at least have left a note for him. 'Oh… thanks anyway.' He drained his glass, nodded a farewell and walked out.

'He wasn't on his own,' the barman called after him, but the door slammed on his words.

It took only a few minutes to walk to Stone Street and along to the bombed-out warehouses. Russell saw the doors gaping open and quickened his step. When he reached it the building was empty. He knelt and, taking a box of Swan Vestas out of his pocket, struck one of the matches on the side and held it close to the ground. He could make out the distinctive tyre tracks of the Bedford lorry in the damp soil.

Back in the car he set off for the stony track where his railway carriage home was. Weeks's own cottage lay not far from it. It was a single-story dwelling, built in the 1920s with whitewashed pebbled-dashed walls and a red, diamond patterned roof. Russell drew up outside but the windows were dark. He hammered on the door but there was just a hollow echo from within. 'Drat!' he said and stomped back to the car. He sat in the driving seat, gripping the steering wheel and thinking hard. Where could Weeks be? He was sure that he would have left a message. Russell knew, or rather he inferred, that the job Atkins had planned was going ahead as scheduled on the Tuesday, two days hence. So why would Weeks go now? He could only assume that the phone call he had been waiting for in the Queen's Head had prompted him to set off early. The trouble was, Russell couldn't go looking for him without causing suspicion and probably jeopardise the gang's plans, something he was unwilling to risk. He could only hope that his constable was safe and would get a message to him as soon as he could.

~o~

'Tommy? Tommy. Wake up,' Weeks said, shaking Atkins's shoulder.

'What?' Atkins shook his head and blinked his eyes open.

'You told me to wake you in 20 minutes.'

'Did I? Oh yeah.' He gave a huge yawn and stretched his arms out. 'Right, cocker. Get this truck turned round and head for the railway station.'

With some difficulty Weeks turned the Bedford. A combination of the heavy steering, limited lock and narrowness of the lane made it a strenuous task. When the lorry was finally facing the way they had come he was visibly sweating. 'You all right, mate?' Atkins asked, with a sarcastic grin.

'Fine thanks, Tommy,' Weeks replied, breathing heavily. 'Where to now?'

'Back on the main road then down to the station. Just park in the forecourt.' Weeks did as he was bid. Atkins's mood seemed to have lightened after his nap. Perhaps it was going to work out all right after all.

They stopped in front of the station and sat waiting, the engine rhythmically ticking over. It wasn't long before they heard the sound of a train pulling in to the platform. It was late in the evening so only a handful of passengers came out through the station entrance. The last one caused Weeks to gasp in astonishment. It was Helen McDermott!

Atkins looked across at him and gave a mirthless laugh. 'That's right mate, Helen. Didn't expect her, did yer?'

She walked across to the lorry; Atkins pushed the passenger door open then shuffled across the seat towards Weeks. Helen climbed up into the cab. 'Hello Tommy.' She leaned over and gave him a peck on the cheek, then smiled at Weeks. 'And hello, *Detective Constable*.'

# Chapter 19

## The previous year

*A flash is a device used in photography producing a burst of artificial light to help illuminate a scene.*

WOLFGANG FELT much better. He had been to the shop and the simple act of breakfasting on fresh bread and butter, plus having milk for his coffee, had lightened his mood considerably. He certainly did not feel so despondent and the suicidal thoughts of the day before were starting to fade.

After studying the letter in detail and considering what Dickens had said he was coming to the conclusion that Doctor Nathaniel Baxter was nothing short of a charlatan. If he had been able to access the funds he might have been inclined to pursue the matter further. The fact that Baxter had told him, when he visited the clinic, that he did not have any personal experience of the procedure he was proposing, only suggesting that he *believed* that others had achieved successful results, did not fill him with confidence. It really did not sound very positive and was less than encouraging. And now that it seemed probable that Dickens would be able to furnish him with a new identity it lightened his load even further. Hopefully, this would mean he would be able to move about without less caution. The quest to free

Ludwig could gather pace. But… he still had to jump the hurdle of delivering Dickens's illicit cargo. And the thought of spending any length of time in the objectionable man's company made him shudder. 'But be positive, Wolfgang,' he told himself, 'It will soon be over.'

Almost on cue, there was a step on the deck, the companionway doors opened and Dickens descended into the cabin. 'Ah, shipmate, just what I fancy, a bit of breakfast.' He helped himself to the bread and butter. Wolfgang gave a wan smile and waited while the other man spread the butter thickly on the chunk of bread he had torn off the loaf. He bit into it with obvious relish. 'Have you made up your mind?' he mumbled, through a mouthful of food.

Wolfgang fetched another cup and poured the man a coffee. 'I think so,' he said. 'You're probably right in your assessment of Doctor Baxter. I have not given up the idea entirely, just put it on hold.'

'Good man. I think you've made the right decision.'

'But,' Wolfgang said, holding up a finger, 'I really do need a new set of documents.'

Dickens finished his bread, sat back and drained his cup. He wiped the back of his hand across his mouth. 'You'll be pleased to hear it's already in hand.'

'Oh really?' Wolfgang was impressed by the speed at which the other man had worked.

'Yes, I spoke to a colleague of mine and he says it shouldn't be a problem. It will cost, of course, but I'm sure we can come to some sort of accommodation.' Dickens winked. 'Now, I think we should prepare for our little adventure, don't you?'

The next day was spent readying the boat for the trip. In spite of his slovenly appearance and the state of the yard, Dickens could be very good at organising when he wanted to. Although he was only slightly built he seemed to be as strong as an ox. Single-handed he manhandled a couple of 45- gallon oil drums on to the after-deck and lashed them securely in place. Next he wheeled a filled drum along the rickety jetty, which, amazingly, held its weight. Then, using a manual pump and a length of hose, he transferred the contents into one drum. Next he wheeled another over and filled the second drum. Once that was completed he examined the rest of the boat, considering how best to stow the cargo. Ludwig looked on, unsettled by the way he seemed to have lost control of his own vessel. To compound his bafflement, Dickens suddenly turned round and said: 'Come on, we've got an appointment to keep.'

'What? Where?'

'You'll find out soon enough. Follow me.' Wolfgang went down into the cabin and returned, wearing his dark glasses and wide-brimmed hat and leaning on his stick. Dickens led the way through the debris of the boatyard and out into the adjacent lane. After they had walked a hundred yards or so, he stopped and rapped on the door of a terraced cottage. The door creaked open and a wizened little man greeted them. Following him down a narrow, dark passageway they were led into a small, white-painted room, the only furniture a wooden chair that had seen better days. The man picked up an impressive camera from the floor. Attached to it was a flash gun sporting a large dished reflector that did its best to dwarf him.

'*Et voila*! Time to have your image immortalised.' Now Wolfgang understood why he had been brought here. 'Off with these,' Dickens said, as he flipped off the German's hat and whipped off his glasses. 'Sit down and watch the birdy.' Obediently, Wolfgang sat on the chair.

The other man stood a few feet away and held the camera to his chest. He peered down into the viewfinder. 'Look straight in ze lens, pleeze.' Wolfgang was so shocked his jaw dropped – the accent was pure German. 'Close ze mouth, pleeze.' Still stunned, Wolfgang did as he was told and almost immediately was blinded by the magnesium flash which left a dark image burned on his retina for some moments after.

Regaining his composure he was just about to address the little German when Dickens bustled up to him, handed him back his hat and glasses, grasped his elbow and started propelling him out of the house. 'Thanks Otto,' he said, over his shoulder, 'let me know when they're ready.'

'But of course, Herr Dickens,' was the last thing the astonished Wolfgang heard before the door closed behind them.

~O~

Back in the yard they made their way towards the boat. 'Now you just go down into the cabin of your lovely craft and make yourself a nice cuppa and have a little rest,' Dickens said. As if on autopilot Wolfgang did as he was told. He didn't have the will to resist. 'And don't you take any notice if you hear noises from the deck. All right, shipmate?' Dickens guided him along the jetty.

When he was sure that Wolfgang had indeed gone down into the cabin, Dickens made his way to the dilapidated shed and scraped the door open. In the corner was a similarly decrepit barrow and, one by one, he wheeled the wooden crates on to the jetty then manoeuvred them on to the foredeck of the boat. Methodically he started stowing the crates in the fish hold, interlocking them like a puzzle. When he had finished, the neat pile was only just above deck level. He wondered if it might make the craft a little nose heavy but didn't think that it would cause too much of a problem. Besides, the oil drums aft would counteract the weight, to some extent. He had checked the forecast for the next few days and it looked as if the weather was going to stay fair. So the journey should be pretty straightforward. Using an almost new square of tarpaulin, he covered the crates and tied it down securely. When he was satisfied with his handiwork he made his way aft and peered into the cabin. Wolfgang was curled up, fast asleep. A cup of cold tea stood on the table. Dickens smiled. He was tempted to sneak down and help himself to the Courvoisier but decided to leave the man in peace. He was going to need to rely on him over the next couple of days, so best to let him get as much rest as could, while he could.

The following morning Wolfgang was in better shape. The long sleep had refreshed him, his leg seemed much less troublesome than of late and he felt reasonably perky. It was early; there was no sound from outside so he decided to examine what Dickens had been doing the day before.

He checked the lashings on the oil drums and was surprised to see that the knots were nearly as good as his own – nearly, but not quite. But they would do. He made his way forward and was again impressed by the neatness with which the tarpaulin had been lashed down. It looked like it would cope with any water that was likely to come over the bow. His heart sank, though, when he thought about what was concealed beneath the covering. But – it was a *fait accompli*. The sooner they made the delivery, the sooner he could return to his quest – and with new papers. He made his way back aft and down into the cabin and prepared breakfast. He was just biting into a crust of bread when there was a familiar step on the deck. This time he was prepared, and, although not exactly welcoming Dickens with open arms, he accepted his presence.

'Ahoy there! Any chance of a bit of grub for your shipmate?' Dickens was carrying a cardboard box of groceries. It was so large he had to peer round the side of it to see where he was going. He put it down on the spare bunk and let out a heartfelt sigh. 'That's the vittles for our voyage,' he announced He plonked himself down next to it and reached into the box. Taking out a brown envelope he threw it down on the desk. 'And this is something, just for you.'

Wolfgang, initially suspicious, leaned forward and drew the envelope towards him. He toyed with it at first and, finding the outside blank, lifted the flap and withdrew the contents. His eyes lit up when he saw the buff cover of a French passport, slightly dog-eared, with the legend, *République Française* and the surname Meunier with his adopted Christian name, Marcel, and place of birth, Strasburg. 'But how? Why Strasburg?'

Dickens chuckled. 'It just struck me that although your French is good, placing you near the German border would explain your accent – if you are ever challenged.'

'That's uncanny. It's just where I would have chosen – somewhere large and anonymous.' Wolfgang gave a rare smile.

'I said I'd help you out – now it's your turn.' Leaning forward, he took some bread while Wolfgang poured coffee into a spare cup.

'When exactly are we off?' the German asked, pushing the cup across the table.

'Tomorrow morning. On the tide.'

'So soon?'

'No time like the present. The glass is holding steady so we should have fair weather all the way.'

'What about navigation? Have you studied the charts?'

'No need.'

'How is that possible?' Being meticulous, Wolfgang was used to plotting his course carefully, allowing for tide and wind.

Dickens beamed. 'We'll follow the coast, heading not quite due west but roughly west-by-south. We know what speed this fine vessel is capable of so, by dead-reckoning, we should be able to work out the progress we're making. Plus at night, we'll have lights to guide us – I've seen the set of fancy charts you've got – so with my confidence and your accuracy...' he guffawed, spraying breadcrumbs across the table. '... we shouldn't go far wrong.'

~o~

There was enough water at six o'clock the following morning to lift *Moonshine* free of the mud in her berth. Dickens was soon on board, tending to the mooring lines, while Wolfgang was in the wheelhouse, starting the engine. The Gardiner diesel burst into life then settled down to a regular thump-thump-thump. Dickens cast off, Wolfgang put the engine into reverse and, with a swirl of churned-up silt, they were off.

After the ropes were neatly stowed Dickens made his way to the wheelhouse, resting his hand lightly on the doorframe while Wolfgang manoeuvred the vessel out of the creek then into the main River Ouse. Once beyond the harbour arm he headed out to sea for about half a mile, gradually turning to starboard until they were heading west-by-south. While he was doing that, Dickens busied himself below and came up with steaming mugs of tea. Since Ludwig had been captured, Wolfgang had become used to doing everything for himself and it came as some surprise that he and Dickens were already working as a team.

As predicted, the weather was fair, the sea, though a little choppy, was not troublesome and they made steady, if monotonous progress. Wolfgang had been used to fairly lengthy trips across the channel from France to England and back, but this was more of a challenge. However they soon fell into a steady routine. Dickens turned out to be a competent seaman and the German was happy to leave him in charge of the helm so he could go below. Before long they passed south of the Isle of Wight, crossing the wake of a Cherbourg-bound ferry, a column of grey smoke issuing from its funnel and blowing astern. By teatime they were off Weymouth and, as darkness fell, Wolfgang studied the chart while Dickens pointed out the navigation lights. They steamed on through the night, each alternating between steering and grabbing some sleep below and at first light they were off the Lizard. Wolfgang hove to, keeping *Moonshine* steady, heading into the swell, while Dickens transferred fuel into the boat's tank.

Once they had rounded Land's End Wolfgang altered course so the heading read north-north-east and they were out of sight of land for the rest of the day. By nightfall Wolfgang was beginning to feel concerned but it wasn't long before they made out the light on St David's Head.

'Change course to due west,' Dickens instructed.

Before day broke on the third day they started seeing lights on the starboard bow, which meant they were off the south-east tip of Ireland, not far from Wexford. 'Right,' Dickens said, 'we need to head west-south-west, but reduce speed. We've made good progress; I don't want to arrive before nightfall.'

Wolfgang slowed the engine until it was just above tick-over and the boat was rolling in the swell of the Irish Sea, barely doing two knots. It was an uncomfortable motion but, after nearly three days afloat, both men had their sea legs and rode it out. By nightfall, when Wolfgang was steering, they picked up the beam from the lighthouse at Roches Point and Dickens said, with a smile: 'I'll take over now. I'm a little more familiar with these waters than you are.' The German was quite happy to relinquish the helm. His companion had shown his ability on the trip and he was sure that the boat was in safe hands.

Dickens obviously knew the area well as he piloted the boat expertly, entering the river at Butlerstown North, passing the beach at Fountainstown, around the Point and into a little creek, where *Moonshine* ran aground on the sandy bottom. 'She'll be fine here. The tide'll lift her before too long. Now, you stay on board, I'm off to find my cousin.' With that he lowered himself over the gunwale and splashed through the shallows to the shore.

Wolfgang sat on the helmsman's seat in the wheelhouse, waiting nervously. Nothing happened for 20 minutes. Then he heard splashing and saw a weak light playing on the shallow water. He could just make out a group of figures pulling something behind them. As they drew closer he could see there were four of them and they had a kind of flat cart, with large pneumatic tyres. 'Right shipmate,' he heard Dickens say, in a hoarse whisper, 'let's have that ladder over the side.' Wolfgang deftly untied the lashings holding the short ladder in place and lowered it over the bow. As soon as it touched the sandy bottom, there was a step on the rung and Dickens's grinning face appeared above the gunwale.

He hauled himself on to the deck and was swiftly followed by an almost identical individual, right down to the beret with the ragged edge and the wispy beard. 'Meet my cousin Seán. Right shipmate, hold this,' he said, handing a torch to Wolfgang.

The two men untied the tarpaulin and peeled it back, revealing the neat arrangement of wooden boxes. Wolfgang kept out of the way; he wanted no part in this, reluctantly shining the torch for them. The pair lifted each crate in turn and lowered it over the side to unseen waiting hands. The whole operation took surprisingly little time and they had only two crates left when Seán stumbled over a piece of rope, fell on his back and dropped the case. It landed on its corner with a crash and split open, spilling the contents. 'Holy Mother of God!' Paddy exclaimed. 'You bloody idiot!'

'Sorry, cousin.'

'No matter, let's get these over the side and hope nobody heard us.' He started handing the Lee-Enfields down to the other two, swiftly followed by the remaining intact case. 'Right,' he said, taking the torch from Wolfgang, 'the tide's on the turn. It won't be long before there's enough water to lift your fine craft off the bottom and we can be on our way. I'll be back in a jiffy.' With that, he followed Seán over the side and with a splash, the men were gone, the weak torchlight bobbing as they dragged the cart to the shore.

Again, Wolfgang waited nervously. The shallow water lapped quietly at *Moonshine's* hull, the only other sounds the distant braying of a donkey and the nearer call of a barn owl. The wait seemed interminable. He started fretting. What if Dickens failed to return? He had no doubt that he would be able to find his way back, but without someone to take a trick at the wheel it would be a hard journey. And was there enough fuel? They'd had to broach the second oil drum before they'd reached shore and he wasn't sure if there was sufficient left for a return trip. Just then, he felt movement beneath him. The tide was starting to lift the boat. Panic now set in. What should he do? Throw an anchor over the side and wait? Or set off on his own?

He felt an occasional bump as the boat lifted briefly, then dropped down on the sand again. There still wasn't enough water beneath the keel to float the vessel, but it wouldn't be long before he would have to make a decision: stay or go. He was just deciding what to do when suddenly all hell broke loose on the shore. There were figures running towards him shouting, torches waving and a number of gunshots rent the air. In a panic Wolfgang dashed to the wheelhouse and turned the key to start the engine. Nothing… just a dull clunk. He tried again, the dread rising as the voices came closer. Once more and still the engine refused to turn. He grabbed the starting handle from its position, hanging on the back wall of the wheelhouse, but just as he was going aft, a peaked cap, followed by an angry face and the burly body of an officer of the Garda, appeared over the gunwale.

$\sim$O$\sim$

'Well, Monsieur Meunier, what have you got to say for yourself?' Inspector Conway asked. Wolfgang shrugged.

They were sitting in a small room in Anglesea Street Gardai station, central Cork. The walls were painted institution sludgy green; a single bulb hanging in the centre of the room gave little light. The room was permeated with an unpleasant odour – a combination of stale tobacco smoke and sweat and a strangely human scent – fear. Wolfgang had been brought to this room a number of times since he had been taken to the police station, several days before. In between he had been locked in a cell, the monotony of solitary confinement only broken when meals were brought to him. Various members of the Gardai had taken turns to interview him. It hadn't amounted to interrogation – yet – but Wolfgang sensed they were starting to become impatient. He had gleaned, from what he had been told, that Paddy, Seán and the other two had got away, with the rifles. The only apparent evidence was the remains of the broken crate they had found on the deck of *Moonshine*. He supposed he could have thrown the pieces overboard before they had arrived but with tide making, they would surely have found them anyway.

'Now listen.' Inspector Conway put his elbows on the table, clasped one hand over the other and rested his broad chin on his knuckles. 'If you're not going to tell us anything else, you're going to be detained under the Prevention of Violence Act, 1939. This could mean an indefinite stay in prison, while we look for more evidence. Are you sure you want that?' Wolfgang said nothing. Conway tried a different tack. 'If you help us, I might be able to help you. If we can prove that you're the innocent party and you were coerced into allowing your vessel to be used for illegal purposes, then it might go well for you. Why don't you tell me who the others were? We know there were several of them. We just need some names.'

Wolfgang folded his arms resignedly over his chest. He could have said a lot, about Paddy Dickens and his cousin Seán. About how he *had* been coerced into carrying the cargo, but… that would mean admitting the reason for the coercion. Which would undoubtedly open up a whole can of worms about his past and he knew he would be in even deeper trouble than he was at present. So, he decided the wisest course of action was to keep his counsel. 'I am afraid I have nothing to say.'

'In that case, it's back to the cells for you.'

And so he remained, incarcerated in Cork prison. He had been allocated a lawyer, who visited him from time to time, but despite the Gardai launching a countrywide manhunt it seemed no further evidence had come to light. Dickens and the guns had disappeared without trace. So, finally, early the following year, he was set free.

# Chapter 20

*The Old Bailey, or Central Criminal Court, deals with major criminal cases from within Greater London and, in exceptional cases, from other parts of England and Wales.*

AFTER WOLFGANG'S capture, *Moonshine* had been impounded. When he was released a kindly junior member of the Gardai took him on a long journey to Minane Bridge, then along the other side of the creek from where he had last seen her. The boat had been moved across the water and was high and dry and in a pitiful state; the topside was green with mould and the hull was caked in mud. The officer handed him a box of basic groceries. Wolfgang thanked him and the man drove off, leaving him on his own. The Guardai had put padlocks on the wheelhouse and cabin and given him keys for both. He knew the Irish were said to be trustworthy but he was still amazed that the locks were intact. He tried the key in the padlock on the cabin and, although stiff at first, it gave and unlocked with a dull click. He pulled the door open and wasn't surprised at the musty smell inside. Nothing smelled rotten – just damp and fusty. It appeared that the Irish police, when turning the cabin over, had cleared out anything perishable. There was a little coke stove forward and amazingly, next to it, a bucket still contained coal. In a short space of time he had a fire going and the kettle singing on the hotplate.

It felt good to be out of prison, back on his own territory. More in hope than anything, he lifted a couple of boards from the cabin floor. Below, in the bilge, were rusty, slimy pigs of iron that constituted the ballast. These heavy weights helped keep the craft on an even keel. But it wasn't these that held his interest. Lying on the floor, to one side of the hole, he pushed his arm up into the void between the back of the locker and the hull of the boat. He smiled as his fingers touched a waxed linen package. He wriggled closer and straining, managed to grasp it and pull it free. Sitting up on the cabin floor he undid the carefully tied knots and opened the package. Still crisp and untarnished were several bundles of banknotes in different currencies – German, French and English, along with his faithful Luger pistol. The Gardai, as thorough as they had been, had failed to uncover his secret cache. He took a number of notes out, and replaced the rest, After retying the package he wedged it back in its hiding place, re-laid the floorboards and dusted himself off.

Everything – mugs, plates, cutlery, glasses – was covered with a thin film of mould. His clothes too all needed washing so, over the next few days, numerous kettles were boiled and the sink was constantly filled with hot soapy water. He rigged up a couple of washing lines between the stubby foremast and wheelhouse and managed to get clothes partially dried in the weak sunshine and gentle breeze, finishing them off by the stove. He did his best to clean the topsides of the boat and reckoned the hull would become cleaner when he next went to sea. When supplies of food and coal grew low, he ventured out and found a nearby farm. The farmer was surprisingly friendly and happy to supply him with milk, eggs, bread and ham. As well as he delivered a load of peat for the stove. When he turned up on his tractor, he took time to look round the grounded boat, stranded above the tideline. 'Were you thinking of putting out to sea any time soon?' he asked.

'I would like to, but I don't see how I can get the boat down to the water.'

'Ah, well, I might be able to help you there,' the farmer said, with a twinkle in his eye. 'Leave it with me.'

'Oh, and I've got a flat battery too. Could you possibly do anything about that?'

The next day, after the previous night's new moon, the man returned with the fully charged battery and two young burly lads who he introduced as his sons. In no time at all they had set to with spades, digging a channel from the stern of the boat towards the watery edge of the creek. Wolfgang kept them supplied with drinks and sandwiches. Later, as the tide rose and started to fill the ditch they had carved out, they began digging out the sand and mud around the hull. As the strength of the tide gathered, the water moved steadily up the channel then crept around the boat, creating muddy eddies that swirled on the surface of the water. The spring tide continued to rise and, with the force of the water, the boat began to strain and shudder until, with a series of loud sucking noises, like giant corks being eased from giant bottles, the hull lifted, to loud cheers from the farmer and his sons. Putting their shoulders to stempost, they grunted and heaved and slowly the boat slid and slithered down the newly created channel and into the water of the creek. Wolfgang was elated. 'How can I ever thank you?' he asked, leaning over the gunwale.

The farmer climbed the ladder, which was still slung over the bow and came and stood close to Wolfgang. 'I'll let you into a little secret,' he said, eyes sparkling. 'When I was a boy, growing up in Cork City, my best friend was called Eamon O'Donovan. We did everything together – we were like brothers. We had lots of adventures, got into lots of scrapes, chased girls; did all the things that lads and young men do. Then we turned 19 and things changed. He decided he wanted to be a soldier. But… did he want to join the Irish Army? Oh no – he wanted to be a squaddie – join the British Army. You can imagine how that went down round here.

'He took himself off to London and joined up. When he came back to see his old ma, he had to wait until after dark and make his way to her house through the back gardens, jumping over the walls and fences. If he'd been spotted he would have been lynched. We met up in secret a couple of times but it wasn't the same – he'd changed. I guess it was inevitable, Cork was always too small for him; the bright lights of London were too much of a draw. But… you know where he ended up…'

'I do?'

'You do,' he chuckled. Wolfgang looked blank. 'You know him as Paddy – Paddy Dickens, boatyard proprietor of Newhaven.'

'Oh.'

'Quite. Not exactly the bright lights of the metropolis, is it? But that's where he put down roots. I didn't find this out until last year when he got in touch. Anyway, I don't think I need to explain what occurred after that. I'm just sorry – and I know that he is – for how you were treated, prison and all.'

'What happened to him,' Wolfgang asked, 'when the police turned up?'

'I can't exactly say. All I know is that he got away, him and his cousin.'

'And you don't know where he is now?'

'It's funny you should say that. I didn't, but then I got a postcard a few weeks ago. You won't believe it but he's back in his boatyard, in Newhaven. So it looks like you've a got a berth for your fine craft, if you're heading back to England.'

Wolfgang looked puzzled. 'But the guns. What happened to them?'

'Ah, now, there's a question. It's said that they found their way up north, possibly over the border – who knows?' His concerned expression lightened. 'Anyway, that's not your problem. I suggest you point your boat east and make your way back to familiar territory.'

~o~

So that is what Wolfgang did. His period of incarceration had only heightened his determination to somehow get his brother out of prison. Particularly now he knew something of what he must be going through. All through his term in Cork jail he was aware that the evidence against him was pretty thin and that sooner or later he would be released. But Ludwig was in a much more perilous position. Because of what he had done – killing three men – it was almost certain that he would be given a death sentence. As far as Wolfgang knew, the only reason that it had not been carried out already was that the victims were ex-Nazis, thus Ludwig remained in prison while the lawyers argued his case. So Wolfgang set off for England with a sense of urgency.

This time he was able to stop at various harbours to refuel and rest. Still he was discreet. Although nearly a year had passed since he had gone on the run there might well be people on the look-out for a small man with a gammy leg, but with his passport and papers giving him a new identity, he hoped to avoid notice.

It took him nearly a week of hopping along the coast until he finally entered the familiar waters of the river Ouse. Motoring up the creek he saw that his old berth was still vacant so he nosed *Moonshine* alongside the jetty, tied off the mooring lines and shut off the engine. It almost felt like coming home.

No sooner had he gone down into the cabin to put on the kettle than there was an all too familiar step on the deck, an 'Ahoy Shipmate!' and Dickens's grubby, beaming face appeared.

Momentarily forgetting the trials of the past few months, Wolfgang grinned and held out his hand. 'Coffee?'

'Don't mind if I do,' Dickens said, settling down on the bunk. 'And if there's a drop of that brandy...' he added, winking. The two sat and chatted for some time. Wolfgang knew that the other man still had a hold over him but, after the gun-running incident, he didn't feel the hold was so strong. Now he had something on Dickens. 'What's your plan, shipmate?'

Wolfgang stared into his empty cup. He was well aware that Dickens was well versed in what he and his brother had done the previous year. He had also probably guessed why he had returned to the boatyard so thought there was no reason why he shouldn't share his plans with him. 'I need to find out where my brother, Ludwig, is being held.'

'I thought as much.'

'And then I have to work out if I can get him out of prison.' He paused, contemplating. 'No, not *if* I can but *how* I can.'

Dickens lifted his mug in a toast. 'That's the spirit. I don't like the idea of a fella's brother being locked up. Especially as it was for murdering Nazis. Hate the bastards.'

'Have you any idea how I can find out?'

'Well, you can't go into a police station and ask, that's for sure.'

'No, I cannot. Even with my new papers, I know I'd look suspicious.'

'True. I'd help you out if I could, but I don't think I'd be welcome in the cop shop either. I suspect the Gardai might have talked to their cousins over here.'

'Then what do I do?'

'Let me think…' Dickens cupped his hand round his cheek, his brow furrowed and he was quiet for a while. The only sound was the falling tide, lapping against the hull of the boat, the cry of a herring gull and the tap-tap of a halyard against a mast. He moved his hands away from his face and stroked his wispy beard. 'The newspapers made a big thing of it at the time. I remember there were pictures of him being put in the back of a Paddy wagon, a blanket covering his head.'

'Excuse me. A Paddy wagon. What is that?'

Dickens chortled. 'Oh, you probably know it as a Black Maria – a sort of armoured police van, with blacked-out windows. Anyway, I think I'm right in recalling that this all took place in London. The case caused something of a sensation at the time. So, I'm guessing it all happened at the Old Bailey.'

'Could we find out there what happened to Ludwig?'

'I suppose so,' Dickens said, thoughtfully. 'It might be a starting point. I'm sure they'll have the trial records there. We would just have to be careful.'

'*We?*' Wolfgang asked slowly.

'You don't think I'm going to let you do this on your own, do you? Anyway, if there's no more of this,' he held up the empty brandy bottle, 'I suggest we adjourn to the pub. I'll introduce you to my local.'

# Chapter 21

*A railway detonator is a coin-sized device that is used
as a warning signal to train drivers. It is placed on the top
of the rail, usually secured with two lead straps,
one on each side. When the wheel of the train passes over,
it explodes emitting a loud bang.*

WEEKS WAS too shocked to speak. Helen's presence not only confirmed his suspicion that she was definitely tied up with Atkins. But far worse, it brought the dread realisation that he had been rumbled. It explained also why Atkins had been acting so strangely ever since he had marched into the Queen's Head earlier in the evening. Which made it even more imperative that he got a message to his DI. But how?

'Come on *Johnny*, time to get a move on.' Atkins nudged him in the ribs with his elbow. Weeks blinked and pushed the gear lever into reverse. There was a nasty crunching sound from the gearbox. 'Careful!' Atkins said. 'Not nervous, are we?'

'N-no,' Weeks stammered, 'I just didn't push the clutch down hard enough.'

Once they were out of the station car-park he drove on, following Atkins's directions, although the route was familiar from his earlier visit to the area. The other two carried on a quiet conversation. Weeks was able to catch only the odd word which made no sense out of context. However, when they pulled up outside the farmhouse he was further puzzled. 'Home sweet home – for now,' Atkins chuckled. Weeks was less surprised though when the round figure of Butcher Bates appeared in the lorry's headlights and opened the gate.

After Helen had climbed out and slammed the door shut, Atkins said: 'Right, drive in. Go round to the back of the house.' Weeks did as he was asked and the lights picked up the open doors of the larger barn. 'Drive in – carefully.' It was tight but the truck just fitted. The driver's door was hard against a post so Weeks had to shuffle across the seats and follow Atkins out of the passenger side, where there was just enough room to squeeze out through the door. With Atkins behind him and Bates in front he had no alternative but to go with them through the open back door of the farmhouse. Waiting inside the kitchen were the familiar figures of Sammy Screwdriver and Laurie Baker. Neither smiled – the atmosphere was distinctly frosty, despite the fire burning merrily in the range.

'Welcome to your new home,' Atkins said expansively. Weeks stood self-consciously in the centre of the room, the four men and one woman all staring at him. 'You led us a merry dance, *Constable* Weeks. Now what are we going to do with you?' Weeks felt his insides turn to water. Atkins looked towards the others.

'I'm afraid *I* can't drive the lorry,' Helen said.

'And we've all got jobs to do,' Baker added, frowning under his fringe. 'Me and you,' he nodded at Atkins, 'have got to deal with the driver and fireman; Butcher's going to handle the guard; Sammy's got to be ready to open up the van. So that only leaves *him*,' he said, disdainfully, pointing at Weeks.

'Tommy, don't you think you'd better tell them about the changes?' Helen said.

'Ah, I was just coming to that.' Atkins's grin was a little forced.

Bates spoke, his fleshy brow furrowed. 'What changes, Tommy?'

'Um, well, it's like this…'

'Come on Tommy, out with it.' Baker was looking worried.

'The job's been brought forward.'

'What?!'

'Just by a day.'

'Just!'

'Now 'ang on…' he held his hands up in surrender. 'This is gonna work to our advantage.'

'How so, Tommy?' Sammy's confusion had rendered his usual restless gaze to one of rapt concentration.

'We don't know who our friend 'ere,' he jerked his thumb towards Weeks, ''as told about our little *escapade*. But if, as I suspect, 'e's told 'is boss Russell, or some other rozzer, they'll be expectin' us to do the job on Tuesday.'

Baker smiled. 'So they don't know about the change of plan?' He paused and the smile turned to a frown. 'But what if the railway people have told the police?'

Helen spoke, 'My contact, the one I met at Victoria station, says the police aren't likely to know. The banks, whose money is being moved, want it kept secret. They're worried that there might be a leak.'

'Fair enough.'

Helen continued: 'But you haven't told them the other thing, Tommy…'

'I was coming to that.' The others listened intently. 'Ah. Hmm. It seems there's gonna be a coach attached to the train.'

'*What!*' Bates exploded. 'A *passenger* carriage?'

Atkins nodded his head. 'So it seems. Something to do with overcrowding or reschedulin' or somethin'...'

'Oh, that's just bleeding marvellous. Passengers to deal with as well. How the hell are we going to manage that?' Bates put his head in his hands and groaned.

'No, it's all right Butch,' Helen said, gently laying her hand on his arm. 'My pal, Simon, has got a railway mate who works down in Brighton. He's going to put reserved stickers on the windows in the carriage to make sure no one gets in.'

'Why's he going to do that then? Sammy asked.

'I'm afraid we're gonna 'ave to give 'im a cut.' Atkins looked slightly bashful.

'Bloody hell! I thought you said we had to stick to the plan, Tommy.'

'I've tried to, believe me. But things 'ave changed beyond my control, ain't they?' He cocked his head to one side, the old confidence returning. 'Any 'ow, there's gonna be plenty of spare dosh to go round. 'Specially now Johnny's agreed to give up his share. Eh, Johnny?' He punched Weeks on the arm, none too gently.

Sammy nodded. 'Fair enough. But it doesn't answer the question: who's going to drive the truck?'

'Oh, Johnny can still do that. It's too late to find another driver and besides, we don't want to involve anyone else. There's enough of us as it is,' Helen said.

'Yeah, but what's to stop him doing a runner?'

'I'll be in the lorry with him,' she said.

'That's all well and good,' Bates said. 'But what happens if he turns nasty, thumps you, kicks you out of the cab and roars off?'

'Oh I don't think that's likely to happen,' she said smoothly.

'Not when he knows I've got this.' With an elegant flourish she produced a Beretta 950 from her handbag.

~O~

Russell had reluctantly decided there was nothing he could do until the morning, so he drove home and parked outside his railway carriage. He used a torch to see his way along the stepping-stone path. Unlocking the front door he was greeted by Aggie, bouncing excitedly up and down like a rubber ball. It was too dark and too late to take her for a walk so she had to make do with a quick sniff around the garden. Russell promised her that he'd get up early and take her out along the beach in the morning.

~O~

That evening Wolfgang and Dickens were sitting in *Moonshine's* cabin. The stove was ticking over nicely and the oil lamp on the bulkhead cast a warm glow. The remnants of a meal they had shared were still on the table, next to a bottle of brandy. Although the Courvoisier was long gone Dickens had replaced it with a cheaper brand. Even so, they had made substantial inroads into the contents.

Dickens was in expansive mood. 'Right, shipmate,' he said. 'This is the plan. Tomorrow morning at nine we get a train from Newhaven to Lewes, and then change for London, Victoria. There will probably be a train that leaves Brighton at about nine-thirty. We should be able to catch that. When we get to London we get on the tube to Blackfriars. After that it's a short walk to the Central Criminal Courts at the Old Bailey. That's where we'll start the search for your brother. What do you think?'

~o~

'Right,' Atkins said, 'what are we going to do with 'im now? We all need a decent sleep and I, for one, don't wanna stay up all night watchin' 'im.'

Baker spoke. 'I've got an idea.'

'Oh yeah?'

'Yeah. When I first came here, I had a look behind that door.' He pointed to the side of the range. 'It might look like a cupboard, but it actually leads to a cellar.'

''An 'ave you been down there?' Atkins asked.

'Not likely! I took one look and decided I wasn't interested – then. But now...'

Atkins walked across to the door. 'Time to 'ave a look then.' He turned the key and pulled the door open. A flight of stone steps ended in a pool of darkness. ''Ere, give us a torch, someone.' Bates handed him one. Atkins shone it down into the opening. While Helen stayed in the kitchen, keeping a watchful eye on the policeman, Atkins gingerly began descending, closely followed by the others. They reached the bottom of the steep steps and stood in the damp room. The floor was wet, the walls weeping, with puddles in places. There was a pile of mouldy sacks in the corner and some broken pieces of furniture; other bits of junk lay in a heap. Atkins shone the torch around but the beam picked up nothing else. 'Perfect. Our driver can spend the night 'ere. Helen can 'ave a room of 'er own, and we'll take the other two bedrooms. Should manage to get a decent kip – if Butcher's snoring don't keep us awake.'

Once they had climbed back up the steps and returned to the kitchen Atkins grinned and said: 'Right, Johnny, we've found you a nice cosy billet for the night. I'm *sure* you'll be comfortable.

'Ere, Laurie. Give 'im a mug of water an' a chunk off that loaf. Don't want the poor lad starvin' to death, now do we?' Atkins gave Weeks a rough shove. 'Get down there, you.' Clutching his bread and water the DC reluctantly went down into the cellar and the door was slammed shut and locked behind him, the darkness complete. He waited while his eyes adjusted and he could just make out a small window, high up in the wall. Despite it being grimy and festooned with ancient cobwebs, the full moon dimly illuminated his cell. He saw the pile of sacks and sat down on them. Water immediately soaked through his trousers. It was going to be an uncomfortable night.

Morning came all too soon. Russell had slept badly; half-remembered dreams had morphed into long periods of restless wakefulness. Despite his fatigue, he was glad to rise from his tangled bedsheets, wash and dress. A grey dawn was only just breaking when he set off in the cold morning air, a delighted Aggie bounding on ahead. They crossed the scrubby meadow, pock-marked with the burrows of rabbits, and climbed up on to the shingle ridge. The cool breeze was fresh on his neck as Russell strode eastward. Below, on the beach, the waves gently rose and fell rhythmically, like a giant breathing. Gulls circled and cried overhead. A trio of cormorants flew in a straight line, low above the sea, seemingly intent on some distant destination. He strode on, his fuddled mind gradually clearing. The little terrier trotted and circled him, sniffing at clumps of newly emerging seakale and valerian, delighted to be outside.

Russell marched on, his swinging arms keeping rhythm with his stride. As he progressed further along the beach, he came close to the shell of the Mary Stamford lifeboat house, standing on the ridge. He felt sad when he remembered reading about the day in 1928 when the crew set off in a howling gale to attend a ship in distress. The rowed lifeboat capsized and all 17 crew were lost. What made the tragedy even more appalling was that those on the ship that the brave men had set out to save had already been rescued. He sighed, said a silent prayer for the men and turned back for home, his mind a little clearer.

Weeks, too, woke from a fitful sleep. He had spent most of the night trying and failing to get comfortable. The damp from the sacks had soaked all the way through his clothes and he was now frozen and shivering. It came as a relief when he finally heard the key turn in the lock and the door opened. 'Come on sleepy 'ead. Time to get up,' Atkins bawled. Weeks mounted the steps to be greeted by the sight of the gang sitting round the table having breakfast. The smell of cooked bacon assailed his nostrils and he realised how hungry he was. 'Give 'im a bacon butty for Christ's sake, before 'e passes out on us.' The sandwich was passed to Weeks, along with a steaming mug of tea that he accepted greatfully. 'Right,' Atkins said, 'do you all know what you've got to do? Or shall I go through it one more time?'

Heads were shaken and there was the odd mutter of 'we're all right Tommy'.

'In that case, let's get going. You,' he said, pointing at Weeks, 'go with Helen and get the truck out of the barn. Butcher, you make sure the doors are closed behind them. Laurie and Sammy, go and check the road is clear and when you have, get the gate open. We're gonna take these.' Unwrapping a large canvas package that had been lying on the floor he handed them sawn-off shotguns that had been concealed within.

Helen stepped forward. 'But they are only to be used as a threat. You are *not*, I repeat, *not* to fire them, under any circumstances.' The men looked uneasily at each other but took the weapons.

Weeks made his way outside and squeezed along the inside of the barn. He climbed up into the lorry, with Helen close behind him. Like the others, they were both wearing shapeless blue boiler suits; Helen's easily concealing her femininity. 'And don't forget *I've* got this,' she said, showing him the pistol. The DC started the engine and backed slowly out of the barn. When he steered the vehicle round to the front of the farmhouse he could see the gate was open and Bates was beckoning him forward. For a mad moment he thought about putting his foot down and going for help. But glancing sideways he saw the dull glint of the morning light on the barrel of the Beretta and thoughts of escape fled – for the time being. He stopped the Bedford in the lane, facing towards Framfield. Atkins climbed up beside Helen and the others clambered over the tailboard and into the back.

Atkins pulled back the sleeve of his boiler suit and looked at his watch. 'Nine-thirty. There's no rush. The train from Buxted will have gone by now so we can get down there and take up our positions. Drive on – but take it steady.' He directed Weeks along Etchingwood Lane, then into Spurlings Lane. After a few hundred yards, where the road turned sharp left he said: ''Ere, turn right and stop by that gate.' Weeks recognised it from his previous visit with Russell and now knew exactly where he was. Bates clambered down from the back of the lorry and opened the gate. Weeks drove through, and then waited while the gate was closed behind the lorry and Bates climbed back inside. They bumped down the track, Weeks keeping the lorry in low gear.

When they reached the crossing, Atkins turned to him and spoke again. 'Now listen. The lads are going to take up their positions. I want you to drive to the other side, turn the truck around and wait for my signal – a short blast on a whistle. Understand?'

'Yes,' Weeks said in a low voice.

' 'Cause if you don't…' he looked towards Helen, who nodded sagely, '…well, I don't need to remind you. Oh, and by the way, you won't need to run down the railway track wavin' a lantern now.' Weeks looked surprised. 'We've got 'old of some detonators an' the lads'll fix three of them on the rails. When they go off the driver'll slow the train down, see the lorry on the crossing, an' stop – without you doin' anything. Get it?' Weeks nodded. 'You stay put in the cab 'til we come back with the loot.'

While this exchange was taking place, the others had left the lorry, the gates were opened and they were making their way to their positions, pulling on woollen balaclavas and leather gloves as they went. Atkins too got out, but before he left, he gave Helen a thumbs-up and Weeks a grimace, then pulled on his mask. Weeks drove forward, over the crossing. He continued down the lane until they reached a gateway so he could turn the Bedford round.

~O~

Russell was in a much better mood as he drove Weeks's car into Collinghurst. The sea air had cleared his head and blown away the tiredness he had felt earlier. He was much more positive about the events unfolding and felt sure that Weeks would be in touch with an update before too long. Maybe there was even a message waiting for him at the station. What was waiting, it turned out, was a nasty shock that was most unexpected.

He parked the car and climbed out. He thought about Weeks, smiled and began whistling *Me and My Shadow*. Aggie trotted along beside him, tail up. She'd had a good walk and been given breakfast and was content with the world. Russell walked into the outer office and wished the desk Sergeant a cheery 'Good morning!'

He was just making his way to his own office when Wickstead called out: 'Sorry, Sonny. Bad news I'm afraid. The Super wants to see you – straight away.'

Russell was surprised. Stout was rarely at the station before nine in the morning. 'Any idea what it's about?'

'Afraid not. But it sounded serious.'

His cheerful mood was rapidly evaporating; a feeling of doom settling around him.

~o~

'I'm afraid I've just received some information that is going to upset your plans,' Stout announced.

'Oh yes? What's that, Sir?' Russell wasn't prepared for what he was about to hear.

'That chap…' Stout looked down at a note in front of him. '… Elsdale, died in the early hours of this morning.'

'What! I thought he was off the critical list; on the road to recovery.' Russell shook his head in disbelief.

'That's what the hospital assumed. It seems he took a turn for the worse last night. There'll be a post mortem of course, but at the moment they think he suffered from septic shock, as a result of his injuries. Anyway, whatever it was, he's dead. And you know what that means.'

'Sir?'

'We've got a murder enquiry on our hands now. I'm afraid you'll have to cancel the stake-out over in Uckfield. This is much more serious.'

'Yes, Sir.'

'And you'll have to let Weeks know, too.'

Russell linked his hands in front of him and took a deep breath. "Er, there's a bit of a problem there, Sir.'

'Oh no, what are you going to tell me now?'

'I'm afraid I can't get hold of my DC.'

'Do you mean he hasn't he come in to work yet?'

'Well no, he hasn't, but there's more to it than that.' Russell explained about the meeting in the Queen's Head and the phone call that Weeks had been expecting and how he had left without leaving a message.

'Where do you think he is now?' The Super's blood pressure was beginning to rise, judging by the reddish tinge that was starting to suffuse his face.

'The lorry that Valiant lent him has gone so I can only assume that he went down early to the site of the robbery.'

'So why the hell didn't he leave a message?' Stout's colour was turning from pink to angry red.

'I don't know, Sir. It's unlike him to go off without saying where he was headed.'

'Bloody hell! What do we do now?'

'If we could leave it for an hour or so, Sir, I'm sure we'll know something by then.'

'Right. You've got exactly two hours. If he hasn't been in touch we'll have to get the manhunt under way. I want the bastard who killed Elsdale.'

~O~

Wolfgang and Dickens caught the train from Newhaven. In less than 20 minutes they were getting off at Lewes station and making their way to the London platform to wait for the connection from Brighton. They were the only passengers waiting and had been standing there for just a few minutes when a train pulled in. 'This must be it,' Dickens said, 'right on time. Hello, what's this?' Behind the engine was a single carriage, with a handful of closed vans and a brake-van bringing up the rear. The carriage had stopped right in front of them and in the windows they could see paper stickers reading *RESERVED*.

'That's strange. Hang on a mo. Look at that compartment.' Wolfgang followed the line of Dickens's finger. In the last window there was no sign. 'Come on, let's get in.' They climbed up into the carriage, Wolfgang receiving a helping hand from his companion. The door was slammed and they flopped down on their seats. 'Look!' Dickens bent down and picked up a *RESERVED* sign that had fallen on the floor. He licked the gummed ends of the sheet and stuck it back on the window. 'There. Now we've got the compartment to ourselves,' he said gleefully. With a 'toot' from the whistle the train set off. Just before ten they were approaching Uckfield. 'Better take precautions,' Dickens said, pulling down the window blind, 'just in case anybody peers into the carriage and sees us.'

~O~

Weeks sat nervously in the lorry, the six-cylinder engine ticking over rhythmically. On the other side of the cab Helen had put on a black pillbox hat with a veil that concealed her features

– no balaclava for her. The pistol lay in her lap. Weeks had been concerned about Atkins and his sudden changes of mood from early on but now that firearms were involved he was really scared. What if one of the train crew refused to co-operate? Knowing Atkins, at best he would be likely to receive a clout round the head with the butt of a shotgun, or at worst... he shuddered.

'Cold, my dear? Or frightened?' Weeks realised that Helen had spoken to him.

'No, I'm fine,' he managed.

'That's good. We don't want you panicking on us.'

He decided to push his luck. 'There's something I don't understand. How come you're involved with Atkins and his gang? You have a lovely house, in an exclusive part of Nottery Quay and, to put it frankly, it doesn't look as if you're short of a bob or two. It's quite a risk, doing this job and it doesn't look as if you need the money. Why are you doing it?'

Helen lifted her veil so Weeks could see face her clearly. She looked directly at him, a huge smile lighting up her face. 'You really don't understand, do you? Atkins and *his* gang? They're *my* gang!' She let out a peal of laughter, deep and throaty. 'Poor Johnny. What *have* you got yourself mixed up in, eh?'

Weeks sat, stunned. He hadn't expected that. He was more confused than ever.

'So you thought young Tommy Atkins was the mastermind behind this operation? That couldn't be further from the truth.' Again, the laughter. 'What did he say to you?' Weeks was about to speak when she held up her finger. 'No, wait. Let me tell you what I think he said: He told you that he'd been the lookout on the Eastcastle Street robbery and that he admired the way Billy Hill had meticulously planned the job. Am I right so far?' Weeks nodded. 'And he told you that he was planning this robbery just as carefully and he's got a mate who works for the railway who gave him the information about the train?'

'That's right.'

'I bet he told you that when he planned the job there were three things to remember: keep it simple, keep it small, and above all else, keep it quiet.' The laugh this time was more of a chuckle. 'Who do you think taught him that?'

'Billy Hill, I assume.'

'Ha! Not likely. Billy called him "that snotty-nosed kid". He was never the lookout on the Eastcastle Street job, he just knew someone who was. But do you know who was involved with it?' Weeks shook his head, totally baffled now. 'Me!' she said, gleefully. 'I'm sure you've read up on the case. You seem the sort to do your homework, so you'll have heard of George "Taters" Chatham?'

'Yes.'

'Well he's a man I admire. He treated both the aristocracy and the police with the same amount of contempt; had no compunction when it came to stealing from one and running rings round the other. He was already well-known – and respected – before that robbery.'

'By you?'

'Not only bright, but insightful, aren't we? I can see why Tommy was drawn to you. Shame you're a copper. You could be a real asset in my organisation.' She saw Weeks's look of astonishment. 'Yes, *my* organisation. Let's just say that George and I were close friends for a while. We were both regulars at the Star Tavern in Belgravia, along with a lot of celebrities and, er, friends from *the underworld*. He was a good teacher and I'm a quick learner.'

'How come Atkins is involved?'

She chuckled again. 'That "snotty-nosed kid" turned out to be brighter than he looked – a bit like you. He did a couple of jobs for me – carried them out to the letter – and proved his worth so I decided to take him on. He'd started to gain a reputation, and respect – amongst the right sort of people: Sammy, Butcher and Laurie among them and I knew I could trust him.'

'Really?'

Helen's face darkened. 'What are you suggesting?'

'Just that his mood can change suddenly.'

She waved her hand. 'I'm well aware of that. He just needs keeping on a tight rein.'

'And do you think you've got that?'

'I beg your pardon?'

Weeks realised he'd overstepped the mark and back-pedalled. 'Sorry! Nothing to do with me.'

'I should hope not,' Helen sighed. 'To think I was just starting to like you.' A blast on a whistle stopped further conversation and she lowered her veil again. 'Right. Time to drive on to the crossing.' Just as Weeks was putting the lorry into gear there was a distant explosion, causing him to nearly jump out of his seat. 'Don't worry, that's the first detonator. Come on, the train will be here soon.' As he drove forward there was another, louder bang, followed shortly by a third, and the train came into sight, a thick column of smoke rising from the engine's chimney. Even over the sound of the lorry's engine, the screech of the brakes on the rails was quite audible. The train slowed to a halt 30 yards from the crossing.

A man, wearing a dirty, faded denim jacket and trousers and with a knotted handkerchief on his head, climbed down from the locomotive, wondering what was going on. Suddenly, the masked figures of Atkins and Baker sprang from where they had been hiding at the side of the track, each brandishing a shotgun. The man immediately put his hands in the air. Baker kept his gun trained on him while Atkins climbed up into the cab. The driver, also dressed in faded, coal-smudged denims and wearing a greasy black cap, was standing at the controls, a defiant look on his face.

Atkins waved the shotgun. 'Come on, out of the cab,' he snarled. The man stood his ground. Atkins pulled the trigger and fired one of the barrels through the cab opening. The lead shot whistled past the driver's ear.

'Bloody hell! You could've hit me!'

'Don't worry, next time I will. Now get a move on!' The man didn't need a second reminder and scuttled across the footplate and down the loco steps, followed by Atkins. 'Right you two, make your way to the brake van – and no funny business.' The four of them started walking along the side of the carriage, coupled behind the engine.

Just as they drew level with the last compartment Baker suddenly said: '*What the...?!*' and pointed upwards. Just at that moment Dickens had raised the blind to see why the train had stopped. For a second his eyes locked with Atkins's who immediately climbed up on the step, turned the handle and yanked the door open.

Seeing the shotgun Wolfgang and Dickens cowered. 'What the *hell* are you doing here? Can't you read? This carriage is reserved!'

'I... we...' Dickens stammered.

'Just get out!' Dickens climbed onto the step and jumped down on to the track but Wolfgang just stood in the doorway, quaking. 'For Christ's sake man! Get down here!'

Wolfgang rubbed his leg. 'I cannot. It is too far.'

Seeing his distress Baker handed his gun to Atkins and climbed on to the step, held on to the grab handle with one hand and with the other, reached out to Wolfgang. 'Come on, I'll help you.' With Dickens reaching up they managed to get him down beside the train. Taking his gun back Baker and Atkins marched the prisoners past Sammy, who was dealing with the lock, and on to the brake van. Meanwhile, Bates had communicated with the guard, who was quite happy to stay quietly where he was. They manhandled Wolfgang up beside him, followed by Dickens and the loco crew. Slamming the door behind them, Bates took a large padlock out of his overalls' pocket and snapped it shut.

'Now they're safely banged up, let's see how Sammy's getting on.' Atkins led the way back along the train. Sammy wasn't getting on too well. The lock was proving trickier than expected. Atkins telling him to, 'get a bleedin' move on!' didn't help and his eyes, the only part of his face visible under the balaclava, started darting wildly.

'Okay, Tommy,' he said nervously, 'give me a couple more minutes and I'll have it done.'

'You'd better,' Atkins growled. 'It won't be long before someone raises the alarm.'

Suddenly with a shout of 'Done it!' the door swung open. The four men climbed inside. There were 40 or 50 mail sacks, neatly stacked.

'How do we know which ones have got the money in?' Bates asked.

'I dunno,' Atkins said, flustered.

'Why don't we take them all?' Baker suggested.

'Good idea. Let's get cracking. They'll soon be wondering why the train hasn't arrived at Buxted so we need to get a move on. Sammy, you stay here and throw the sacks down. The rest of us'll take them up to the lorry.'

Atkins and Baker each carried two sacks and the stronger Bates carried three. For the last trip, Sammy helped and they were all shifted within five minutes. Helen had had the presence of mind to get Weeks to drive the lorry forward on the level crossing so they could dump the sacks behind it. Then, it was only a case of throwing them into the back of the truck and, when it was done, climbing up after them. Once all four were inside, jammed up against the sacks, Atkins banged on the tailgate and shouted: 'Go Go Go!' Weeks shoved the stick into first gear and with a roar from the engine they were off. Encouraged by Helen, and her pistol, he drove much faster back up the rutted track than the stately pace at which they had come down. The men in the back had to hang on for dear life. In a few minutes they had reached the gate, Atkins jumped down and swung it open so Weeks could drive through, stopping only to let him climb in again. In no time at all, they had reached the farmhouse. Again the gate was opened, Weeks drove the Bedford into the barn and everyone piled out. Reaching up into the back of the lorry Sammy started to haul one of the sacks out.

'No! Leave it!' Helen said. 'Let's get in the farmhouse and lie low. There's bound to be a hue and cry when they find the train, so let's leave the loot until nightfall.' Obediently Sammy pushed the sack back; they closed the tailgate on the truck then shut the barn doors.

'Hang on,' Baker said, 'shouldn't we do something about the tyre tracks in the yard. Just in case someone comes snooping?'

'Good idea,' Helen agreed. 'See what you can find in one of the outbuildings. There must be a rake or broom or something.' After a quick search a hay rake and a worn bass broom were located. Baker and Bates set to and soon the dusty yard was track free.

Once inside the farmhouse the mood was euphoric. 'We've done it!' Atkins exclaimed, upending a bottle of whisky straight into his mouth.

Helen grabbed the bottle. 'That's enough Tommy. There'll be plenty of time to celebrate later – when the heat's died down. Let's just act nice and civilised for now. Here, have this.' She handed him a bottle of Courage Light Ale.

Atkins took it and said, sheepishly: 'Sorry, Helen. Of course you're right. I just got a bit carried away.'

'That's okay. Just remember, we're not out of the woods yet. Hopefully, they'll assume that we've hightailed it as far away as possible. They won't think that we've stayed so close to the site of the job. But you never know, they may well go over this area with a fine-toothed comb. We want this place to look derelict and unoccupied so they won't poke their noses in. In the meantime, what are we going to do with him?' She pointed her thumb towards Weeks. 'Our tame copper. We don't want him giving the game away, now do we?'

'Only one thing for it, I suppose.' Baker nodded towards the cellar.

'Afraid you're right,' she said. 'Off you go. We'll bring you a mug of tea when the kettle's boiled.' Baker opened the cellar door and Weeks, shoulders drooping miserably, reluctantly descended the damp, stone steps.

Weak sunlight filtered through the high, grimy window giving Weeks just enough illumination to see the extent of his cell. Apart from the musty sacks, where he had spent an uncomfortable night, there was just the mound of broken furniture. He picked up a chair leg and poked around in the heap, hoping there was some unbroken or usable piece so he could get up to the window, but he was out of luck. Whoever had lived here before wasn't in the habit of throwing anything of value away; it really was all just a pile of sticks. Dejected, he slumped down wearily on the sacks, oblivious to the damp. How the hell had it ended like this? He couldn't see how Atkins – or rather, Helen – could let him go now he knew so much. Atkins had hinted that he had no room for any baggage. Weeks remembered that he'd said: "I tend to dispose of me bags when they're no use to me anymore." He shuddered at the thought of his possible fate. He looked up toward the window, willing it to be closer than it was.

The cellar was surprisingly spacious, with the ceiling a good 10 feet above the floor. He sighed and idly looked round again. Then he noticed a deeper shadow on the farther wall and got up to investigate. The shadow turned out to be a recess in the wall, about two feet wide, the back sloping up at an angle. As he stepped towards it, something crunched under his feet. He bent and picked it up. Coal. It was a coal chute! This meant that there must be a hatch at the top. He began to feel quite excited at the prospect of possible escape but, just then, he heard the key turn in the lock of the cellar door and he scuttled back to the sacks.

'Grub up,' Bates said, as his ample form filled the doorway.

He put a mug and tin plate down on the top step and was just about to close the door when Weeks asked: 'Any chance of a light?'

'Cor blimey, you'll be wanting a feather mattress next. Hang on, I'll see what I can find.' Weeks waited patiently and was delighted to see the big man return with a stub of candle. He lit it, dripped some wax on the plate and stuck it down, dropped a box of matches next to it then the door was closed. Eagerly Weeks climbed the steps, picked up the mug and plate and carried them carefully back down. He took a quick sip of the tea, which was satisfyingly hot, then took the plate and candle over to the coal chute. However, his heart quickly sank as he held the flickering light high above his head. It looked as if there was a hatch at the top of the chute, but no light showed round the edges – that probably meant it was stuck fast, he realised. To add to that, the recess sloped back for only about five feet, before going up straight. Without a ladder, there was no way of reaching the hatch to see if it was moveable. Gloomily, he made his way back to the sacks and pinched out flame on the wick, to conserve the candle. He chewed on the spam sandwich and sipped at the tea. With his hopes of escape dashed, he struggled to keep what fate probably had in store for him out of his mind.

# Chapter 22

*A **Charcoal burner** is someone whose occupation is
to manufacture charcoal. Traditionally this is achieved
by carbonising wood in charcoal pile or kiln.
It is one of the oldest human crafts.*

Russell looked at his watch. His two hours were nearly up and there was still no word from Weeks. Briefly he drummed his fingers on the desk, then sat back and started whistling the Dream Weavers' *It's Almost Tomorrow*. He'd just reached the second chorus when the door burst open, Aggie barked in surprise and Sergeant Wickstead's head appeared, his moustache bristling. 'Sonny! There's been a train robbery!'

The DI shot out of his seat. 'Where?'

'Over Uckfield way.'

'*What?*'

'A mail train apparently. It was carrying cash up to London.'

Russell put his hands over his face. 'Oh God! That's why Johnny went off early.'

'Sorry?' Wickstead looked baffled.

'Nothing. I'd better go and see Stout.'

'Yes, I think you had. I saw him just now – face like thunder.'

~O~

'What the *hell* is going on?' The voice matched the face. 'You said the raid was happening on Tuesday, and today is Monday. How come you got that so wrong?

'I've no idea, Sir. As far as I knew it was planned for tomorrow.'

'So now we've not only got a murderer on the run but a gang of train robbers on the loose, too. The Chief Constable is going to go spare when he finds out.'

'At least they're connected...' Russell said, lamely.

'*What*?!' The Superintendent looked about to explode.

Russell ploughed on: 'Baker, who is *possibly* involved with the death of Elsdale is part of the gang that was planning the train robbery.' Stout's eyes actually bulged, but his teeth were clenched so tight no sound came out so Russell continued: 'I've a feeling that Weeks may have been coerced into going off early. Otherwise, I can't understand why he hasn't been in touch. It's not like him at all.'

Stout regained the power of speech. 'I don't care what's like or not like him – at all. I just want this mess sorted out,' he thundered.

'Yes, Sir.'

There was a tin of cheroots on the desk; the Superintendent opened it and took one out. He placed it between his lips, produced the Zippo from his pocket, and lit the end, sucking greedily. He inhaled deeply then blew out a column of blue smoke. This seemed to have a calming effect and he went on in a more moderate tone. 'You'd better get Parker and Barrow to go with you over to Uckfield. Tell Lewis to get over there with his boys, there may be some fingerprints or other evidence – if we're lucky – though the way things are going I doubt it. And take a constable. The mid-Sussex police are already there and they've set up road blocks around the area. I had to sweet-talk their Superintendent and explain that you were already involved with the case. Luckily – for you – they're in the middle of a major incident at Lingfield, over at the racecourse, so they're stretched already. He was reasonably happy for us to take over. You'd be advised to get there as quickly as you can – and grovel.'

~o~

Reluctantly, Russell was sitting in the visitor's chair in Detective Inspector 'Bonnie' Parker's fusty office. 'So your DC has gone AWOL then?' Parker gave a Cheshire cat smile, the Capstan Full Strength held loosely between his lips sending a shower of ash down his grubby, crumpled jacket. He took the cigarette out of his mouth and rested it in the overflowing ashtray, a curl of acrid smoke rising towards the ceiling.

'I'm not sure that's strictly true,' Russell countered.

'Well, whatever's happened to him, it's left you in the shit, hasn't it? And you need our help to dig you out.'

'I guess so.'

'Stout said that you'd cocked up with the day of the robbery.'

'Not exactly...'

'Really? It sounds to me that you thought it was going to happen tomorrow, when actually it happened today,' he chuckled.

'Yes, but I didn't know that until this morning.'

'Because, as I said, your DC has gone AWOL,' he said triumphantly. Russell decided not to respond. 'I'll tell you what though...' Parker continued.

'What's that?'

'If we're going over to Uckfield, I don't want that mutt in my car.' He picked up the cigarette and pointed it towards Aggie, who was sitting obediently at her master's side.

'That's fine,' Russell said, sniffily. 'I'll go with Constable Beaumont so you and DC Barrow can enjoy each other's company. I'll see you there.' Standing, he turned and left the office without another word.

~O~

'So, do you think they've got Weeks, Sir?' PC Beaumont asked. He was driving the Wolseley.

'That's what I'm afraid of,' Russell replied. 'He's always so reliable; I can't believe he'd go off without letting me know what was happening. I can only assume he didn't get the chance to communicate before he went off – probably under duress.'

'How much do we know about what's happened in Uckfield, Sir?'

'The information is a bit sketchy at the moment but it appears that the gang managed to stop the train on the line between Uckfield and Buxted. They'd parked a lorry – presumably the one "loaned" by Captain Valiant – on the level crossing, and the train had to stop. They got the crew off the locomotive and locked them, and the guard, in his brake van. Oh, and there were two passengers as well.'

'Really? I heard it was just a goods train.'

'It was supposed to be, but because of overcrowding, or scheduling or something, they'd attached a carriage.' He frowned. 'The funny thing is, the first officer on the scene said there were reserved stickers in the windows so no one was supposed to have been on it.'

'Who raised the alarm?'

'It was the stationmaster at Buxted. He was suspicious when the train didn't arrive. He left it five minutes or so, in case it

had been legitimately delayed, before ringing his counterpart at
Uckfield and found it had left the station. He then sent one of his
staff up the line where he discovered the train, and then found
the crew locked in the brake-van. He ran back to the station; they
stopped the next down train and rang the local police. Apparently
they arrived quite quickly but had to radio for someone to bring a
pair of bolt-cutters so they could get the padlock off.'

'What about the lorry?'

'That was long gone. Once they got the van open they released
the crew and the two passengers who were shaken but unharmed.
They should all be waiting for us to interview them.'

~o~

Weeks decided to have another root around in the pile of
broken furniture. Moving several pieces of wood he uncovered
a coil of thin rope. Looking more carefully he found several,
fairly straight, lengths of timber between three and four feet
long. He wondered if he might be able to fashion a ladder of
some sort. But before he did he thought he would see if the
hatch at the top of the coal chute would move. Using a piece
of broken glass he cut a length of mouldy rope off the coil. He
lashed the ends of two pieces of wood together, making a rod
which almost doubled their length. Going back to the recess
in the wall, the DC pushed the rod upwards until it pressed
against the bottom of the hatch. Nothing happened so he
shoved harder. After a few moments of straining he feared the
rope or wood would break. Then there was a slight movement
and suddenly a clatter; the rod shot upwards and daylight
appeared at the top of the chute. He stood still, holding his
breath, certain that the noise would have been heard. But after

waiting a few minutes, all remained quiet. Now he felt as if he was getting somewhere...

He lashed another couple of three-foot lengths of wood together then started tying shorter pieces across to make rungs. He had just enough useable rope, the last few feet being so mouldy that it snapped easily. Weeks stood back to admire his handiwork. He now had a crude, but serviceable ladder, six feet long. By standing on the topmost rung, he reckoned that he would be tall enough to get up to and through the hatchway. Elated he carried it across to the recess and propped it against the sloping back wall. Gingerly he climbed the ladder and near the top, found he was close enough to reach up and slide the hatch fully open. Climbing higher, he was delighted to find that he could put his head out through the opening and look round the yard. But, his hopes were dashed, when he tried to force his shoulders through the narrow gap. He wasn't a big chap but the hatch was just too narrow, even for his slender body. He pushed and strained but just couldn't get through. Then, with a last almighty heave, the lashings on his makeshift ladder just couldn't take the strain, several broke and the structure collapsed, dumping him on the floor. He cracked his head, saw stars and passed out.

Then it started to rain.

$\sim$o$\sim$

'It's raining boss,' Bates said, peering round the corner of the sack hanging across the window.

'Come away from there!' Helen hissed. 'You never know who's going to be looking at the house.'

The big man hung his head, crestfallen. 'Sorry.'

The mood had turned from elation to one of disgruntled frustration. The members of the gang were desperate to get their hands on the mailbags. They really wanted find out how much money they had stolen. Helen, however, was determined that they should keep a low profile; not draw attention to themselves. She knew that if she allowed them to start taking the sacks out of the lorry before nightfall they would be bound to be indiscreet; make too much noise or show themselves. So she insisted that they stay indoors, however frustrating it might be. In any case, the rain would help. Not only would it hamper any search but would help to wash away any traces they may have left that would lead to their hide-out.

'Anyone got any cards?' she asked.

'I have,' Bates said.

'Then get them out and let's have a game. We can play for matches. Then when we've got the loot the winner can take his share.'

'Good idea,' Sammy said,' a rare smile flitting across his weasel face. They cleared the table and sat down, an up-ended wooden box providing the fifth seat. Soon a serious card school was underway. Cigarette smoke filled the room but Helen allowed no drink stronger than beer. Bates appeared to have a definite knack for the game, his pudgy features easily transforming into a 'poker face'. Before long there was a pile of matchsticks in front of him and a sly grin playing around his lips. As the day wore on the rain continued to fall steadily.

~O~

'Let's get out of this weather and into the carriage,' Russell said. They had arrived in Hempstead Lane and Beaumont had parked the car by the level crossing. There was no sign of Parker and Barrow. The two local constables who had remained, plus the driver, fireman and guard, were glad to escape the downpour. First, Russell addressed the PCs: 'Tell me again what happened to the two passengers.'

The older of the constables spoke. 'We took their statements and let them go. They said they had an important appointment to keep.'

'But surely you should have kept them here until we arrived?'

'We did get their names and addresses.'

'Let me see.' The man handed over his pocketbook. Russell read the notes: 'James Joyce and Victor Hugo.' He tutted. 'I don't suppose one of them was Irish by any chance?'

'Yes, he was.'

'And the other one French?'

'He was,' the policeman said excitedly. 'How did you know?'

'You don't read a lot of literature, do you?' Russell asked.

'No, I'm afraid not. Why?'

Russell sighed. 'Because they are the names of two of the most famous writers of the past couple of centuries.'

'That's quite a coincidence.'

'Somehow, I don't think so. I dare say we'll find these addresses are false too.' The PC looked crestfallen. 'Perhaps you can describe them?'

He perked up. 'Yes, I could do that. James Joyce…'

'The one who called himself that…'

'Yes, okay. Well, he was quite small, about five foot six, maybe 40 or 50 years old. He was scruffy, with a threadbare jacket and trousers and a beret on his head that had seen better days.'

'What else did you notice about him?'

The other constable spoke. 'Grubby is probably the best description. His face was lined and he seemed to have dirt ingrained in the creases.' He thought for a moment. 'Oh yes, he had a funny wispy beard, that he kept stroking as he talked.' Beaumont jotted down these details.

'And what about the other one,' Russell asked.

'He was definitely French – well foreign, anyway.'

'Why do you say that?'

'His accent. Although his English was good, it was rather *too* perfect. And now I come to think of it, the way he said things, wasn't quite, well, *English*.'

'Describe him.'

'He was small, too. Smaller than the other bloke. He was dressed more smartly though – clean jacket and trousers, though they looked well-worn but foreign, somehow. And he was wearing a wide-brimmed hat and dark glasses.'

'And he had a stick. One of those thumb sticks – with a notch in the top,' the other constable added.

'Why would he need a stick?' Russell asked.

'Because of his leg.'

'What about his leg?'

'Oh, one of them was gammy and when he sat, his trouser leg rode up and you could see he was wearing one of them irons.'

Beaumont and Russell exchanged a glance. 'As if he'd had polio?'

The PC smiled brightly. 'Yes, that's right.'

'So, let me get this straight,' Russell said slowly. 'He was small, dressed in foreign clothes, with a gammy leg and a foreign accent?'

'Correct, Sir.'

'*Ye gods and little fishes!* It sounds like you've just set free one of the most wanted criminals we've come across.'

'Sir?'

'Don't you remember that case last year? Three Nazis were killed in rather grisly ways...'

'I do, Sir. Wasn't one of them keelhauled or something?'

'That's right.'

'And another whipped with a cat o' nine tails?'

'You remember then?'

The PCs face shone. 'And the third, made to walk the plank?'

'Correct.'

'We had a good laugh about that, I can tell you.' Seeing Russell's face darken he quickly added: 'It was a rather bizarre way to bump off those Nazis, you must admit, Sir.'

'That's as maybe. But do you recall the outcome?'

'Didn't someone get caught for it?'

'A German, Ludwig Müller.'

'A good result then, Sir.'

'No, it wasn't' Russell said firmly. 'Not only did my DC, Weeks, almost lose his life but the mastermind, Müller's brother, Wolfgang, is still at large. *And you've probably just let him go free!*'

'Oh...'

'Yes, oh.'

'But we weren't to know. They weren't even supposed to be on the train.'

'Possibly not, but you still should have kept them here until we arrived.'

'Yes, Sir.'

'Right, wait here, while I talk to the train crew.' Russell turned to his constable. 'Beaumont, go back to the car and get on to the mid-Sussex police. Tell them to look out for Müller and the other man. They should be easy to spot. They're on foot so shouldn't get too far.'

~O~

'Blimey shipmate, that was a lucky escape.'

'You can say that again.' Wolfgang and Dickens had found shelter in an old charcoal burner's hut in the woods near Hempstead Lane. Both had been sweating when the police turned up and released them from the brake-van. Wolfgang, especially, was convinced that he would be recognised but, whether it was the apparent slowness of the constables who had interviewed him, or the fact that his disguise actually worked, they had not realised who he really was. 'Thank goodness it was not that Detective, Russell, or even worse, his junior, Weeks. They would have known me straight away.'

'A lucky escape then, shipmate. Anyhow, what are we going to do now? We can't stay here. For one thing, we've got no vittles and two, I wouldn't be surprised if they don't send a search party up here soon.'

'We'll have to abandon our visit to London, won't we?'

'For now, I suppose. Although I still think we should go at some time. Meanwhile, we need to get back to Newhaven so we can lie low for a bit.'

~O~

The engine driver was still shaken and deaf in both ears after Atkins had fired the shotgun in the cab. The fireman was less traumatised so Russell started by interviewing him. 'What can you tell me about the men who held up the train?'

'Not a lot, I'm afraid. They were all wearing masks.'

'What about their clothes?'

'They were all dressed the same – in blue boiler suits – like mechanics wear.'

'Do you recall anything about the individuals, their build and so on?'

The man paused for a moment. 'Difficult to say, the overalls were rather shapeless and baggy. I think three of them were of average build although one was much bigger – his boiler suit was rather tight. Sorry, I can't tell you any more.'

'Ah well. Thanks, anyway.' Russell turned to the engine driver. 'Can you add anything to what your mate said?' The man looked blankly at him.

Constable Beaumont leaned across and spoke to Russell. 'He can't hear you, Sir. The gunshot. You'll have to speak up.'

'Of course.' He raised his voice. 'Can you tell me what you saw?'

The driver smiled in comprehension. 'Oh, I heard that! Well it was strange…'

'In what way?'

'Before the gunman climbed into the cab I took a look at that lorry that was parked on the crossing. It looked ex-army. Anyway, I could see two people in it. The passenger wasn't very clear, wearing some sort of veil, I think, but I could see the driver quite clearly, and he wasn't wearing a mask.'

'Can you describe him?'

The man turned his head sideways and put his hand up to his ear. 'Pardon?'

Russell asked again, louder. 'Can you describe the man?'

'Oh yes. He was young with a mop of dark hair.'

'Weeks!'

'Sorry?'

'Never mind. You've been very helpful.' Just as Russell had suspected, it looked like his DC had been taken under duress and had been used in the robbery. The thing was, where had they taken him now? He was more than a little worried. Weeks knew what all the gang members looked like and would easily be able to identify them if they were caught. No...*when* they were caught – he must remain positive. Although he wouldn't voice it, for him, the stolen money was not as important as finding his DC. He needed to discover where they had taken him, and quickly. He turned to the train's guard.

'Can you tell me any more about the men who held up the train?'

'Not really. Only that one of them, the one I first saw, was much larger than the others. Oh, and they were all wearing gloves. Sorry I can't tell you anything more.'

There was a rap on the carriage door. Beaumont opened it and they could see the fingerprints man, dressed in oilskin and sou'wester, standing in the rain. 'Hello, Lewis. Good to see you although I'm not sure there will be much for you here.'

'We'll see what we can find, Sonny. You never know what clues they have left. Oh, by the way, Bonnie and Clyde have just turned up. They're sitting in their car. Afraid of getting wet, I expect,' he said, grinning.

~o~

'Blowed if I'm going out in this,' Parker said, lighting another cigarette.

However, his DC, Barrow, decided he'd had enough of sitting in the smoke-filled car, with the windows closed. 'I could go and have a word with Russell. See what he's found out – if that's all right, Sir?'

'You go ahead. I'll stay here in case anything comes across on the radio.' Barrow got out of the car, opened the back door and grabbed his gabardine raincoat and hat and quickly pulled them on. He hurried along the side of the track and knocked on the carriage door. Beaumont opened it so he could climb up inside.

'Hello, constable,' Russell said. 'Where's your boss?'

'Ah, he's in the car – just in case there are any messages.'

'Staying in the dry, eh?' Russell chuckled, and then went on to recount what he had gleaned from the train crew.

Barrow said: 'I, rather we, wondered what you'd like us to do, Sir.'

'I suppose you could go up Hempstead Lane. The lorry was pointing in that direction – away from the town – so I assume that's the way they went. Drive up there slowly and see if you notice anything out of the ordinary. It's possible they may have dumped the lorry and the wood would be as good a place as any to do it. See if there's a track off the lane.'

'Righto, Sir.'

'Also keep an eye out for two men on foot – both small, although one walks with a limp and has a stick. Oh, you might remember him – Wolfgang Müller.'

Barrows eyes widened. 'The one who nearly did for Weeks!' he exclaimed.

'The very same. Our friends here…' he nodded towards the two constables, '…let him go.'

Back in the car, Barrow told Parker what Russell had said.

'Well, bugger me. Old Wolfgang's back. He was last heard of sailing into the sunset in France. Thought we'd seen the back of him.'

'It seems not, Sir. Anyway, Russell suggested we drive up the lane – see if we can discover anything.'

Parker blew a column of smoke towards the windscreen. 'Wild goose chase, if you ask me. That gang was pretty slick. They'll be miles away by now.'

'I suppose we could have a look, Sir. And maybe we might see the other two.'

'Oh, all right. If we must. But don't expect me to get wet unless I really have to.'

The gates were still open and Barrow drove over the level crossing. 'The railway authorities will be getting twitchy about the line being closed, won't they, Sir?'

'Tough luck. It's a crime scene and we can keep it closed for as long as we want.' They drove on up the lane, Parker complaining about being bumped about. Suddenly Barrow stamped on the brakes. Parker shot forward. 'Bloody hell! What are you playing at?!'

'Sorry, Sir. Look.' The constable pointed to the left. A track, even more rutted than the one they were on, snaked off into the woods. 'Shall I take a look?'

'Might as well. Let me know if you find anything. I'll stay here – by the radio.'

Barrow raised his eyebrows. 'Righto.' He got out of the car and started along the track.

'Listen! What's that?' Wolfgang asked.

'Mother of God! Sounds like a car. Let's get the hell out of here,' They stumbled out of the hut and into the trees. There was a thick tangle of holly bushes. 'Behind there. No one will be able to see us but we can keep an eye on what's going on.' Crouching down behind the evergreen hedge they waited, their clothes getting wetter by the minute. Presently they saw a figure wearing a hat and a raincoat appear along the track and go into the hut.

'*Gott in Himmel!*'

'What is it, shipmate?' Dickens was startled by Wolfgang's muttered outburst.

'I have left my stick in that hut.'

'Oh,' Dickens said lamely. 'With any luck they won't notice.'

The newly emerging leaf canopy gave little shelter and Barrow was glad to get into the charcoal burner's hut and out of the rain. The interior was gloomy and it took a few moments for his eyes to adjust. It was a crude affair, he realised. Roughly circular, it was shaped like a bell tent, with chestnut poles leaning in to meet at the apex, but the outside was cloaked in sacking and grassy turfs instead of canvas. However, the hut was surprisingly weatherproof. He looked around. There was nothing of note, just a few pieces of whittled wood, a small bench and some old sacks. He poked at the pile with his shoe and kicked something hard. Reaching down he uncovered a smooth length of wood. He almost dismissed it, thinking at first that it was of no consequence, but when he examined it more closely, he realised it was a walking stick, with a distinctive V at the top. He ran back to the car and tapped on the passenger window.

The window opened a crack. 'Found anything?' Parker asked, boredom in his voice. Barrow triumphantly held up the stick. 'Is that all?'

'But, Sir. It's a thumb stick! That's what Wolfgang had, according to one of the local coppers who talked to him.'

'I see.' Parker huffed. 'I suppose you want me to help you look for more clues.'

~O~

From the safety of their hiding place Wolfgang and Dickens saw the man, still carrying Wolfgang's stick, return with a companion and go into the hut. 'They're the police', the small German said.

'Too right, shipmate. Time to make ourselves scarce.'

'Wait a moment,' Wolfgang said, putting his hand on the other man's arm. 'They've left their car in the lane...'

A cunning look passed across Dicken's face. 'You're right.'

'But what if there is another policeman waiting in the car?'

'I think that's most unlikely. They usually hunt in pairs. Come on.' Keeping low, they skirted the hut and made their way back to the track. Sure enough, the car was standing there, unattended, with engine conveniently ticking over and the wipers tracing a lazy path across the windscreen. 'Quick! Get in.' Climbing into the car, they pulled the doors to, being careful not to slam them and Dickens drove carefully up the rutted track, keeping the revs low so as to make as little noise as possible. He had to get out at the top to open the gate, and then set off along Spurlings Lane. Less concerned about making a noise now they were away from the hut, he put his foot down and they sped along, turning left into Etchingwood Lane. They passed by the derelict farmhouse in a haze of spray, the wipers barely clearing the windscreen.

~O~

'Blimey! Did you see that?' Baker dropped the corner of the sacking covering the window.

'I told you not to look out the front!' Helen snapped.

'But it was the police – I swear it! Going like the clappers!'

'That's good then, ain't it,' Atkins said. 'Means it's just as we thought. Told you they wouldn't think we'd stay so close to where we did the blag.'

'Well done you for finding this place, Tommy,' Helen said, smiling.

'Can we go and look at the loot now?' Sammy asked.

Helen's smile turned to a frown. 'I told you. Not until dark. That's only one police car, there could be more to follow.'

~O~

Keeping to the lanes and heading east for a couple of miles they reached the outskirts of Blackboys. Dickens slowed the car. Rounding a bend they could see a roadblock ahead, with two police cars blocking the way. '*Mein Gott!*' Wolfgang exclaimed. 'What do we do now?'

'Leave it to me, shipmate. They won't be expecting us to arrive in this. You keep quiet. Just let me do the talking.' He drove up to the roadblock and wound the window down a crack; the rain was still falling heavily. A uniformed policeman wearing a helmet with a cape over his shoulders approached the car. He bent and peered through the crack. 'Any sign of the lorry, officer?' Dickens asked, no trace of Irish accent in his clipped tones.

'Nothing so far, Sir.'

'Hopefully they're still in the area. Keep your eyes peeled. Can you let us through? We've got to get back to HQ.'

'Of course, Sir.' The policeman signalled to his colleague, who reversed one of the police cars out of the way, then waved them through.

'Phew! That was close.'

Wolfgang grinned. 'Well done. You would have taken me in too, with that accent!'

# Chapter 23

*The Bank of England £5 note was issued in 1793 to
replace gold coin during the French Revolutionary Wars
and remained in circulation essentially unchanged
until 21 February 1957*

'THERE'S NOTHING else here,' Parker said, poking half-heartedly with the stick. 'Might as well go back to the car.'

'Shouldn't we have a look around outside, Sir?'

'What, and get soaked?'

'But Russell said…'

'Forget what Russell said. *He's* in the dry – and that's where we should be. We can get uniform to do it when we get back.' With that, he turned up the collar of his raincoat and set off. They retraced their steps and found their way back to the lane. When they arrived, Parker stood and looked around, baffled. '*What the…?*' he exclaimed, realising the car was no longer there. 'The bastards! They've nicked it!'

'Russell is going to be furious.'

'Never mind Russell. We need to get back pronto and report that the car has been stolen.'

They arrived at the railway line, dripping wet; DC Barrow miserable and resigned, DI Parker soaked and fuming. When they reached the carriage Parker told Russell, through gritted teeth, what had happened. Russell managed to supress a smile but could not resist saying: 'Last year, Ludwig Müller stole a police car from under your nose and now his brother's done the same.' Parker did not respond but the thunderous look on his face spoke volumes. Russell just had to add: 'I wonder why they've picked on you?'

Parker looked fit to explode but managed to keep a lid on it. 'Anyway, you'd better tell the local force to look out for a stolen police car,' he said grudgingly.

'Will do.' Turning to the uniformed constable Russell said: 'Beaumont, can you go to the car and ring mid-Sussex headquarters?'

'Yes, Sir.'

'And you two, take off your wet coats and sit down. We've got to plan what to do.'

~o~

The rain continued to fall relentlessly. At the back of the farmhouse a cast-iron downpipe had come adrift from its bracket and had swung sideways. So, instead of the water going into a drain, it was discharging the contents of the gutter down through the coal chute and into the cellar. If the hatch at the top had remained in place it would have flowed harmlessly across the yard, but after Weeks's efforts the water was now forming a pool around his body. The door at the top of the steps opened, the light from the candles in the kitchen too weak to penetrate beyond the first couple of steps

'Weeks?' Bates called out. 'There's some grub for you here.' Receiving no reply he turned back to the kitchen. 'He's not answering. Shall I go down?'

'Nah,' Atkins replied. 'He's probably 'avin' a kip.' With that, Bates put the plate and mug on the broad top step and closed the door. Weeks lay, oblivious to the rising water. When the ladder had broken and he had banged his head he hadn't fallen flat out but was slumped against the back of the chute in a sitting position. Even so, the water was creeping up round his thighs, pieces of wood and sack were starting to float around the floor. And still the rain fell.

'It's getting dark. Can we go and get the mailbags now?' Sammy asked, hopefully.

Helen lifted the corner of the makeshift curtain and looked out. Because of the rain the light had left the sky early. Nothing was visible but the silvery stair rods falling from the sky. 'Okay. But be *careful* and be *quiet*. And keep your gloves on!'

Donning coats and hats the men made their way silently out through the back door and across the yard. Once the doors to the barn were open, they dropped the tailgate of the Bedford, Sammy climbed up inside and started handing the mailbags down to the others. They had to make several journeys, carrying the bags through the steady rain, but soon they were all heaped up in the kitchen. Wet coats and dripping hats were discarded and just as they were about to start undoing the string round the top of the bags Helen said loudly: 'No! Stop! We need to have a system or we're going to get in a muddle.' The men stood back. 'Right, that's better. Now, open them carefully; we've got plenty of time. If they've got money in, put them over there.' She pointed to the corner of the room by the threadbare sofa. 'Any of the others, put over there by the table. Now you can start opening them – but *don't* take out any cash until they're sorted.'

Her commanding voice had a calming effect and they all set to carefully, opening the bags, without disturbing the contents and putting them in their respective piles. After a while, the sacks containing just mail formed a large heap, while there were only about 10 containing cash.

'Why don't we look through the letters?' Bates asked. 'There may be cash or postal orders in them.'

'No!' Helen said emphatically. 'We leave them alone. It's too risky – too easy to trace. Let's concentrate on the cash.' The table in the kitchen was cleared of plates and cups and gradually became covered with stacks of bank notes. Drawing the chairs, and box, up to the table the five of them sat and patiently counted the money. It was surprisingly quiet, just the sound of rain falling outside and the rustle of paper. The cash was sorted into 10-shilling and one pound notes, plus a further pile of white fivers. It took some time, with Helen jotting down the amounts on a notepad. Eventually, it was all counted and she added up the total. 'Not bad for a morning's work,' she said, sitting back and smiling.

'How much?' Baker asked, eagerly.

'I make it £58,275.'

Sammy whistled. 'Wow! So how much is that each?'

Helen jotted down some more figures. 'That's 10 grand each, after expenses of course.'

Bates furrowed his brow, then broke the silence. 'What expenses?'

'Well...' she said, 'there's my contact at the station who gave us the gen on the train, his mate at Brighton, who sorted out the carriage, then various other odds and ends. Don't worry, it's all accounted for.'

'What about him, down there?' Baker pointed to the cellar door.

'Him? Weeks? He gets nothing of course.'

'Apart from his just desserts,' Atkins chortled.

'Quite. We need to decide what to do with him. He knows us all, plus he knows where I live, or rather, where I used to live…'

'What do you mean, "where you used to live"?' Baker asked.

'You don't think I'm going back there, do you? It was all very nice but I only rented it. I'm going somewhere different.'

'Oh, yeah? Where are you off to then?' Sammy asked, his eyes sliding around nervously.

Helen chuckled. 'I don't think I'm going to say. The less you know about what we all do from now on, the better it will be for all of us. It's been great fun, but I think this is where we go our separate ways; where our friendship ends.' And, before anyone could protest, she said, 'Right, let's sort the money out and put it into individual bags and label them so we know whose is whose. We don't want it getting muddled up with the other bags. Then it's time we had a party to celebrate. And don't worry about overdoing it, we're not going anywhere until nightfall tomorrow.'

After they had divided the cash, they put the bags in the corner, away from those that contained letters. Then the bottles were opened. The evening went from civilised toasts to hearty congratulations to raucous singing and joke telling. It was the early hours of the morning before, bleary eyed, they started setting off for bed. No one had noticed that although Helen had kept her glass topped up, the level had hardly gone down. She had joined in the laughter and frivolity with as much gusto as the rest of them but remained stone-cold sober. Atkins was the last of the men downstairs. 'Thanks very much for all the help you've given me. I couldn't have done it without you.' She reached forward and pecked him on the cheek.'

He looked a little bashful. 'Are you sure this is where it ends, where we say goodbye?' he asked.

'Afraid so, Tommy. You don't need me. If you want to do another job I'm certain that you're quite capable of doing it on your own. Anyway, you get off to bed. I'll have a tidy up down here before I turn in.'

'Okay. Night, Helen.'

'Night, Tommy. Pleasant dreams.' She waited until she was sure that he and the others were settled; the only sound, Bates's stentorian snoring. Then, making as little noise as possible, she went out of the door and spent a few minutes in the barn. Once back in the kitchen she began working on the mailbags.

~o~

Weeks woke in darkness, panicking. He had the mother of all headaches; he was sitting in water, soaked from the waist down and had no idea where he was. Gingerly he stood and edged blindly along the wall. As his feet moved through the water, pieces of floating debris threatened to topple him, but he managed to keep his balance. Then he bumped into something fixed and solid – a step. Leaning forward and balancing with his hands he ascended the stone staircase until he came to the top, broad step, where he touched a plate. Feeling along its surface his hand touched something soft. He picked it up. Bread. He realised how hungry he was and in a few bites it was gone. Feeling round again his hand came to a cold cylinder. It was a mug. He lifted it to his lips and tasted tepid tea. Even so, he drank it down, still with no idea where he was. His headache seemed to become worse after his exertions. He put his hands either side of his head and groaned. The pain became overwhelming and he slumped on to the step, unconscious. He knocked the tin plate and it clattered down the stone staircase.

Helen heard the noise, alarmed that someone was coming downstairs. Then she realised it had come from the cellar. Cautiously, she unlocked the door and opened it. The sight of Weeks lying in a crumpled, sodden heap, with a trickle of blood on his neck, made her heart freeze. She crouched down and put the back of her hand to his cheek. Warm, thank God. Putting her hand round the back of his head she could feel an egg-shaped lump through the thick hair. Gently she shook his shoulder. He groaned. She shook him a little more forcefully. He blinked and struggled to sit up.

'Where am I?' Slowly as his eyes focused Helen's face swam into view. 'Who are you?' he said.

'Don't you know?'

'No. Why, should I?'

'And you've no idea where you are?' He shook his head. The effort seemed to be too much, he slowly toppled over and his eyes closed again. Helen got to her feet and fetched a dry blanket, returned and draped it over the sleeping figure. Her smile was one of relief. It looked like they wouldn't have to silence him after all.

Dickens turned right on to the Lewes road and they drove south. Within half an hour they were approaching the outskirts of the town and the rain was easing. 'There's a bit of waste ground between the railway tracks and the river. We'll dump the car there and make our way to the station. It's not far. D'you think you'll be able to make it?' He glanced at his companion.

Wolfgang gave a wan smile. 'I should think so, although I wish I hadn't left my stick behind.'

'Don't worry, my friend, I'll give you a hand.'

Just as Dickens had said, they reached a patch of scrubby land, covered with straggly grass, spindly trees and untidy bushes. He drove the car in as far as he could then switched off the engine and they got out. For good measure he locked the door and threw the key into the nearby water.

'But won't they be looking for us in the railway station?' asked Wolfgang.

Dickens chuckled. 'Judging by how inefficient they've been so far, I doubt they will yet. However, I have a plan that should fool them. When we get there, you wait outside while I get the tickets.' The rain had finally stopped and after a short while they reached the station and climbed the steps of the footbridge. 'You stay here and I'll come and get you.' Holding his head high and squaring his shoulders Dickens marched up to the ticket office, passing a uniformed policeman who didn't appear to give him a second glance. He bought two tickets for Brighton and went back to join Wolfgang.

'Right,' he said, 'this could be tricky. There's a bobby standing by the ticket office. He doesn't seem to be looking out for anyone but we need to be careful.' They stood for a while, watching until the PC walked across to the vacant ticket window, leaned down, and started chatting to the clerk. 'Come on. *Now!*' He gripped the little German's elbow and steered him to platform four. They descended the steps and waited until the train came in.

There was only a handful of passengers and they paid the couple no heed. Once on the train the two men sat quietly as it pulled out of the station. 'But why are we going to Brighton?' Wolfgang asked eventually.

'We're not,' Dickens whispered. 'That's part of my plan. When the police enquire at the ticket office they'll think Brighton is where we've gone. But we're going to get off at Falmer and double back.'

Wolfgang gave a rare smile. 'Oh, I see.'

In only a few minutes the train pulled into Falmer station and they left the carriage and crossed the footbridge to platform two. Soon another arrived, they found empty seats and, within 15 minutes, the train was pulling into Newhaven station. Luck was with them again as the ticket collector was absent. They walked out of the station unchallenged. Crossing the bridge over the river, it was only a short walk before they were back at the yard.

'There we are shipmate. Told you my little ruse would work. Now all we need to do is lie low for a few days, then we can resume our quest to spring your brother.'

~O~

The detectives sat in the carriage discussing what they planned to do, until it became too dark to make out each other's faces clearly. Because of the rain, night had come early and it was decided there was little point in continuing the search. Scant progress would be made until daylight and besides, the railwaymen were keen to move the train so that normal services could be resumed. Lewis and his team had dusted the van for prints and looked around for clues but were doubtful if they would come up with anything. The robbers had been too careful.

'So, tomorrow,' Russell said, 'we start at the crack of dawn.' Parker groaned. 'Oh come on, it's not been a bad day for you. Oh, apart from losing your car.'

'All right, all right. You've had your fun. What do you want me to do?'

'To start, I think you and Barrow and a couple of the local PCs should go house to house around Framfield; knock on a few doors and find out if anyone has seen anything. The roadblocks are in place and the local force is checking the railway stations in the area. I'm going to get the police up at Victoria station to haul this Simon H fellow in for questioning. If nothing else we can get him for aiding and abetting and, you never know, he might be able to help us track down the villains. I think that's about covered everything for now. I suppose you'd like a lift back to Collinghurst? I'm afraid you'll have to share the car with my *mutt...*'

~o~

Despite Dickens's confidence to the contrary the policeman at Lewes station *had* spotted him. When he spoke to the clerk he found that the Irishman had bought two singles to Brighton. He telephoned ahead to warn the police to keep an eye on the passengers leaving the train on platform eight. It wasn't long before he received a call saying that there had been no sign of the fugitives. Then he struck lucky. He rang the stationmaster at Falmer who informed him that two figures had alighted from the Brighton train, crossed over the bridge and caught a train in the opposite direction. The policeman speculated that they had gone all the way to Newhaven and, sure enough, when he telephoned it was confirmed. The ticket clerk he spoke to said he'd had to leave his box briefly but, as he came back, he saw two small figures – one scruffy, the other limping – go through the barrier and disappear into the night. The PC called Collinghurst police station and passed the information on.

~o~

When they arrived at the station, Russell was glad to see the back of Parker and Barrow. The conversation had been stilted but the atmosphere had been thick with the fumes from the full-strength cigarettes that Parker insisted on smoking. However, as Russell walked through the foyer, Wickstead called him over. 'I've had a message from a particularly diligent officer,' he chuckled. 'He should go far.' He then went on to report what he had been told.

'At last! Something positive,' Russell exclaimed. 'We'll get some uniforms knocking on doors around Newhaven station first thing in the morning. See if we can flush them out.'

~o~

Morning came, and with it more news, good and bad. The bad news was that Simon H had not turned up for work and no one knew where he was. The good news was that Parker's car had been found abandoned close to Lewes station. That tied in with the observant policeman's report. Russell agreed to drive Parker and Barrow there to collect the car. After they had dropped the two detectives off, he and Beaumont went over to Newhaven to see how the house-to-house was progressing. So far, the PCs knocking on doors had failed to turn anything up. Then one constable thought he had struck lucky. A small German man answered the door of a terraced cottage. Excitedly, he called the DI over. But when Russell saw that the man was well into his seventies and nothing like Wolfgang he shook his head. 'Afraid not,' he said and they moved on to the next house.

When the German had closed the door he almost ran down the passageway to the telephone. 'Paddy?' he said, 'they are on to you. The police have been asking questions. I suggest you get out – and get out fast. You had better tell your friend, too.'

Standing in his office Dickens slammed the phone down and cursed. 'Bloody hell! And I thought we were in the clear.' Pulling open drawers he stuffed a handful of papers into a bag, went into his living quarters and grabbed some clothes. Looking round, possibly for the last time he thought, he sighed then made his way quickly to *Moonshine*. At first, Wolfgang was pleased to see him. Somehow they had become, if not friends, then tolerable acquaintances. But when he heard what Dickens had to tell him, the smile disappeared. 'What are we going to do?' he asked miserably.

'Only one thing for it, shipmate. We'll have to set sail.'

'But the boat is not ready,' Wolfgang protested. 'I don't know if the battery is okay; I haven't topped up the fuel; the engine probably needs servicing…'

'No time for that, my friend. We've got to leave and leave now. Come on, get the engine started.' He took a knife out of his pocket. 'I'll deal with the mooring ropes.'

The engine started easily and, although the tide was nowhere near full, there was sufficient water under the keel to enable Wolfgang to reverse the boat out of the berth, turn her in the creek, and then they were on their way.

It was fortunate that they had taken a spare key with them but it still took a while to extricate the police car from the undergrowth. Parker insisted on driving while Barrow had the unenviable task of putting his shoulder to the bonnet and pushing. Eventually, after much swearing from Parker, the car was free from the bushes, the wheels could grip solid tarmac and they could set off for Framfield. When they arrived, a couple of uniforms were waiting for instructions. 'Right, lads,' the DI said, 'you start knocking on doors here in the village and we'll go and do the same at the outlying farms and houses.'

'What is it we need to know, Sir?' one asked.

'Just ask if they've seen any suspicious characters hanging around – maybe using the phone box. Or indeed, if they've seen anyone they don't recognise. Pretty straightforward, even for you chaps, eh?' Parker smirked. A look passed between the two constables but he didn't notice. 'Right then. We'll see you back here later. Perhaps you'll actually turn something up?' With that he levered himself into the passenger seat of the car and Barrow drove off.

'Bloody cheek!' one PC said to the other. 'Just because we let that sodding foreigner go.'

Over in Newhaven the policeman carried on making enquiries of householders and business owners located around the railway station. It was a chilly, damp day and it seemed like a thankless task until, just after lunchtime, they struck lucky across the river in Bridge Street. Russell happened to go into the New Bridge Inn and asked if either of the two men they were seeking was known and found the landlord more than helpful. 'You must be talking about Paddy Dickens.'

'You know him then?'

The landlord roared with laughter. 'Know him? He helps keep me in business!'

Russell beamed. 'I don't suppose you know where he lives, do you?'

'I do. He's got a boatyard on the creek at the back of Denton Island. If you can call it a boatyard – it's more of a junkyard.'

'What about the other man. Have you seen him?'

The landlord thought for a moment. 'Now you come to mention it, he did bring someone in recently – another little bloke.'

Russell didn't want to lead him so he asked, simply, 'Do you remember anything particular about him?'

'What, you mean apart from the wide-brimmed hat and thumb stick?' His eyes twinkled.

'Go on.'

'He had a gammy leg – walked with a limp.'

'And you say they came in together?'

'Just the once – seemed as thick as thieves – heads together, plotting. They were sitting just there.' He pointed to a corner table.

'When was this?'

'Let me think… Oh yes, I remember. Day before yesterday.'

'Oh really?'

'Yes, they must have spent a couple of hours in here then snuck off without me noticing. Ain't seen either of them since.'

'Thanks, you've been a great help.' Russell gathered together the uniforms and told them what he had just heard. They set off for the creek. It wasn't long before they found what they were looking for.

A small, tar-washed single-storey building stood at the entrance to a yard containing a jumble of rotting hulks, leaning sheds and haphazard piles of timber, chain and rope. A crudely painted sign declaring OFFICE was nailed to the door. Russell tried the handle. It was unlocked. He pushed the door open. The interior was a continuation of the chaos outside, but open drawers and scattered papers suggested that someone had left in a hurry. 'Spread out and see if you can find anyone in the yard,' he ordered the policemen. 'I'll have a look round in here.' He went through a door at the back of the office into what was apparently living accommodation. The chaos continued but he felt certain that the occupant had not long left.

There was a shout from out in the yard. Russell made his way to where the sound had come from. One of the PCs was standing by a wooden jetty that looked as if a strong wind would blow it over. He held out a much-darned woollen sock. 'And look, Sir,' he said. A mooring rope was belayed round a timber upright, one end neatly whipped, the other, roughly cut. Russell bent and examined the knot. It was expertly tied, almost like a signature. He guessed at once who it belonged to – Wolfgang!

Meanwhile, the policemen going door-to-door in Framfield were having less luck. One householder thought she had seen a masked man with a gun riding a bicycle down the high street but her neighbour pooh-poohed it. Said she was a bit simple in the head and read too many detective stories. Another man said he had seen a stranger going into the phone-box but, when questioned further, couldn't remember exactly when it was, He thought it might have been some time the previous year. Dispirited, the policemen decided to interview the landlord of the Hare and Hounds. Although he could offer no help he did pull them a couple of pints, which cheered them up considerably.

Parker and Barrow were faring no better. They had headed east out of the village, where the houses were grander and further apart. Most times, Barrow was sent to make enquiries while his boss sat in the car, dozing – it *had* been an early start. They drove up to a couple of farms and Barrow had to get out into sticky mud and other substances, Parker complaining about the smell when he returned. They were driving along Etchingwood Lane when Barrow stopped the car suddenly and reversed back up the road. 'What the hell are you playing at?' Parker asked angrily.

Barrow brought the car to a standstill at the side of a rickety farm gate, with a sad-looking farmhouse at the end of a long drive. 'Nearly missed this one, Sir.'

'Bloody well should have done. Doesn't look like there's anyone home, or has been for some time. I suppose *I'd* better go and have a look.' Grumbling, he heaved himself out of the car, walked over to the gate and stared at the forlorn building. He rattled the padlock. 'Locked,' he said, dropping it. 'Bloody waste of time if you ask me. They'll be miles away by now.' He slumped back into the car. 'Drive on. And no more emergency stops, okay?'

~O~

It was mid-morning and Helen was sitting at the table, drinking a mug of tea. Atkins was the first of the gang to come down. Considering the amount of alcohol that had been consumed the previous evening, he didn't look too bad.

'I've been thinkin' about what you were sayin' last night,' he said.

She looked up. 'Oh, really?'

'Yeah. Are you serious about goin' off and leavin' us?'

'You'll get along just fine without me,' she said, smiling warmly.

'But I thought we was a team.' Maybe it was the hangover but his sad eyes made him look miserable.

'Tommy,' she said, taking his hand, 'you'll be fine. You've learned well; the others respect and look up to you. Besides, with all that money,' she glanced across to the pile of sacks, 'you don't need to do anything for some time.'

'I s'pose not.' He still looked like a scolded puppy.

'Come on, have a cuppa. That'll perk you up.'

The others came down, one by one, much the worse for wear. Sammy looked like death warmed up and asked, in a hushed voice, if Helen had any aspirins. For once, his eyes were not darting all over the place, they just remained blurrily unfocused. Bates went to the sink and drank several mugs of water from the tap, one after another; Baker poured himself some tea and sat down, quietly nursing the mug. Time passed with little being said until they heard a car go past, stop with a screech of brakes, a little way up the road, then reverse back to the gate.

'What the hell is that?' Baker said, stiffening.

Helen gingerly lifted the corner of the sacking covering the window and risked a sneaky look out. Holding her breath she watched as a stocky man, wearing a crumpled suit and a trilby, got out of the car, walked up to the gate, lifted the padlock and shook it. He stared at the farmhouse. Helen remained stock still.

After a moment the man dropped the padlock and walked back to the car, said something to the driver then got in and they drove off. She started breathing again. 'Looks like we're in the clear lads. I'm pretty sure that was the law. I don't think they'll be bothering us.'

'Does that mean we can go now?' Sammy asked, his eyes back to performing their usual gyrations.

'Of course not!' Helen said, crossly. 'We still wait until it's dark.'

Baker spoke: 'When we do go, are you coming in the van with us?'

Enunciating carefully, as if speaking to a slow child, she said: 'I told you, this is where we part company.' Seeing his face, she added: Don't look so downcast, I'm sure you'll have more *adventures* with your pals. You just don't need me anymore.'

'How are you planning on leaving here?' Bates asked, his fleshy face creased with concern.

Her laugh was musical. 'Don't you worry about me. I've arranged my own transport.' No one thought to enquire who was picking her up and how they came to know about the hide-out.

'Ain't you forgetting something?' Atkins enquired.

'What's that, Tommy?'

'Our friend down there.' He pointed at the cellar door.

'Ah. I think that's been sorted out for us.'

'What do you mean?'

'I looked in on him last night and it seems as if he's had a fall.'

'Is he dead?' Sammy asked quickly.

'Don't be daft. Of course he isn't. He's had a bump on the head and...' the laugh was more deep throated this time, '...he's lost his memory.'

'How can you be sure?'

'I saw him last night and he had no idea who I was or where he is. I checked on him this morning and he was fast asleep. But just to be on the safe side, I'll look in on him again later.'

'We don't need to do anythin' drastic then?' Atkins asked.

'No, I don't think so. We'll leave him here when we go.'

'Yes, but you said you didn't think the law would be troubling us,' Baker said.

'Yes, that's right.'

'So if no one comes looking, he might die.'

'I've thought of that. Once I'm away from here, I'll make an anonymous phone call – let the police know where he is.'

~O~

Wolfgang had opened the throttle wide on *Moonshine* until she was creaming along with a bone in her teeth doing nearly 15 knots. When they were a mile or so off the coast, Dickens said: 'Don't you think you should ease off now?'

'I've got to keep her going flat out,' Wolfgang said. 'We need to get as far away from here as possible.' He was quite agitated.

Dickens reached across and pulled the throttle back. 'No, there's no need. We're far enough off shore, we don't know where we're going and we don't want to run out of fuel,' he said, taking control of the situation.

Wolfgang relaxed a little. 'Very good. You are probably right. Where do you think we ought to go?'

'While we were making our getaway I've been giving that some thought. I wonder if we should go to the place where we're least expected.'

'Where's that?' Wolfgang asked.

'Compass Point.'

'You have to be joking!'

'No, shipmate, I'm deadly serious.'

'But they're bound to look for us there!'

Now that the speed had been reduced *Moonshine* rode the waves easily; she really was a good sea boat. 'I don't think so. They're not to know that we haven't much fuel so they'll probably think we'd go back across the Channel – to where you were before, or somewhere near. Didn't you say that the policeman, Russell, has a *comrade* in Boulogne?

'Yes, Bruissement.'

'He'll tell him to keep a look-out on the coast along the *Cote d'Opale*.'

'How can you be sure of that?'

Dickens gave a laugh. 'I'm starting to work out how his mind works. The last thing he'll consider is that we'll be taking *Moonshine* back to her home port. Especially as she is not *Moonshine* anymore.' The laugh turned into a deep-throated chuckle. 'And didn't you tell me that you know some old ferryman there, the one who found the boat for you?'

'Jack Spratt.'

'That's him. You said he could be easily persuaded, with a bribe or two.'

'He *could*. But I am not so sure now.' Wolfgang remembered back to their last encounter, the previous year. Spratt had told him where his brother was being held, immediately after his arrest. He was remembering too, how the ferryman had asked for more money. Wolfgang had refused, threatening him with a gun. 'No, I am not so sure,' he repeated quietly.

'I don't think we've got any alternative. Wherever we go, the police will be on the look-out for us. This could be the best, worst option, if you see what I mean.'

'I suppose so.'

'We could wait until dark to go in…'

'I will check the tides and see if that is possible. There is a sand bar across the mouth of the estuary and there is only enough water for a certain time either side of high tide.'

'Right. We motor along steadily, that will conserve fuel. If we're there too early, we'll just sit it out, well off-shore, until it's time to go in. How does that sound?'

'All right, I suppose.'

'Right then. Let me take a trick at the helm while you brew us some coffee.'

~O~

'I knew this would be a waste of time.' Parker slumped in his seat. He had got out of the car only a handful of times, leaving his DC, Barrow, to do the lion's share of the legwork: visiting outlying farms and properties and asking the same questions, over and over again. The uniforms in Framfield had experienced the same lack of success, but at least they had enjoyed a pint and a pork pie in the Hare and Hounds, courtesy of the landlord. The two detectives drove back to the village and met with them, outside the village store.

'Get us a packet of fags, will you?' he said to Barrow. 'I need to have a chat with these lads and see what they've come up with.' By the time his DC came back with the Capstan Full Strength, Parker had learned that the PCs had gleaned nothing either and he decided to call it a day and agreed to take them to their police station, *en route* back to Collinghurst. When they arrived they all went in to the station; Parker needed a pee. Just as they were about to leave, the desk sergeant called out: 'Why don't you stop for a bit. One of the lads is going for fish and chips. You're welcome to join us. Might be a beer or two as well,' he said, giving them a wink.

Barrow looked at the DI. 'What do you think, Sir?'

Parker shrugged. 'There's no rush to get back. I suppose we could.' Then, to the sergeant: 'How much do you want? Presume there's a kitty.'

'Couple a bob each should do it.'

Parker fished two half-crowns out of his pocket. 'Here you are. Keep the change.' Looking at the sergeant, Barrow raised his eyebrows. He wasn't used to this level of generosity from his boss.

'Thanks, Inspector. Come and have a brew while you wait.'

Motoring steadily along, Wolfgang and Dickens watched the coast slide by; Beachy Head lighthouse appeared to port, then the Royal Sovereign light ship, just visible to starboard. It was off Hastings that the trouble began. Although they had kept the engine ticking over at the lowest revs to maintain steerage, there was even less fuel than Wolfgang had feared. First the Gardiner diesel started missing a beat every so often. He pushed the throttle forward, increasing the revs, but the intermittent misfires became more frequent, then, with a cough and a splutter, the engine stopped. Wolfgang tried to get it going again but the starter motor just whirred and the engine turned over without firing.

He sighed. 'That's it then.'

'Are you sure, shipmate? Haven't we got any spare diesel oil?

'I told you the tank was low but you insisted on leaving,' the German replied angrily.

'We had to go when we did,' Dickens insisted. 'Otto said the police were just round the corner and would have caught us, if we'd stayed.'

'That is all very well. But what are we going to do now?'

'I don't suppose we could launch the dinghy and tow *Moonshine*?'

Wolfgang snorted. 'You *do* realise how much she weighs?'

'Yes, but I'm a powerful rower.'

'Perhaps you are, but I think you will find that the tide is making us drift faster than you can row.' Indeed, while they had been arguing, they had drifted further along the coast.

Neither said anything for some time then Dickens put his hand to his ear. 'Listen!' The thud of an engine was unmistakable. 'Look!' he pointed astern. The blurred shape of a boat was just visible, the engine note growing louder and the hull larger as it drew nearer. When it was closer they could see it was the harbourmaster's launch.

As it came within hailing distance a figure stepped out of the wheelhouse. 'Ahoy there. Are you in trouble?'

'Do not say anything,' Wolfgang said quietly.

'Don't be silly, shipmate. We need help. You make yourself scarce. I'll do the talking.' As soon as Wolfgang had gone below Dickens cupped his hands round his mouth and shouted: 'Any chance of a tow? Bit of engine trouble.'

In a few moments, the launch came alongside and the man threw a rope across. 'I'm going into Compass Point; will that do?'

'That's perfect. That's where I was heading anyway.'

'Are you on your own?'

'That's right, shipmate. Just me, on me tod, feeling a bit embarrassed.'

The man laughed. 'Happens to all of us at some time. Have you got that line secure?'

Dickens tied the rope off on the Samson post on the foredeck and threaded it through the fairlead on the bow. 'Right you are. All done.' The man went back into his wheelhouse, motored forward slowly until the slack was taken up then opened the throttle a little so that they were moving at a respectable speed.

They reached the entrance to Compass Point, just as the tide was gathering and there was sufficient water to cross the bar at the mouth of the river. When they reached the quay, the man, who was not the harbourmaster, but a mechanic testing the engine, jumped ashore, secured his craft then helped Dickens do the same with *Moonshine*. 'You best talk to Jack Spratt, the ferryman. He should be able to help you out with fuel.'

'Thanks a million, I'll do that.'

'Anything else, give me a shout. I'll be over there.' He pointed to a sign that read *MITCHELL'S BOATYARD*.

Once he had checked that the mooring lines were secure Dickens went down into the cabin where Wolfgang was sitting on one of the bunks. 'I am really not happy about this,' he said miserably. 'If we had come in at night it might have been different. But in broad daylight....'

'To be sure you're worrying too much, shipmate. You know that the boat looks quite different, painted black, and as long as you keep your head down, and let me do the talking, we'll be fine. Now let's have a brew, and then I'll go and find this ferryman chappie.'

~O~

Captain Salt wandered across to the quay and looked out, surveying the view. As the tide came in, it lifted the fishing boats and pleasure craft off the muddy bottom; those out in the estuary started to swing to their moorings. Herring gulls and black-headed gulls sat bobbing on the water and he could hear the distant mournful bubbling cry of a curlew and the urgent piping of oystercatchers. He looked down and saw that a new boat was moored below the ferry steps. Then he looked more closely and wondered if it *was* a new boat – something about the lines looked familiar. Just then, a figure came out of the cabin, stepped across the gunwale and started climbing the ferry steps. 'Good afternoon,' the man said. 'And a fine one it is, too.' The accent was Irish, Salt noted. 'D'you know where I can find a fella by the name of Jack Spratt?'

Salt took the pipe out of his mouth. 'Why, of course. That's his shed there.' He pointed to a black, tar-painted hut, raised on timbers, with lengths of wood, oars and rope lying around it. 'You could try knocking but I'm not sure what sort of reception you'll get. He's probably having a kip; doesn't tend to get up until there's enough water to row across to the other side. That's his ferry there.' He pointed to a neat, pale-blue dinghy moored forward of *Moonshine*. 'Anyhow, what brings you here?'

''Tis a bit embarrassing really. We...' he quickly corrected himself, '...I mean I, ran out of fuel and the man in the harbourmaster's launch kindly towed me in.'

'Oh, that'll be Stan, he works for Mitch Mitchell. I'm the harbourmaster – he's been doing a bit of maintenance on my boat. Jolly good mechanic, if you need one. Which you might, if the injectors on the engine need bleeding.'

'I'll bear that in mind, if I have a problem.'

'Where are you bound?' Salt asked.

'Er, Dover.'

'Today?'

'That's the plan. Anyway, thanks for your help. I think I'll see what sort of mood Mr Spratt is in.' He walked across to the ferryman's hut and knocked on the door.

Salt stood looking down at the boat. He tapped his pipe out on the top of a wooden bollard then brought out a soft leather pouch from an inside pocket. Putting the pipe in the pouch he pushed some tobacco into the bowl and thumbed it down firmly. He produced a box of matches, took one out, struck it on the side of the box and held the flame to the bowl of his pipe. He sucked greedily until a gout of grey smoke issued from the side of his mouth.

Dickens knocked again, more loudly this time. An angry muffled voice came from inside. 'Bugger off! Can't you read? Ferry's closed!'

'I don't want the ferry.'

'Why are you knockin' on my door then?' There was the sound of shuffling and more grumbling from within, then the door opened and Spratt appeared. He was wearing a threadbare jersey and baggy grey flannels tucked into a pair of well-darned woollen socks. Startling blue eyes peered bleary from a weather-beaten face. 'What be you wantin'?' he asked suspiciously.

'Sorry to trouble you but I need some fuel,' Dickens said, in his most placatory voice.

'S'pose I can help. 'Ow much d'yer want?'

'I don't rightly know. Say 10 gallons?'

'Got any cans?'

'I'm afraid not.'

'Grr. Don't want much, do you?'

'I'll pay for your trouble.'

'Too right you will. Wait here.' He went back inside and Dickens could just see, in the gloom, Spratt sitting down and pulling on a pair of wellingtons, the tops rolled over. After much grunting, he stood, pushed past Dickens, stomped down the steps and disappeared into another shed. In a few moments he came out bearing two battered jerry cans. He handed them over. 'That'll be three quid – and I want them cans back!' Dickens reached into his pocket and produced three, one pound notes and gave them to Spratt, who held each one up to the light. He looked at Dickens from under his flat cap. 'Ain't seen you afore. Not from round 'ere, are you?'

'No, just passing through.'

'Hmm. Don't forget to bring the cans back. Leave 'em on the step.' With that he went back inside his hut and slammed the door.

Dickens made his way carefully down the ferry steps – the lower ones slippery with seaweed. Back on board *Moonshine* he undid the engine hatch, unscrewed the fuel filler cap and, putting a metal funnel into the opening, carefully poured in the contents of the two cans. When he'd finished, he returned the two empty cans and went back to the boat. 'Come on,' Wolfgang said, as Dickens entered the cabin and carefully closed the companionway doors behind him, 'Let us get out of here.'

Dickens held up his hand. 'Not so fast. If we hightail it out of here straight away it'll look suspicious. Let's just sit here for a little while, then we'll go.'

Captain Salt had been unobtrusively watching all the exchanges and as soon as Dickens had dropped out of sight he examined the boat more closely. He looked at the transom, but there was no name, although it looked like one had been hastily painted out. He walked along the quay and looked at the boat from the bow. He was sure she looked familiar, but he didn't remember her being painted black. He frowned, concentration furrowing his brow. Then he had it. 'Well I'll be damned!' he said quietly to himself. 'I'd better ring Sonny. He'll want to know about this.'

~o~

Russell had just walked into the police station when Wickstead called out: 'Phone call for you, Sonny.'

Russell walked up to the counter and took the handset that the desk Sergeant was holding out. 'Hello? Oh, Captain Salt. Really? Are you sure? Right. I'll come straight over.' He handed the phone back to Wickstead, a big grin spreading across his face. 'Best news I've had for a long time! He turned to PC Beaumont, who was standing waiting patiently. 'Come on, lad. Back in the car. We need to get down to Compass Point – pronto!'

~o~

Salt returned to the quayside just in time to see Dickens climbing up on to the quay. 'Off already?' he asked.

'No time like the present. As I said, I'm headed for Dover. Be nice to get there before it's too late.'

'Sounds like the engine started okay.' The Gardiner had settled down to a steady beat.

'Yes. Just had to prime the injectors then she roared into life.' He started untying the mooring lines.

Salt was doing his best to delay *Moonshine's* departure but was struggling to slow it down. 'Why in such a hurry? The tide's only just making and there'll be plenty of water when you get there.'

Dickens continued loosening the ropes. 'Aye. Just feel it's best to get under way. Want to take it easy, just to make sure.'

Salt tried one more tack. 'Might it not be wise to leave it, until you've had enough time to check the engine is running all right?'

Dickens paused and listened. 'Sounds all right to me. I think I'd know if anything was up, don't you?' Anxious to start the journey he was beginning to suspect that Salt might be deliberately delaying him. He finished untying the warps, threw the stern line untidily down on to the afterdeck and looped the bowline round the bollard. He jumped down on to the deck, pulled the line in behind him and, with a wave to Salt, began turning the boat. The tide was coming in swiftly and the boat slewed sideways, travelling back up the river, before Dickens got the bow pointing seaward. Even at half throttle *Moonshine* barely made headway against the current so he gave the engine more revs and she began moving slowly down the estuary, a large bow wave breaking either side of the vessel.

She hadn't gone more than a couple of hundred yards when Salt heard a car approaching at speed. The Wolseley rocketed over the level crossing – the front bouncing high on its springs – and into the yard, screeching to halt surrounded by a plume of dust. Russell and Beaumont tumbled out and ran to where Salt was standing. 'Where is she?'

Salt pointed down the channel. 'There! They're getting away!'

'Not if I have anything to do with it! Quick, get Stan. We need to get after them!' Salt ran to the boatshed while the two policemen climbed down the ladder and into the launch. By the time Stan had joined them, the engine was running and the warps were untied. *Moonshine* was some distance away and Dickens had obviously opened the throttle fully as she was now creating an even larger bow wave. 'Can you catch her?' Russell asked.

'I'll give it my best shot,' Stan said.
'If Wolfgang's aboard, I don't want to lose him again!'

# Chapter 24

*A flare gun, or Very pistol, is named after
an American naval officer, Edward Wilson Very.
It is a single-shot, snub-nosed pistol
that fires flares.*

SALT'S LAUNCH had a good turn of speed and was highly manoeuvrable but was as much subject to the fierce flood tide as the other craft. Consequently, they started nearly a quarter of a mile behind *Moonshine*. Stan had taken the helm, with Beaumont next to him while Russell and Salt stood braced, either side of the wheelhouse.

'I knew I'd seen that boat somewhere before.' Salt had to shout to make his voice heard above the sound of the engine and the water, rushing along the hull. 'Stan did too, but didn't realise it was *Moonshine* at first – I guess he was too busy making sure he towed her in safely.'

'What on earth do you think it's doing back here?' Russell asked.

'I've no idea,' Salt replied. 'It's very odd that the Irishman is aboard – on his own.'

'But are you sure that he's alone?'

'That's a point, I don't know. I just assumed…'

'Müller could be skulking below. He knows that someone would be bound to have recognised him at the Point if he had shown his face.'

'True. But what's that Irishman doing with his boat?'

Russell laughed. 'Oh, I can help you with that. We're pretty sure he owns a rundown boatyard in Newhaven and calls himself Paddy Dickens although I suspect that's not his real name. Also our *friend* Müller has been travelling in his company using the alias of a Frenchman, Monsieur Marcel Meunier.'

Salt's bushy eyebrows rose and his blue eyes sparkled. 'So if we catch them, it'll be two birds with one stone...'

'No, not *if* we catch them, but *when* we catch them!' Russell leaned into the wheelhouse. 'Can't you make this thing go any faster Stan?'

'I'm doing my best, Inspector. We are closing on them, look.' He pointed forward. The gap was nearer to 300 yards now. However, *Moonshine* was approaching the mouth of the river and once in the bay would be free of the tidal surge. Plus, the sky was just beginning to darken. It was frustrating for those on the launch. Although they were slowly gaining on the other craft there was nothing more they could do.

'Look! They're turning!' Russell shouted. Sure enough *Moonshine*, just clear of the harbour mouth, had turned sharply to port, angling across the troubled water covering the sands and sunken forest of Shell Bay.

'Hells teeth!' Salt exclaimed. 'They'll hit the bottom if they're not careful. It's really shallow in places at the best of times, let alone this soon before high tide.' By now, the launch too had reached the entrance and those on board could quite clearly see the other boat heading diagonally across the bay. Suddenly, it juddered to a halt. 'She's aground!' exclaimed Salt. Dickens appeared from the wheelhouse and was joined by the figure of another man who had come up from the cabin.

'It's Müller!' Russell shouted. 'I'd know that little runt anywhere!' Both figures bustled back into the wheelhouse and they could hear the engine roaring; the propeller sending up a spray of mud and seawater, but the boat didn't budge. Although the launch was of much shallower draught, Stan had taken the precaution of reducing the speed to a walking pace but they were still closing on the other vessel. When they were within 150 yards, *Moonshine*, the engine still racing, juddered, then slowly began to edge backwards. The launch was now close enough for those on board to see the rope that Dickens had earlier carelessly thrown on to the afterdeck. It was actually hanging over the transom and into the water. Suddenly, with a jerk, the craft's rearward progressed ceased, there was a loud bang, the engine roared even more, then suddenly stopped and a puff of smoke came from astern.

'Hah! The rope's caught round the prop!' Salt exclaimed. 'Now they're done for!'

PC Beaumont came out of the wheelhouse and stood on the foredeck, legs wide, rolling with the motion of the boat. 'Do you want me to get ready to board her, Sir?'

'I think we'd better be cautious, lad. Now they're cornered we don't know how dangerous they're likely to be.' Almost immediately, lighting the gloom, there was a bright flash and a crack from *Moonshine*. Beaumont let out a cry and grasped his shoulder, tumbling to the deck. 'Quick! Get down! They're firing on us!' Salt and Russell ducked below the gunwale and Stan, swiftly closing the throttle, crouched down in the wheelhouse.

'What now?' Salt asked.

'Let's get Beaumont in the wheelhouse. Find out how bad it is.'

'I'm all right, Sir,' the PC said feebly. 'It's just a flesh wou…' and he passed out. Salt had taken a large white handkerchief out of his pocket and was holding it to Beaumont's shoulder where it slowly turned crimson.

'They can't go anywhere,' Russell said. 'Let's get him sorted out before we do anything else.'

'I've got a first aid kit here, Inspector,' Stan said, and produced a large wooden box with a red cross painted on it.

Salt grabbed it. 'Leave him to me,' he said. 'You plan what you're going to do next.'

~O~

'Can we set off *now*?' Sammy asked.

Helen cautiously lifted the corner of the window covering. 'Better give it another half hour.' Just then there was the sound of a car stopping, then a 'toot' from the road. She raised the sacking again. 'Ah, my lift has arrived.'

'But I thought you said "give it half an hour"?' Baker said.

''Well…' she said slowly. 'Maybe it's dark enough now. Can you give me a torch?' Baker handed her one. She switched it on and flashed it briefly through the window. 'There, now he knows I've seen him.' Atkins was about to speak but she held her hand up. 'Don't ask who he is. The less we know about each other from now on, the better. Right, let's check on Mr Policeman. You lot stay back, just in case.' She unlocked and opened the cellar door and shone the torch inside.

Weeks was sitting on the top step with the blanket wrapped round his shoulders. 'Hello. Who are you? Are you coming to take me away?' His speech was slow, but clear.

'How are you feeling?'

'Oh, all right, thank you.'

'How's the bump on the head?'

He reached up with his hand. 'Oh that. Don't know how I did it. Do you?'

'I think you fell.'

'Oh… Where is this place, anyway?' he looked puzzled.

'Don't you know?'

'No idea. I just know that it's a bit damp.' He started to get up. 'Can I come in there?'

'Not now. Someone will be along to get you later. Are you hungry?'

'Not really. But I could do with a drink.' He held out the mug.

'Wait there. I'll be back in a moment.' She took the mug and shut the door. 'Quick, fill this up.' Baker took the mug to the sink, filled it with water and handed it back to Helen. 'Keep out of sight.' She opened the door again.

Weeks was just standing there. He meekly took the mug. 'Have you come to get me?'

'No, not yet. It won't be long. Will you be okay?'

'Oh I'm fine,' he said weakly, 'now I've got a drink.' He smiled and took a gulp.' Helen gently closed the door and turned the key.

'I see what you mean,' Bates said. 'Away with the fairies.'

'Saved us the trouble of silencing 'im anyway. Shame, I was looking forward to fixin' 'im. Led us a right merry dance,' Atkins growled.

'Not us, Tommy, *you*. We told you he was a wrong'un, but you wouldn't listen,' Baker said.

'Now listen 'ere…' Atkins said angrily, squaring up to the little man with the odd haircut.

'Boys, boys.' Helen stepped between them, quickly defusing the situation. 'Falling out now isn't going to help anyone.' Turning to Baker, she said: 'Why don't you help me carry my stuff to the car while the others get the van ready?'

'Okay.'

'I'll say goodbye then.' She shook hands formally with each of them. 'I won't see you around, but be lucky. Oh, and I'll make that phone call about our *guest*. Right, Laurie, off we go.'

They made their way out of the front door while the others went through the back. She was carrying the mailbag with her share of the raid in it while Baker carried her suitcase. 'Blimey!' he said, as they walked up the drive. 'What have you got in here? Weighs a ton!'

'Oh you know. A girl always likes to have plenty of everything,' she said coyly. Baker worked his magic with the padlock and swung the gate open, wide enough for them to get through. Standing in the lane was a sports car resplendent in British Racing Green. The roof was up so Baker couldn't see who was sitting in the driver's seat. Helen spoke. 'Thanks for everything. I'll put these in here.' Turning the handle she opened the lid of the boot and swung the bag in. Baker put the suitcase in, too. It was a tight squeeze. Helen closed the lid and leaning forward, gave him a peck on the cheek. 'Take care,' she said, opened the passenger door and climbed in. As soon as she'd slammed the door shut, the car roared off, leaving Baker standing in the lane feeling somewhat fazed. He shook his head slowly and went to join the rest.

Bates had driven the van out of the small barn and the others were bringing the mail bags through the back door. Baker could see they were carrying far more than the four they had agreed; the one each containing their share of the loot they had labelled. 'What's going on?'

'We're takin' all the bags,' Atkins said.

'But Helen said to leave the other ones.'

'Tough. She's ain't here no more so it don't matter.' He paused. 'Anyway. Who picked 'er up?'

'I don't know. I couldn't see. Nice car though, nearly new Triumph TR2.'

Atkins whistled. 'Blimey, that's a bit flash.'

'Yeah, and we're going off in a van.'

'Quit moaning. You'll be able to buy a brand new TR3 if you want.'

'I suppose so.' Baker still wasn't happy about the additional mail bags so he pressed on. 'Helen said the contents of those bags could be traceable.'

Atkins would not to be dissuaded. He put his face close to Baker's. ''Ow does she know? 'Til we open 'em we won't know what's in 'em, will we?'

'I suppose not.'

'Let's get 'em loaded an' then we can push off.'

~o~

'What's the plan, Sonny?' Salt was kneeling on the floor of the wheelhouse of the launch, dressing Beaumont's wound and making him comfortable.

'First of all, how's the patient? Should we turn back and get him to hospital?'

'I don't think so. I agree with him that it's just a flesh wound. I think he passed out with shock but he's come round and is quite coherent.'

'As long as you're sure.'

'Yes, I am. What's more important is to catch those two.

What are you going to do?'

'The trouble is, they're armed; well, at least one of them must be.'

'And we're not...'

'Quite.'

'So even though they're now stuck on that sandbank, we can't get any closer?'

'Look!' said Stan, pointing. 'She's moving!'

Salt sat up and peered over the gunwale. 'It's the tide! It's lifted her off the bottom. She's drifting towards the shore.'

'If they get into shallow water they'll be able to wade to the beach, then we'll lose them in the dunes,' Russell said. 'We've got to get nearer to them.'

'Hang on,' Stan said, 'they're stuck again.'

'So they are. If *only* we had a weapon. If we get any closer they'll fire on us again.'

Salt looked thoughtful, rubbing his chin. Then he said: 'Hold on, I've got an idea. Stan, haven't we got a Very pistol on board?'

'We have, Captain. Hold on a minute.' He went to the back of wheelhouse, opened a locker and took out what looked like a small, stubby handgun.'

'What's that?' Russell asked, frowning.

'Its purpose is for firing flares, so it's not very accurate. But I've heard it can be used as a weapon at close range. We could try to get nearer. Who's the best shot?' Salt said.

'Beaumont, actually, but he's obviously not up to it. How about you?' Russell asked.'

'Used to be good, but my sight's not what it was.'

'I wasn't bad in the Army, but I haven't fired a gun for a long time. Stan?'

'I reckon I could have a go. Who's going to take the boat in?'

'I can manage that,' Russell said.

'Better get a move on,' Salt broke in. 'Looks like they may be about to launch the dinghy.

The two men in *Moonshine* had indeed made their way to the dinghy, which was lashed on the deck, and seemed to be untying the ropes holding her down. Russell was steering the launch slowly towards her and, when they got within 50 or 60 yards, there was a loud *bang!* then a ping and a whine, as a bullet ricocheted off the corner of the wheelhouse. Russell was safe inside; Salt was kneeling next to Beaumont but Stan, standing, ducked automatically. He crept forward and crouched behind the gunwale. By raising his head he could peer forward through the bow fairlead. The sky was darkening and it was growing gloomy but he could clearly see the silhouettes of the two men frantically trying to free the dinghy. When they were within 20 yards, another shot ricocheted off the hull, just below his position. The flash from the muzzle showed him where the gunman was standing and, in one swift movement, he stood, aimed and fired the Very pistol.

Suddenly, *Moonshine* was lit up as if by a spotlight. There was a scream from the deck. The flare bounced off and sizzled in the water, still glowing bright white. Russell opened the throttle and the launch bore down on the fishing boat. He slammed the engine into reverse at the last moment but even so there was a sickening crunch as they hit *Moonshine* and the launch jerked to a standstill. Stan was over the bow in a trice and pinning one of the figures to the deck. The other was still screaming. Russell followed quickly and saw that it was Wolfgang, smoke coming from the centre of his jacket. Russell grabbed a bucket with a length of rope tied to the handle, swung it over the side, half filling it with water and threw it over the prone man. He screamed even louder for several seconds and then went quiet.

'He may be a wanted man but we've got to get him to hospital,' Russell said. 'He's in a bad way.'

'And we need to get this one seen to as well,' Stan added, still straddling Dickens.

'Yes, quite right. I'll get Salt to throw over the handcuffs so we can secure him. I presume there's a VHF radio on the launch?'

'Of course.'

Russell called to the other vessel. 'Salt.'

'Yes, Sonny?

'First of all, Beaumont should have a pair of cuffs on him. Pass them over can you, please? Then radio the station and get them to send an ambulance and a police car to the Point.'

Once Dickens was cuffed, they gently manhandled Wolfgang on to the launch. He groaned but did not regain consciousness. 'We don't have time to tow *Moonshine* back. You'll have to collect her later, Stan.'

'Okay Inspector. I'll make her secure for now.' He threw the anchor over the bow, so that the craft would not drift out to sea. Picking up the revolver that was lying in the scuppers, Russell directed Dickens across to the launch. The journey back would be quicker because, although the tide was not running so swiftly, they were travelling in the same direction as the flood.

As they motored back up the river, Salt used the radio to contact the station. 'Yes, two injured, one with a gunshot wound, the other's got a nasty burn,' he said. 'How long?' A pause. 'We should be back in about 10 minutes. What's that?' another pause, longer this time. 'Right. I'll tell him.'

'What was that?' Russell asked.

'Apparently there's been an anonymous message about Weeks...'

'*Really*?'

'You're to ring the station as soon as you get back to your car.'

~O~

'Right, is that all the bags stowed now?' Atkins asked.

'I think so, boss,' Sammy said.

'I'm still not happy about this,' Baker's face looked like a smacked arse.

'Tough. Listen... You can either stay 'ere and whinge 'til the law comes callin' or go with us. Which is it to be?'

Baker thought for a moment and let out a long sigh. 'I suppose I'll come with you.'

'Get in the van with Sammy then.' Baker climbed into the back, making himself as comfortable as possible, amongst all the mail sacks. Atkins slammed the door and turned the handle. Walking round to the front he got in the passenger side and shut the door. 'Right, Butch. Let's get out of here.'

~O~

The launch came alongside the jetty just as the ambulance arrived, bells clanging. Russell stopped briefly to speak to the crew, then dashed to the car and radioed the station. 'So, what's the news about Weeks?' he asked.

Wickstead was manning the phone. 'A woman rang – cultured sounding – said we'd find him in the cellar of a farmhouse in Etchingwood Lane, just outside of Framfield.'

'But Parker and Barrow are supposed to have searched that area.'

'That's right, but you know them…'

'Ye gods and little fishes! Can't they be trusted to do anything right?'

'What do you expect of Bonnie and Clyde, Sonny?'

'Quite. Any idea where they are now?'

'They haven't come back here yet. Shall I ring the Uckfield nick and find out if they've seen them?'

'Yes, that's a good idea, Sarge. Call me straight back can you? I'm a bit worried about Weeks. It'll take me the best part of an hour to get over to Framfield. It'd be easier if someone from there could go.'

Russell sat in the car, drumming his fingers on the steering wheel. He was loath to set off until he had heard back from Wickstead but was frustrated by the delay. After a few minutes the car radio crackled into life. 'Sonny?'

'Yes, Sarge? Any news?'

Wickstead chuckled. 'They were still there. Eating a fish supper – and probably sinking a beer or two.'

'Typical! Can you ask them to get over to that farmhouse?'

'Already done, Sonny. They're on their way with a couple of PCs from the station. I spoke to the desk Sergeant. Apparently, their Super gave Bonnie a right flea in the ear for missing it.'

'I should think he did. They should have pensioned that pair off years ago. I just hope they get to Weeks quickly. I'm really worried about him.'

~O~

Bates put the van into gear, and was just driving towards the gate when he stopped. 'Hang on, there's something wrong.'

'What do you mean?' There was panic in Atkins's voice.

'I think we've got a flat tyre.'

'Bloody hell! Is that all? *Christ*! I thought something terrible had happened. Come on, let's have a look.' Sure enough the nearside rear wheel was down on its rim.

Sammy and Baker had to get out of the back again and the mailbags needed to be heaped to one side so they could get at the spare wheel. Bates got the jack and cursed as it would not fit under the sill because of the extra weight. So they had to take the mailbags out and pile them on the drive. Then, when the van was jacked up, he found the nuts were corroded on to the wheel and he couldn't shift them. 'For crying out loud!' Atkins exclaimed. 'Are we ever going to get away?'

Bates was flustered and breathing heavily. 'I need a lever. A bit of pipe would do.'

'For Christ's sake! Go and find something.' Bates went off with a torch while the others stood around, smoking. Finally, he came back with a length of galvanised gas pipe that he had found in the barn. He fitted it over the end of the wheel brace and using his considerable weight on lever, the first nut suddenly came free, and he tumbled to the ground.

Atkins could not suppress a laugh. 'Come on Butch. Quit clowning around. We've got to get off.'

Bates stood up, a hurt look on his fleshy face. 'I ain't clowning around,' he said indignantly.'

'Sorry, mate. It was just funny, that's all.'

Bates harrumphed and finished undoing the other nuts. The wheel came off easily and the spare was soon in place. Bates retightened the nuts then lowered the jack. 'Oh, no,' he said miserably.

'What's the matter now?' Atkins snapped.

'You won't believe it – the spare's flat.'

'Jesus! I thought this was your pride and joy. Don't you look after it?'

'Course I do. It's just one of them things.'

'What do we do now?' Sammy asked.

'We'll have to pump it up – see if it holds air,' Bates said.

'I suppose you *have* got a foot pump?' Atkins asked.

'I think so. Give me the torch and I'll have a look.' Bates rummaged around in the back of the van for what seemed like an age but was actually only a couple of minutes. He finally emerged triumphant. Even so, it was not a great pump. Even with them taking it in turns, it was nearly 10 minutes before the tyre had enough air in it.

'Hoo-ray,' Atkins exclaimed. 'Right. Let's get the van repacked and get this bloody show on the road. I'm starting to get nervous now.'

~O~

Parker's ears were still stinging from the dressing down he had received from the Uckfield superintendent as they drove away from the police station. 'Worse than bloody Stout,' he muttered to himself. 'Thought he was bad enough.'

'Sorry, Sir?' the PC enquired, wrestling with the steering as the car screeched round a tight corner.

'Nothing,' Parker grumbled. 'You just concentrate on the road. Get us there in one piece.'

They were approaching Framfield when the PC, who knew the area well, took a sharp left, throwing Parker sideways. Barrow and the other PC slid one way across the back seat then almost immediately slid the other way as he took a right. Parker was about to speak but kept quiet. Soon they were rocketing along Etchingwood Lane when Barrow recognised where they were and yelled: '*Stop!* We've just passed it!' The PC stood on the brakes and Parker all but broke the screen with his forehead. As soon as the car had stopped, they all jumped out and shining torches ahead of them the two PCs and Barrow dashed back, Parker trailing behind. They reached the farmhouse and stopped in amazement. Inside the open gateway, illuminated by their torchlight, was a Morris van with four men hastily stowing mailbags in the back. The men were equally surprised and for some moments there was a Mexican standoff. Nobody moved for several seconds then all hell broke loose.

Bates wrenched the driver's door open, clambered behind the wheel, started the engine and attempted to drive off, but in his hurry it stalled and the van just shuddered; Atkins tried to grab a shotgun from out of the back of the van but it became tangled with a bag and, as he struggled, a PC was on him. Sammy stood, petrified, his eyes all over the place, submitting meekly as the other PC clamped handcuffs on his wrists. Baker made a run for the gate, dodged Barrow but collided with Parker, who ended up flat on his back in the dirt. Baker would have got away, but just as he turned along the lane a second police car came tearing round the corner, two PCs leapt out before it had stopped and pinned him to the ground. Soon, all four robbers were rounded up and stood, handcuffed and resigned, waiting for the police van to arrive.

Meanwhile, Parker had picked himself up and, grumbling, did his best to brush the mud off his suit and raincoat. It didn't make a lot of difference. 'Come on,' he said to Barrow, 'let's find this cellar.' The front door was locked so they made their way round to the back. The kitchen was littered with empty beer bottles, dirty plates, saucepans and mugs. Saucers overflowed with cigarette butts. They found the cellar door and Parker unlocked it. Weeks was sitting on the top step, bewildered, a faraway look on his face. He still had the blanket wrapped round him. Parker took pity. 'Hello, lad, how are you?'

He looked up, his eyes slightly unfocused. 'Have you come to take me away?'

'Yes, lad, that's right.'

Weeks smiled dreamily. 'The nice lady said someone would come for me. Is she still here?'

Parker frowned. 'Lady? What lady? They were all men here, weren't they?'

'I didn't see any men – just the lady. She had glasses and nice eyes.'

'Helen McDermott, Sir,' Barrow said. 'Russell told us she was involved with the gang.'

'Did he?' Parker thought for a moment. 'Oh, yes. I do recall something about that now. Anyway,' he was all business-like, 'let's get this chap out of here and off to hospital. Better let Russell know he's okay.'

~O~

Russell received the news with relief although he was concerned about Weeks's mental state. He rang the hospital his DC had been taken to and was reassured that the amnesia was probably only temporary, caused by the bump on the head. Apart from that he appeared to be fine. Russell promised to visit as soon as he was able. Meanwhile, he had Wolfgang and Dickens in custody. He was going to let them stew while he went over to

Uckfield to see Atkins and his cronies.

When he arrived he found that Bates and Sammy were in separate cells but was told, that for some reason of his own, Parker had decided to have both Atkins and Baker together in the interview room. Russell opened the door. 'Can I have a word?'

Parker stubbed out his cigarette and got laboriously to his feet. 'Just keep an eye on them,' he said to his DC, 'I'll be back in a minute.' Closing the door behind him, he said, 'What is it, Russell? Can't you see I'm in the middle of an interview?'

'That's what I want to speak to you about.'

'Oh, yes?'

It's not usual to interrogate two prisoners at the same time...'

'Are you questioning my methods?'

'I suppose I am.'

'Well don't!' Parker said crossly. 'I know what I'm doing.'

'Okay. Well do you mind if I sit in? It is my case, after all.'

Before answering Parker took a battered packet of Capstan Full Strength out of his pocket, withdrew a crumpled cigarette and lit it. Blowing smoke towards the ceiling, he sighed. 'I suppose not. Just don't interfere. It *might* have started out as your case. But as I'm sure you've got your hands full with those other two over at Collinghurst. I'm actually helping you out.' Russell raised his eyebrows but didn't reply. Parker spoke again. 'Come on then. You'll have to stand, as it's a bit cramped. I'd be grateful if you'd keep your mouth shut and let me do the talking.' Refusing to rise to the bait, Russell just nodded.

Parker sat back down at the table and took a long drag on his cigarette. 'Right. Can you explain what you're doing with a van-load of mailbags?' Atkins and Baker sat without speaking, their arms folded across their chests. 'Okay, tell me what you were doing at the farmhouse?' Again, silence. There was a knock at the door. 'What is it?' Parker asked tetchily.

A PC poked his head round the door. 'Can I speak to you for a moment, Inspector?'

Parker looked round. 'Is it important?'

'Could be, Sir.'

'All these interruptions. We're never going to get anywhere. Do you want to find out what this man wants, Russell?'

'Of course. Leave it to me.' He walked out and joined the PC in the corridor and leaned against the wall. 'What is it lad?'

'We've just been looking through those mailbags we took out of the van and we're a bit puzzled.'

'Why's that?'

'We haven't found any money yet.'

'What?'

'So far they really are just mail bags, filled with letters and parcels.'

'That's definitely a bit strange.'

'What's even stranger is that four of the bags have labels with names on them; Tommy, Butcher, Laurie and Sammy.'

'And no cash?'

'Not a penny.'

'Then where is the money?' Russell looked thoughtful. Then a slow smile spread across his face. 'Helen...'

'Sir?'

'I think I know where the money has gone. Now for some fun.' He stood upright and reached for the door handle.

'Before you go in, Sir. There's just one other thing.'

'What's that?'

'You know that Elsdale, the man who fell on the wooden spike, didn't make it, Sir?'

'Yes, that was sad. I only met him briefly but he seemed quite a nice chap. What of it?'

'I don't think they know – in there.'

'Oh. That is interesting. Thanks for telling me.'

Back in the interview room Parker had still made no progress. The two felons continued to remain silent. 'What did the constable want?' Parker asked.

'Oh, he told me a couple of interesting things. Do you mind if I say something to the prisoners?'

Parker slumped back in his chair. 'Feel free. I'm not getting anywhere with them.'

'Right, thanks.' Russell addressed Atkins: 'It seems the bird has flown – with the loot.'

Atkins scowled and spoke for the first time. 'Bird? Loot? Dunno what yer talkin' about.'

I haven't got the exact figure but the raid on the train should have netted you over fifty thousand pounds.'

'Still don't know what yer on about.'

'I think you do. We've looked through the mailbags and the trouble is, the money's not there anymore.'

Baker sat up abruptly. '*What*?'

'Shut up!' Atkins growled.

'But…'

'I said keep it shut!'

'Not much of a robbery when someone else goes off with the cash,' Russell continued.

'What are you on about?'

'Yes, what are you driving at?' Parker added.

Sonny smiled. 'It seems that four of the bags had name tags on them, two of them yours.' He pointed to Atkins and Baker. 'But they contained nothing but letters.'

'*Whaaat!*' Atkins said, jumping to his feet.

'Sit down!' Parker commanded. Barrow got up and pushed Atkins back in his seat.

Parker turned to Russell: 'Come on then, tell us what happened to it.'

Russell walked over and leaned forward, resting his knuckles on the table. He looked straight at Atkins. 'All along we thought this was *your* job. *You* were the brains behind it. But that's not the case, is it?'

'I don't know what you mean.' Atkins muttered and folded his arms again.

'I think you do... Yes, you were heavily involved in the organisation. It was you who brought the gang together. Yes, it was you who found the farmhouse hideaway and, I suspect, you who supplied the sawn-off shotguns we found.' Atkins stuck his jaw out belligerently but said nothing. 'But someone else was the main boss. And she's got all the money.'

'Why, the dirty, double-crossing, b....,' Baker began.

Atkins silenced him. 'I said *shut it!*'

Parker was watching with interest but hadn't spoken so Russell walked round the table and went on: 'I've got another bit of information you might be interested in.' Atkins showed no response, but Russell continued: 'Yes, it's a rather sad piece of information. Your friend, Dave...' Atkins looked up then. '... Dave Elsdale. Well I'm afraid he didn't make it.'

Now Atkins reacted. '*What*? Waddyer mean, didn't make it?'

'He seemed to be recovering but two days ago, he died.'

'*What!*' He leaped out of his chair, knocking it to the ground, turned and put his hands round Baker's throat. 'You bastard! You killed him!' Choking, Baker tried to prise the hands off but

Atkins clung on tightly all the time yelling: '*Bastard! Bastard!*' It took the combined efforts of Barrow and Russell to pull him away and force him back in his chair where, to prevent further attacks they linked his arms behind him with handcuffs.

Baker sat, massaging his throat. 'I didn't mean to kill him, he just fell,' he said miserably.

'You pushed him. Helen told me.'

'But not hard.'

'It don't matter. He was my best mate. An' now he's dead.' Atkins bared his teeth and hissed, ' *I'll get you for this!*'

He tried to stand but Russell roughly pushed him back down. 'So, not only have you lost your best mate, but you've also lost all your money. Now, are you going to start talking?'

The revelations had opened the floodgates and both men started freely answering the questions put to them. When Baker told them about the Triumph sports car that Helen had gone off in Russell left the room, saying: 'It's probably too late but I'll get the description circulated and tell them to look out for it at the ports.'

~O~

As they approached the ferry terminal at Dover, Helen turned to the man in the driving seat. 'Do you know, Simon, I'm really going to enjoy spending all that lovely money with you.' She snuggled up to his shoulder. 'Where shall we go? Monte Carlo?'

He put his arm round her shoulder, steering with one hand. 'Anywhere you like, my darling. The world is your oyster.'

A worried look crossed her face. 'You don't think I made that phone call too soon, do you?'

Simon laughed. 'No. The speed they work at it'll take them ages to find out where you left that copper. When they do, he won't be able to tell them anything anyway.'

'But what about Tommy and the others?'

'Oh, they'll be well away by the time the police get to the farmhouse. I'll tell you what. They're going to be furious when they find out you switched the mailbags!'

She was quiet for a while. 'There's something I didn't tell you.'

The tone of her voice made him wary. '*What* haven't you told me?'

'I, um, arranged it so they'd be delayed in leaving.'

'Ha! What did you do?'

'I let the tyre down.'

'Is that all? That wouldn't take long to sort out.'

'I let the spare down, too.'

He laughed. 'I'd love to have seen their faces when they discovered that.'

'But maybe they didn't get away before the police turned up.'

'They're bound to have done.'

'But what if they didn't?'

'So what? You don't feel sorry for them, do you?'

'No, of course not. But what if they tell the police about me going away with you?'

'I think that's highly unlikely. Stop worrying.'

They had now reached the customs control booth. Simon handed over their passports. The uniformed man peered in through the car window and examined him and Helen carefully. Despite her normally calm demeanour, she could feel panic rising. After what seemed an age the man nodded and handed the passports back. Simon drove on. She could feel sweat trickling down between her shoulder blades. 'Are you all right, darling?' he asked.

'I think so. I don't know what came over me. I was convinced he was going to stop us.'

'You're worrying too much. As I said, Mr Plod will take forever to work out what really happened. And by then we'll be miles away.' They joined the queue of vehicles waiting to board. The ferry was festooned with lights, lit up like a Christmas tree in the dark. It wasn't long before they were driving up the ramp and into the hold. Soon they were on their way across the Channel, to a new life.

~o~

'Tell me Johnny, how're you feeling?' Russell was sitting at Weeks's bedside in the hospital. He was leaning forward, a look of concern on his face. A brown-paper bag of grapes – unopened – sat on the side cabinet.

Weeks had a bandage circling his head; his unshaven face was pale, but his eyes were clear. 'Not too bad, thank you. Are you a doctor? I don't remember seeing you before.' His brow was furrowed with puzzlement.

Russell chuckled. No, I'm not a doctor. Are you sure you don't know me?'

Weeks stared at the other man. 'Mmm. You do look familiar – I think.'

'I reckon you need a bit more rest. Then I'm sure you'll remember.'

'Yes, you're probably right. I do feel a bit sleepy.'

'I'll leave you in peace then, but I'll come back tomorrow.'

'That'll be nice.' With that Weeks closed his eyes, lay back on the pillow and turned his head away.

Russell quietly got up and left the room. Outside, in the corridor, he found a doctor. 'Excuse me, Can I ask you about Johnny Weeks?' He pointed back toward the room.

'Are you a relative?'

'No, I'm DI Russell, his boss.'

'Ah, I see. What did you want to know?'

'He didn't recognise me. Is that normal?'

'He has had a nasty bump on the head. But you shouldn't be overly concerned. People suffering from amnesia can take a while before they start returning to normal. But nine times out of ten they regain complete recall.'

'Then I shouldn't worry?'

'No. I'm sure he'll be fine. Come back tomorrow and maybe he'll realise who you are.'

# Postscript

'I'VE JUST heard from a customs officer at Dover, Sonny. A Triumph TR2 in British Racing Green drove on to the Boulogne ferry half an hour ago.' Wickstead said.

'Who was in it? Russell asked.

'A man and a woman.'

'I don't suppose he remembers their names?'

'Sorry Sonny, he doesn't.'

'Then it might not be them, damn!' He paused. 'Wait a minute though. Get on to the ferry company. They're bound to have a record of the tickets.'

A few minutes later Wickstead called him over. 'The booking clerk at the ferry company has just been in touch. The tickets were in the names of Helen McDermott and Simon Hargreaves.'

'Bingo!'

'But the ferry's gone now.'

'Yes, but it hasn't arrived yet. Get me Inspecteur Bruissement's number in Boulogne.'

~o~

After a smooth crossing, when they had enjoyed a meal in the first-class restaurant, Helen and Simon made their way down to the car deck. Arms round each other, they were blissfully happy.

Once back in the TR they joined the queue of cars, disembarking from the ferry. As they drove down the ramp they were waved over to one side by a Gendarme. 'Anything the matter?' Simon asked.

There was a tap on the passenger window. Helen wound it down. A smiling face with a luxuriant moustache peered in. 'Mademoiselle McDermott, I presume?'

THE END

# Blood on the Tide

**A DI Sonny Russell mystery**
**Chris O'Donoghue**

**WHEN A** gruesomely mutilated body trussed up in a distinctive fashion washes up on a lonely stretch of the south coast in the 1950s, DI Sonny Russell is soon struggling to unravel an intriguingly knotty puzzle. And as more bodies, similarly tortured, appear he begins to realise that, for some at least, the war is far from over.

A trail of intrigue leads him to Europe where he befriends a French detective and together they set out to track down the villains.

Blood on the Tide is a story of the sea and boats, murder and Nazis that begins in a sleepy coastal backwater and takes the reader through post-war France and Germany.

# Blood on the Strand

### The third DI Sonny Russell mystery
### Chris O'Donoghue

**IN A RAGING GALE** a heavy crate is washed up on the beach near Compass Point. DI Sonny Russell and his sidekick DC Johnny Weeks happen upon it while braving the weather near Sonny's home. Puzzled, they go to get help to recover it, but when they return it has gone. So begins a thrilling and dangerous search for stolen Nazi plunder. It leads the detectives, ably assisted by an eager young policewoman, Nettie Sharpe, on a twisting trail that encompasses Hastings fisherman, their iconic net huts, ruthless foreign criminals and the shady side of antique dealing. BLOOD ON THE STRAND is a story of intrigue and drama, set on the sleepy south coast in the post-war mid-fifties.

*Chris O'Donoghue has kept up the suspense and action in this, his third Sonny Russell story. Sonny and his sidekick Johnny Weeks are joined by a WPC to solve the riddle of stolen Nazi treasure.'*

*'Great to return to familiar characters and see them evolve, as well as meeting new ones. Some unexpected twists and interesting plot.'*

*'Another good Sonny Russel mystery from Chris O'Donoghue. I recommend this series of books, proper 50s police detective work.'*

# Blood on the Cards

### The fourth DI Sonny Russell mystery
### Chris O'Donoghue

**A TRAVELLING FAIR** brings fun, laughter and excitement - but when one comes Nottery Quay it brings gruesome death too. The resident fortune teller is found with her throat cut in a damp and dirty WWII pillbox near the Royal Military Canal. The owner of the fairground comes under suspicion but, when a second body is found, DI Sonny Russell begins to have his doubts. Falling foul of his bombastic boss Superintendent Stout yet again, he is taken off the case and replaced by the bumbling duo Bonnie and Clyde. However, assisted by his French opposite number, Inspecteur Guillaume Bruissement, and his ever faithful sidekick DC Weeks, he pursues his own investigation. So begins a gripping tale which criss-crosses Sussex and Kent and ends in a thriller chase along the canal, with disastrous consequences...

*I've been enjoying the DI Sonny Russell series and this book doesn't disappoint. The feel of the time is present and the story was nicely engaging. I've grown to love the characters and you can't help rooting for them. A great read.*

*This is the 4th book in the "Blood on the" series and is a gripping read. Held my attention till the end as I did not cheat and read the last chapter halfway through the book. No skim reading, good twist at the end with the clues being in the story if you pay attention. Cannot wait for book number 5.*

*Have read the three earlier books and enjoyed this fourth book in the series just as much as the others. Especially interesting when you live in the area in which the series is set. Hope there are more stories to come.*

*A real page turner with good characters and some plot twists, I think this may be my favourite of the Sonny Russell series.*

# Blood in the Garden

**The fifth DI Sonny Russell mystery**
**Chris O'Donoghue**

**SUPT STOUT IS DESPERATE** to improve his standing in the community by joining the prestigious Nottery golf club and, when two people connected with it go missing, he sees a matchless opportunity to improve his chances. He puts DI Sonny Russell, on the job - much to the officer's disgust.

Russell has more interesting conundrums: why hasn't dependable WPC Nettie Sharp reported for duty? An antique dealer finds a body in the boot of his car. Whose is it? Is the suspect attempting a foolhardy escape? How much does an unhelpful landowner really know about his wife's disappearance?

As all the strands gradually untwist Russell manages to solve several mysteries - with a cocktail of shocks along the way.

*Chris O'Donoghue trained in industrial ceramics at Bournemouth Art College and worked at Poole Pottery and Cranbrook Pottery in Kent before setting up on his own in Rye. He later specialised in model making and sculpture.*

*When much of the kind of work he did began to be made in the Far East, Chris, having always loved the outdoors, decided on a change of direction and started gardening. His design ability led him to create three medal-winning gardens at the Chelsea Flower Show.*

*A lifetime's passion for the sea, crime novels, the simple pleasures of the Fifties and railways – he is well known on the model railway scene – led him to combine all three in this, his fourth published book.*

The first five DI Sonny Russell mysteries

**BLOOD ON THE TIDE**
**BLOOD ON THE SHRINE**
**BLOOD ON THE STRAND**
**BLOOD ON THE CARDS**
&
**BLOOD IN THE GARDEN**

are available from Amazon
or direct from the Author
chrisodonoghue.blogspot.co.uk
www.chrisodonoghue.co.uk

The sixth DI Sonny Russell mystery
**BLOOD ON THE DUNES**
Will be published soon